Deadly Detail

Deadly Detail

Don Porter

Don G Porter (signature)

Poisoned Pen Press

First Trade Paperback Edition 2007

10 9 8 7 6 5 4 3 2 1

Library of Congress Catalog Card Number: 2005925323

ISBN: 978-1-59058-418-7 Trade Paperback

Poisoned Pen Press
6962 E. First Ave., Ste. 103
Scottsdale, AZ 85251
www.poisonedpenpress.com
info@poisonedpenpress.com

Printed in the United States of America

Chapter One

We broke out of the overcast at three thousand feet over the Tanana Valley. The Tanana River below us looked like a silver ribbon winding along the edge of the Nenana Hills, then turned to a loose braid where boat-shaped islands divided it into multiple channels. Trees along the creeks were beginning to show streaks of yellow where early frost had tinged them. Fairbanks made a smudge against the hills on the horizon twenty miles ahead. I cancelled my IFR clearance and turned on the CB radio. My passengers, administrative types from the Kuskokwim Community College in Bethel, were to attend a conference at the University of Alaska. I had their schedule to thank for our afternoon departure and evening arrival. That made a welcome excuse to spend the night in Fairbanks, and the best way to do that was a visit with Stan and Angie.

I tuned the CB radio to channel nine and gave Stan a call. He lives out on the Chena Hot Springs Road beyond telephone service, so he keeps the CB on. I still had enough altitude for the line-of-sight transmission, and he came right back at me.

"Alex, hey, buddy, are you in town for a while?"

"Overnight. Can I buy you and Angie some dinner?"

"Alex, this is a godsend. We need to talk, bad. But don't come here, this isn't for Angie's ears."

"What's the matter? What the devil have you been up to now?"

"Not on the radio. Can we meet somewhere?"

"Sure. I'll be landing in ten minutes, just have to drop off some passengers. If the company pickup starts, I can be at the Rendezvous Club in an hour."

"That's really great, Alex. See you there."

My passengers almost ran for the terminal, swinging attaché cases behind them, and turned left toward the restrooms. A vacant tie-down between a Cessna 172 and a Piper Pacer in the general aviation area was close to the nest where the company pickup was rusting beside the Sea Airmotive hangar. Bushmaster is based in Bethel, but the charter business is statewide, so we keep vehicles in Fairbanks and Anchorage. The door squeaked pitifully and popped open with a cloud of dust. Mold and a metallic odor of decay wafted out, but after some serious pumping on the gas pedal and a generous application of choke, the old International pickup came out of hibernation and sputtered to life.

The Rendezvous Club where we planned to meet was on the Steese Highway on the other side of town. That meant a tour of the city for me, but Stan would be coming in from the Hot Springs Road, so it was the closest place for him.

Airport Road had almost gone off duty for the night. Two Checker Cabs on their way to pick up my passengers were the only traffic, so the pickup rattled and smoked along at a good clip. Birch and aspen trees beside the road were starting to turn fall colors with yellow leaves tipping low branches. Those were interspersed with dark green spruce, and over all rested a mantle of quiet and calm. Houses and businesses were spread out with trees between, and none of the buildings were taller than the trees. Even the new strip mall was single-story, its multiplex theater barely taller, and none of it disturbed the peace.

I should have been settling into the ambiance that makes Fairbanks forever a small town, in spite of ambitions and aspirations. Perhaps it's the feeling of a tiny cluster of people huddled together with hundreds of miles of primeval wilderness around them. Problem was, I couldn't shake the feeling that something was very wrong. I kept going over our conversation, and the more I thought about it, the more it seemed like real urgency in Stan's voice. I had the feeling that he was relieved to hear from me, a release of tension, and that just wasn't like him. He's always glad to hear from me. We go back years together with the special bond that comes from sharing failed hopes and unrealistic dreams. Mostly, I couldn't imagine what he needed to talk about that Angie shouldn't hear. In the old days, when he was prospecting on the Kuskokwim River, there would have been plenty of things to keep from Angie, but I thought all that ended when they hooked up in Fairbanks.

Grubstaking prospectors is the Alaskan version of a trip to Las Vegas. You pour in money, knowing there isn't one chance in millions that it'll come back, but you enjoy it anyway. I had a reasonably stable income and access to float planes and helicopters. Stan had the knowledge and drive to dig up mountains of dirt and gravel, and the optimism to expect gold in each new scoop. He was self sufficient in the wilderness, wherever a hunch took us and I dropped him off. I contributed groceries and transportation. His share was blood, sweat, and calluses.

I stayed on Airport Road past the edge of town and turned toward the Chena River on Noble Street. Hotels, service stations and grocery stores joined the single-family dwellings. The Fairbanks skyline, the aluminum-clad cubic block of the Northward building, and the twelve-story green cement monolith of the Polaris building loomed ahead. Those constituted Fairbanks' bid to join the twentieth century.

Not that Fairbanks was asleep. The nightclubs and strip joints out on South Cushman would be jumping, and the native bars on Second Avenue would be a barely controlled riot, but I bypassed those and used the Wendell Street Bridge to cross the river. A new Piggly Wiggly grocery store, with attached bowling alley, served the Island Homes subdivision, so Fairbanks was expanding, albeit minimally. The town ended, trees and hills took over, the Steese Highway started its lonely trek to the Arctic Circle, and the last bastion of civilization was on my left. A dozen cars were scattered around the gravel parking lot outside the Rendezvous Club. Stan's pickup wasn't in the lot, so I wandered inside.

The club was a rambling jigsaw of log buildings and frame afterthoughts spliced together, and like all Fairbanks bars, it had no windows. In summer, twenty-four-hour daylight would detract from the atmosphere, and in winter you're probably in the bar trying to forget what's outside. In early fall, at eight o'clock, the sun was near the western horizon, but going sideways rather than down.

It was deep twilight inside, the stage not yet lighted. Jack Tiemeyer was warming up the piano at the back, but using a gooseneck reading light. That would change in an hour when the hostesses, or *B-girls* in the Fairbanks vernacular, started taking turns with their dance routines. The term for the dancing, by the way, is *exotic*, not lewd and lascivious.

The air was heavy with disinfectant, tobacco smoke, and alcohol. Tables on the right sported a few couples, deep in conversations, or otherwise absorbed with each other. The forty-foot bar was populated in fits and starts. The first two stools supported a couple of gray-whiskered old-timers in plaid shirts and overalls hunched over shot glasses. Farther along, working stiffs or bandits in twos and threes waved beer bottles and bantered. I passed those to plunk down in a vacant stretch, and Satch leaned over to swipe the area with a bar towel.

Satch was a Fairbanks institution: head of a hawk, body of a bear, and no hair apparent. He knew his customers and what they drank, but I'm an out-of-towner so he was waiting for me to name my poison.

"Captain Morgan and Coke." He nodded and bent to the shelves below the mirror for the rum. He dumped a generous shot into a barrel glass, added ice, and ran Coke from a nozzle. He had just set it in front of me on a little paper coaster and I was reaching for it when a bejeweled hand came from behind me and covered the glass.

"Don't drink that. It'll kill your kidneys. Let's you and me get a thirty-dollar bottle of champagne and take it to a table."

She rubbed her breasts across my back when she came around, a cloud of dime-store perfume enveloping a drugstore counter of Revlon and Maybeline. An attractive brunette lurked under the paint and bangles, but no one is ever going to penetrate that far. You can flirt with her, and pretty much anything else you want, if you have enough money, but you'll never be invited beyond the facade. She rubbed herself past my shoulder and settled on the stool beside me with soft warm thigh contact.

"Hi, Jody. Maybe later? I'm meeting a friend." I keep cash rolled in my left front pocket and the bill on the outside was a ten. I would have preferred a five, but it was too late; she'd seen the ten. It was a bribe to make her go away without causing a fuss or burning bridges. "Here, this is just to keep your motor running, but really, not now. You go powder your nose or something."

"Okeydokey, but you don't know what you're missing." She stuffed the bill into her garter and managed to rub me with most of her anatomy while she climbed off her stool. She wandered back to a ringside table to wait for her next victim.

Jody is one of the more attractive, and aggressive, hostesses. She claims to have a degree in mineralogy, but that may be her way of saying she's a gold digger. Anyway, she never wants to talk about minerals or mining. Her favorite subject is what a big, strong, handsome man you are, and if that isn't enough, she segues to how tough it is for a single woman to survive in Fairbanks.

The door opened bringing a flash of light and whiff of fresh air, and it was Stan, hair a little too long, not recently shaved, but still a striking figure. His six-foot, hundred eighty-pound frame, and his damn-the-torpedoes stride were unmistakable, but the rugged profile you'd expect on an actor or an insurance salesman was marred by an uncharacteristic frown. He spotted me and made a beeline. Satch followed him down the bar and set an open Budweiser for him.

Stan clapped me on the shoulder while he sat, a gesture half-way between a hug and a handshake. "Damn, I'm glad you're here, Alex. I can't get my head straight. I don't know whether to be terrified or just have a good laugh, but either way I feel better with you in my corner. Maybe you can talk some sense into me, but if things get rough, I want you beside me with your pistol in your hand."

He was referring to an unfortunate incident a few years back. Bushmaster had kept a helicopter in Aniak that summer so it was an easy run upriver to drop Stan at a likely looking creek above Chuathbaluk. He was doing great, keeping the gold dust in a pint jar instead of the usual film canister. I'd just dropped off the week's groceries when two scruffy types from Chuathbaluk came stomping out of the brush, packing rifles and carrying a sign. In capital letters, the sign proclaimed, PRIVATE PROPERTY NO TRESSPASSING. That was a crock. We were legally on government land. They were planning to plant their sign, back it up with rifles, and scare us off. I jerked my revolver out of my belt; Stan already had his in his hand. Loud enough for the claim jumpers to hear, I said, "You take PROPERTY, I'll take NO." We both shot, the sign flew out of the guy's hand and flopped on the ground behind them. It lay there with a bullet hole in the center of each O; the men and the rifles disappeared into the brush. They weren't looking for a gunfight. They were hoping we'd run away scared, and when we didn't, they did.

I picked a different incident to kid Stan about. "You, terrified? Aren't you the same Stan who faced down a grizzly bear with nothing but a .38 revolver?"

"That was different. Bears are predictable. These are guys I don't know, and if you can believe this, I'm scared just because of the look one gave me. I know, looks can't really kill, but he wanted to—might be planning to." He sampled the beer, set it down, and shook his head like he was trying to wake up.

"Well, are you going to tell me what's going on, or are we playing twenty questions?" I took a sip of my drink, cold, rich, plenty of fizz with an undertone of alcohol. It was ambrosia, and long overdue, kidney killer or no.

Stan took another sip and half turned toward me. "I've been working as an expediter for a couple of pipeline subcontractors.

I needed to send a small engine into Anchorage for repairs, but I got to Interior Air Cargo a little late. The outside door wasn't locked, so I carried the engine back to the freight desk, filled out the paperwork and left it there so the engine would go out on the morning flight."

"Sounds like security's a little lax."

"Hey, this is Fairbanks. We don't even lock our cars. Anyhow, when I walked back past the office, the door was open and two guys were just inside talking. They obviously thought they were alone. I only saw one of them, and when he saw me you'd have thought he'd been struck by lightning."

"So, you overheard something you shouldn't have?" We both sipped again, but it was ritual, busy work. I don't think Stan realized he was drinking, or where we were. He was too distracted by the image in his head.

"That's the weird part. I wasn't paying attention to them. Angie has been working at Channel Two, so I was late picking her up, already thinking about dinner. I've been trying to remember what they were talking about, but all I can recall is the flash of eye contact. You know, if you meet a bear in the woods, he's weighing his options, will run away if he can. Those eyes were like a wolverine, the instinct to attack and kill with no thought involved."

"So you just kept walking?" Satch checked on us, saw we weren't keeping up the usual pace, and wandered back to his strategic spot near the center of action.

"Yeah, I walked straight out to my pickup and went to meet Angie, but I can't shake that look. Alex, I don't mind admitting, I'm scared."

"You must have heard something?"

"I heard...."

The front door burst open and three guys dressed as carpenters stomped in. They were talking loud, laughing, obviously on their second or third bar of the evening, and they headed straight for us. That's a problem with Alaska, and Fairbanks in particular, you recognize everyone you meet and most want to be friendly. Two of the newcomers sat on Stan's left, the other came around and sat on my right. Satch was already there, doling out two Budweisers on the left, a Michelob on the right. I couldn't put names to these guys, but it didn't matter. They'd absorbed enough alcohol to make everyone bosom buddies. The one beside Stan raised his bottle in salute, chugged almost half of it, but couldn't wait to pass the news.

"Hey, did you guys hear about Molly getting busted?"

I shrugged. "You mean this week, or last? What did she do this time, solicit the police chief in his office?"

"No, no, this is really good. See, Oley was trying to sober up in the Coffee Cup Café. She latched onto him and dragged him up the back stairs at the Nordale and into her room." That was as long as he could go without a drink; he had to stop and chug. I glanced at Stan and he was getting agitated, hands almost fidgeting, toying with his beer bottle. He'd worked himself up to confide, maybe embarrassed himself a little, and wasn't taking the interruption well.

The two straight men were swilling and grinning, urging the spokesman on. "Well, see, Oley had just got his pants off when two detectives busted in the door." He sipped fast, but couldn't wait for the punch line. "So, Oley is standing there, naked and all, but the cops didn't go for him. They went straight to the closet and pulled out these two teenyboppers."

That wasn't specific enough for the guy on his left. He chimed in, "Real youngies, man, like high school. San Quentin quail for sure." He lifted his bottle and drained it. Our narrator took over.

"See, it turns out Molly was teaching them the trade. She had them stashed in the closet to watch."

The one on my right stopped sucking his bottle long enough to insert, "She should have asked me, man. I'd have taught them the trade for free." He went back to nursing and the narrator took over.

"See, the thing is, if Oley can't convince the DA he didn't know the girls were in the closet, we won't see him no more for prob'ly twenty years."

Stan gave me the elbow and extricated himself from the confab. "Hey, Alex, we're late. We'd better hit the road."

"Right." I stood and Satch materialized in front of us. I did the math, dropped a twenty on the bar. "Round for our buddies here. Sorry fellas, gotta split."

Stan strode toward the door. I was right behind him but Jody caught me in the doorway with a bear hug and stood on tiptoes for a kiss. "My motor's in overdrive, big boy. I get off at three."

"Right, thanks."

Stan was crunching across the gravel toward his pickup, but Jody was glued to my arm. "You won't forget?" She strained up for one more kiss, booze, tobacco, chalk-flavored lipstick, and tongue like an agitated snake.

"Sure, I'll tattoo three o'clock on my forehead." I shook her off and started after Stan. I had ten feet to go and was already reaching toward the door when Stan started his engine. The door shot toward me, knocked me halfway back across the lot, and a belch of flame felt like it seared off my face.

Chapter Two

I must have been out for a while. I found myself sitting on the gravel, leaning against the rough logs beside the step. The lot was full of noisy people milling around, cop cars and a fire truck rotated red-and-blue flashes across the scene. Stan's pickup was a smoldering wreck. I couldn't even look at it.

My head was in black fog but struggling out, and the first cogent thought was, *Angie.* I suddenly had the feeling that I needed to get to her, fast. I wobbled to my feet. Everything was sore but apparently nothing was broken. The crowd had its back to me so I slunk behind them to my pickup, using the logs for support. My forehead felt wet. I swiped it with the back of my hand and it came away bloody, but sticky and congealed, not flowing.

The engine started on the first revolution, and I turned left on the Steese. I burned the new paving, fishtailed onto Hot Springs Road with a shower of gravel, and blasted into the hills. I didn't know why, but the feeling that I needed to get to Angie was a palpable presence, and it was shoving down on the gas pedal.

Angie is spawn of the Kuskokwim, specifically the Demoski clan from Crooked Creek. She grew up in a one-room log cabin with the smell of the river always with her and counting the seasons by its changes. By the time she was ten years old, she was braced in the back of a riverboat, helping to pull in driftnets full of salmon. The river was in her blood, and probably a lot of her blood was in the river. She grew into a tall, slender figure with flowing black-silk tresses from her Athabaskan Indian ancestors, but a touch of Russian genes had softened her features into that classic beauty you see in magazine ads for tropical vacations. She'd been waitress and maid at the lodge in McGrath the summer Stan had filtered the black sand and rubies, but barely a thimble full of gold, out of Alexander Creek.

Instead of camping on the creek as usual, Stan had headquartered at the lodge, borrowed a riverboat, and commuted to his digs. I figured at the time that Angie had a lot to do with that. When they met in Fairbanks that winter, maybe by design, they melded like gold to mercury. Stan forgot about prospecting and worked odd jobs around Fairbanks. Angie was obviously the best thing that ever happened to him.

Their cabin site in the woods was probably picked because the Little Chena River came right to their backyard. The Little Chena isn't much, compared to the Kuskokwim, but it is a river. It marks the seasons with freeze-up and break-up, and is home to grayling and seasonal salmon.

The pickup floated on its springs when I topped the final hill, no shock absorbers, of course. I stood on the brake and threw gravel to make the turn through the woods into their driveway. It was getting dark, but Angie hadn't yet started the generator to turn on lights. She was framed in the big picture window wearing jeans and plaid shirt, and she was radiating anxiety.

I slid to a stop ten feet from their steps. She had the door open before I got to the porch, but was staring at me in shock. "Alex?" It was a question. It hadn't occurred to me how bad I must look. My face had that tight painful feeling like the second day in the Miami sun, and I realized the strange stench I'd been ignoring was burned hair.

"Where is Stan?" She was trying to see past me, like maybe he was in the pickup. She already knew the answer, but was obviously clinging to hope.

"Angie, I'm so terribly sorry." My expression must have said it all.

She screamed and crumpled. I caught her and guided her onto the couch. She sat forward, elbows on knees, hands covering her face, and rocked like an autistic child. It might have been easier if she'd been sobbing, but her shock was too deep for that. I put a hand on her shoulder. "Angie...."

"What happened, Alex?"

"It was a bomb in his truck. It was instant, he never felt a thing." That was the only comfort I could offer.

"But, why, why, why?"

"Angie, I don't know, but I promise you this. I'll find out, and whoever did it will wish they were already in hell."

She slammed her fist down on her knee. "Damn, men are so *stupid.* He picked me up from work looking like he was seeing ghosts, and he kept telling me that nothing was wrong. He didn't want to worry me, right? Damn him, that worried me ten times more, and now he's...gone?" She jumped up and ran for their bedroom.

I just stood there. Sobbing from the bedroom was the sound of abject grief, but she obviously wanted to be alone. The realities were finally sinking in for me, too, and I didn't need an audience to watch me rub my eyes. The stone fireplace on the left had a birch fire already laid, waiting for a match to turn it into the centerpiece of a cozy evening. I kept glancing at the door, still expecting Stan to come bursting in, light the fire, and bellow for Angie to come give him a kiss. Sudden death, often violent, is very much a part of life in the Arctic, but is normally due to accidents. My mind was refusing to accept what I'd seen.

Stan and Angie had built the double-studded, double-insulated house with its ten-inch-thick walls to last a hundred years. The three doors on the right were the spare bedroom, the bath, and the master bedroom at the back, next to the kitchen and dining table. The front bedroom had always struck me as a nursery for future use, but now....

Gravel crunched when a car stopped out on the road, and that was strange. I stepped to the big double-paned window. Twilight was deepening, but slowly. Sun above the overcast would be scooting sideways along the horizon, so there was just enough light to show the figures striding down the lane.

They were two uniformed city cops, but why had they parked out of sight? Then I noticed that one was carrying a rifle. What the devil? Cops should come to break the news to Angie, but they couldn't have been that fast. Maybe they followed me. Maybe it's a crime to leave a scene like that, but they hadn't been in my mirrors.

They paused forty feet from my pickup. The tall one gestured, the one with the rifle turned between the trees to circle the house. The tall one drew his automatic but held it out of sight, almost behind him, and strode toward the door. Did they think I was armed and dangerous? I opened the door, hands up, palms out.

"Hi, officer, I'm not armed. What's the problem?"

He was obviously surprised to see me. He stopped dead and stared. They must have come for Angie, but with weapons drawn and circling the house? I suddenly realized that he wasn't wearing a badge, and he was swinging his automatic up toward me. I slammed the door and dove for the carpet. Two .45 slugs punched through the door, throwing splinters, and slammed into the wall behind me.

Turk, Stan's eighty-pound husky, set up a frantic ruckus of barking and snarling in the backyard. I crawled for the bedroom. Angie was lying on her belly on the bed, hugging a pillow. Her eyes will haunt me forever: red rimmed, tears brimming, but they were empty.

The shots and my scrambling across the carpet on all fours jerked her back to the present. "What's the matter, what's happening?"

"I don't know. Where's Stan's shotgun?"

"It's in the closet."

The shotgun and a .30-06 hunting rifle were leaning against the back of the closet. I grabbed the twelve gauge, pump action, three shells, and jacked one into the chamber. Turk was outside the bedroom window, growling and lunging at his chain, concentrating on the woods past the end of the house. Stan had set a pole in the middle of the backyard and Turk was tethered to a ring on top of it.

"Is Stan's canoe still on the riverbank?"

"Yeah, it's there. Alex, what is happening?"

"Angie, I haven't the foggiest, but two guys are here to kill us. Grab your jacket and crawl, don't walk, to the back door. When you hear me shoot, run for the canoe, and leave the door open." She got the message, grabbed a denim jacket from a hook behind the bedroom door, hunched down and ran. I raised the window sash. The twelve-gauge belched an explosion of fire and smoke and splintered the top of the pole. Turk's eyebolt ripped loose and he was into the trees like a shot.

I was setting a new personal best, but it was a long fifty-foot run across the yard to the riverbank. It was almost dark, but I could see Angie crouched down wrestling to turn over the canoe. The sounds of cursing and crashing brush were coming from the trees on the right, much too close. I handed Angie the shotgun, grabbed the canoe, flipped it over, and shoved the craft into the water. Angie scooped up two paddles that had been under the canoe, cradled them and the shotgun, and scrambled in on elbows and knees. I shoved us out into the river, grabbed the shotgun out of Angie's bundle, and sprawled on top of her. Two shots came from the woods, a yelp from Turk, then silence.

Angie lay flat on the aluminum canoe bottom. I raised up on my elbows and stuck the shotgun over the side, but realized that if I fired over the side, recoil would roll the canoe. Trees were moving by fast; we drifted toward mid river. Stan's clearing disappeared behind us and nothing moved along the bank. I turned around carefully, propped the gun on the rear seat where it would be safe to shoot over the stern, and waited.

The river gurgled. A splash and an angry slap ahead of us was a disturbed beaver. Cold water had turned the aluminum hull to an instant icicle, and the air was heavy with moisture, smelling of wet dirt and dead leaves. The canoe slowly turned crosswise to the current. Birch trees on both banks were dark and silent.

Chapter Three

I'd been wishing it were darker, now we could have used some light. In fall, the river was low but still clipping along at ten miles per. Angie sat on the front seat with a paddle; I was at the rear, but we weren't trying to make time, just trying to steer. Shores were black now, the ragged silhouettes of trees barely darker than the sky. Water was just a little lighter than the banks, a twisting, roiling rope reflecting overcast sky. The temperature had dropped twenty degrees when the sun went down, and I guessed it was near freezing.

The Little Chena seemed to be turning constantly. The insides of curves were gravel bars, the outside crumbling banks with fallen trees waiting to impale us. Sometimes it was thirty feet across, sometimes the trees almost met overhead. Mostly, we were steering by sound. Mid river was deep and silent. When we heard water rushing around rocks or splashing against snags, Angie dug in and paddled around them. I tried to keep us aligned with the current.

In a straight line it might be ten miles to the junction with the main Chena, then another ten to Fairbanks, but the way that creek was twisting, it was probably twice that. Good that no roads come near the river until town. Also good that there had been some frost so we weren't fighting swarms of mosquitoes.

Angie screamed, "Look out!" and fell backward off her seat. I ducked, and a fallen birch whacked me in the head and scraped across my back.

"You okay?" She was lying on her back looking up at me.

"Yeah, I'm fine, but if you hadn't hollered, I'd have been knocked off the stern." The bow hit something, shuddered, and we turned sideways. We were caught by another birch that had fallen into the water and the current was trying to shove us under it or smash us against it.

The tree, maybe four inches in diameter, was still attached to the right bank, and we were snared in the branches. "Grab something, push us this way." We were shoving, like climbing a tree sideways. The canoe wanted to roll, the river was furious at being blocked. We were stuck, black water boiling up with a hungry roar, inches from swamping us. The pressure seemed to be crushing the canoe. We scrabbled frantically at branches and the trunk, moved a few inches backward toward mid river.

"Again, together, *push*." We slid a few more inches, branches bending and breaking like pistol shots. Water drops slapped us, so cold they seemed to burn our skin. The stern cleared the branches and swung to drag us downriver. Broken branches scraping across aluminum sounded like giant nails on a blackboard, but we pulled free and were racing again, now backward.

I was still trying to sit up, digging leaves out of my hair and collar, when the stern plowed into gravel with a crunch and stopped. A whinny like a startled horse erupted right beside us. A black silhouette of moose that looked the size of a mountain reared up and spun away. He crashed into the brush and was gone.

I reached over the side and found three inches of freezing water over gravel. "Sit tight," I whispered. "Maybe we should stop and think while we're still able." I crouched, held onto the sides, stepped over the back seat, and over the stern onto dry gravel. "Okay, come on."

"Alex, I lost my paddle."

"Least of our problems."

I steadied the canoe while she climbed past me, then pulled it up onto the rocks. I could still smell the moose. He was sporting some powerful musk, and I guess that smells good to lady moose. It reminded me of childhood on the farm and horses in the rain.

"How you holding up?" I asked.

"Nearly frozen, but not drowned."

With our frantic gyrations on the water, I hadn't noticed how wet we were. When we stopped moving, the cold air took over and suddenly had us shivering. My hands felt like clubs and seemed to be permanently curled to fit the paddle.

"Let's find some wood and build a fire." I tried to pretend the situation was normal and survivable. "I don't suppose you thought to bring hot dogs?"

Angie joined me in the game. "Damn, I'm so forgetful, but I might have enough branches in my hair for a campfire." She dropped down to crawl along the gravel bar, feeling for driftwood. I turned toward the trees and ran smack into a medium-sized spruce. Spruce usually have dead branches at the base, and this one did. I broke off an armload of tinder-dry dead stuff without getting my eyes poked out.

Branch tips fanned out into lace. I wadded a snowball of the tiny twigs, held my lighter under it, and it blossomed to blessed light. By the time I'd built a teepee of branches over the tinder, Angie was back, dragging several chunks of driftwood. Our fire lit a circle of canoe, black rushing river, dry gravel bar, and trees. Angie sat down on the gravel, cross-legged, leaning toward the fire, but she was shivering spasmodically, her teeth chattering. I knelt behind her, opened my windbreaker, and pulled her against my chest. It was brotherly and practical, and that's the way she took it. She leaned into my embrace, and the shivering subsided.

"Talk to me, Alex. What's going on?"

"Right now, what we're doing is trying to stay alive. If we swamp the canoe, we'll be dead. Even if we swim out, which is highly unlikely, with wet clothes and nearly freezing temperature, we'd be gone without a trace. It's probably twenty miles to Fairbanks, at least five back to the cabin. And if we go back, we might get shot."

"But why? Why on earth would anyone want to hurt Stan?"

"Pure irony. Someone thinks he overheard something that he shouldn't have. The irony is, I don't think he really caught anything damning. He wasn't even sure what they thought he overheard, and he never got a chance to tell me even what that might have been. What we know now is that these guys are desperate and deadly. They must have monitored our radio conversation and our plan to meet. Stan was in the club less than ten minutes, so they must have been waiting in the lot for him.

"The other irony is that I owe my life to Jody. She saw me with a roll of cash and when I started to leave the club with bankroll intact, she panicked and tried to climb my frame in the doorway. Otherwise, I'd have been in the pickup with Stan."

Angie shivered and snuggled closer, but it wasn't the cold. "And you think the guys at the cabin came to kill me?"

"Yes, I do. They assume that Stan told you whatever it was. They know he went to the club to talk to me, so now I'm part of the imaginary threat. Those guys were dressed as cops, probably just so you would open the door, but they weren't wearing badges, so let's hope to heck they weren't real cops."

"If they weren't real cops, where did they get the uniforms?"

"That's the scariest part. Angie, these guys are professionals. Putting a bomb in a truck in a matter of minutes took skill and practice. Cop uniforms are generic until they put on patches and badges, so they're probably tools of the trade. They might have even worn them while they worked on the truck. No one would have questioned them."

The moose must have been lurking. Maybe he came for a drink and we interrupted him too soon. He did some snorting and stamping just outside the firelight. We'd made a problem for him. His experience had taught him that this was a safe place to drink, but we were in his way. He was reluctant to take the chance and scout another drinking spot. Since it was a night for ironies, that was another. His instinct to return to known safe spots is exactly what gets him killed. Hunters find where he drinks, or where he sleeps, and wait for him. I wondered if that principle applied to us and Stan's cabin. I helped the moose by tossing a rock at him. He grunted and crashed away.

I released Angie from the hug and got up to tend the fire. One of the chunks she'd found was cottonwood, six inches thick and four feet long, that had been chewed off at both ends by beaver. I banked the fire against it, added branches and chips until it flared up, then used the light to gather more wood. My Casio said twenty-three hundred, which translates to eleven o'clock. I was guessing four or five hours until daylight would let us onto the river safely.

I found several more beaver-severed logs, so a dam must have burst, probably during spring flood. With enough wood to keep us warm for several hours, I sat down beside Angie again, lightly brushing shoulders.

"Are they going to kill us, Alex?"

"Not if we can help it, and every hour that goes by is to our advantage. We didn't know we were in danger, and Stan wasn't even sure there was a problem at all. Now, I'll recognize at least one of them and we'll be on guard. The good thing is that they won't recognize you. They may have gotten a glimpse of me at the club or the house, but I was cleverly disguised as a disaster survivor so they might not know me if I clean up my act."

Angie nodded and turned her back to lean against me. "Hold me, Alex. Just hold me and don't talk. I want to pretend that you're Stan. Do you know how wonderful it is for a woman to have a man like him? I thought we were safe against the whole world."

I slipped my arm around her and pulled her close. The fire burned down, the shadows deepened. The river made swishing and gurgling noises. Angie was sobbing quietly. Each in our own way, we were mourning Stan. Angie's hair held the perfume of the life that was gone, the slender strength of her a touchstone in the wilderness, the assurance that life could, must, go on.

The moose slipped out of the woods, almost silently in spite of his four-foot rack. He'd moved thirty feet downstream and ignored us. He took a long drink, raised his massive head, and faded back into the trees.

Chapter Four

By four o'clock I could see across the river and make out shapes of trees, rather than silhouettes. The overcast was still solid, but turning from black to charcoal gray. I let the fire go out, scattered the embers, and rolled our smoldering hearth log into the river. The canoe was dry, shotgun and one paddle leaned against the back seat. I shoved it halfway into the water and steadied it while Angie got settled in front, then shoved us out and vaulted aboard.

We'd wound around two bends, and we seemed to be racing. If I'd realized how fast we'd been moving in the dark, I'd have stopped sooner. We'd covered perhaps a quarter mile when we saw a flash of blond wood caught in a tangle of brush ahead. I backed water hard, steered next to the bank and grabbed a root. We slid to a tentative stop against the crumbling mud. Angie saw her paddle, scrambled up the slope, and risked her life to reach out and grab it.

She slid down the bank, resumed her seat, dug her paddle in like a trooper, and together we steered around the brush pile and followed the current. Hopper Creek came in from our right and the river channel broadened and straightened. In another twenty minutes we were spewed out into the main Chena River and headed for Fairbanks on what looked like a highway.

With the river thirty yards wide instead of thirty feet, we relaxed and drifted. The water seemed to have stopped and the banks were gliding by. It was almost silent, just the occasional murmur or hiss when something submerged ruffled the surface. Angie leaned her paddle against the seat, wrapped arms around her shoulders and hunkered against the cold.

If the sun had been out, it would have been a postcard moment. Birch and aspen were tinged with yellow, occasional patches of blueberry bushes dark red, all counter-pointed by green spruce. Fairbanks can be gorgeous in the fall, but it's an abbreviated season. Some years it's less than ten days from the first tinge of color to a stark white blanket. I took a couple of strokes to keep us straight with the current. The swish of paddle was replaced by an almost subliminal hum.

It got louder fast, rising and falling as the river turned, but unmistakably a boat was coming upstream. My scalp got that tingling, urgent feeling.

"Quick, Angie, right-hand bank." We both dug in, raced for the shore. A four-foot-wide sandbar fronted a two-foot-high dark loam bank. We buried our nose in sand. Angie jumped out and steadied the canoe while I hunched forward. We each grabbed a side, boosted the canoe over the bank, and shoved it into the trees. We had just scrambled up after it when a boat came around the next bend, moving upriver fast.

It was small, but had a canvas canopy, like the boats you see towing water-skiers around Harding Lake. In the north, the usual riverboats are eighteen feet long and six feet wide with flat bottoms for sliding over sandbars. They're capable of hauling a ton of salmon in the spring, or a couple of moose in the fall, workboats, not pleasure craft.

I hunkered down behind the canoe to keep the aluminum from showing, and we watched through leaves while the boat passed. Definitely two men, definitely with rifles, but we couldn't be sure of much else. The boat raced on up the river. When it disappeared around the next bend, I climbed down onto the sandbar to listen.

The sound was steady for a couple of minutes, then slowed and seemed to come from the left, so they had turned up the Little Chena. I crouched down next to the water and smoothed the cut our bow had made, then brushed away the footprints and climbed back up the bank.

"Let's drag the canoe farther back so it won't show."

"They're looking for us, aren't they, Alex?"

"Maybe…no, probably. I think they turned up the Little Chena. Thing is, we're ripe for paranoia." I picked up the front of the canoe, Angie the back, and we half carried, half slid it thirty feet into the brush. I grabbed the shotgun and we slipped back to the edge of the trees.

Angie's denim jacket and jeans were reasonably inconspicuous. My dark green windbreaker was fortuitous, not intentional good management. We sat on the cold ground and listened for maybe ten minutes before we heard the motor again, this time slow and quiet.

"Alex, they couldn't have gone all the way to the cabin."

"They didn't. They found our campfire. I scattered it enough to be sure it was out, but not enough to hide it. Sorry, put that on the long list of things I haven't thought of lately."

The boat came around the last bend, moving slowly down the middle of the river. We flopped on our bellies and I jacked another shell into the shotgun.

"Are you going to shoot them, Alex?"

"No, darn it, and I probably should. Angie, they could be moose hunters out scouting for a blind. We don't know that they're after us, don't even know if the phony cops who came to the cabin are the same ones who bombed Stan's truck, or if any of them were the guys Stan heard. If they beach the boat and come for the bank with weapons, I'll cut them in half, but we don't want to blow away a couple of innocent hunters."

We stopped talking. The boat passed slowly, mid river, one passenger watching each bank, and continued around the next bend.

"Did they spot us?" Angie was concerned, not frightened. I realized I was seeing the culmination of generations of her ancestors who had faced possible death on a daily basis. If lives were at risk, and if I couldn't have Stan, then she was the next best partner.

"They didn't even bobble, so if they saw us, they're the greatest poker players since Dan McGrew. Let's get the boat in the water."

We'd been on the water again for less than ten minutes before my internal radar was screaming at me.

"Angie, we've got to get off the river. We could come around any bend and run smack into them. If they dropped off one man on the bank with a rifle, we'd go by like wooden ducks in a shooting gallery."

Both of us were feeling urgency and paddling fast. Angie answered over her shoulder, "How about the Chena Slough? Can't be more than one or two bends ahead, and that runs right next to Badger Loop Road."

"Great, let's go for it." We hugged the left-hand bank, rounded a deep bend to the south, and paddled like mad out of the river, through an eddy and into the slough. With almost no current in the backwater, we scooted upstream, plowing a swath of ripples through mirror-still water, riffling reflections of overhanging trees. Houses appeared through the trees on the bank, then a thick stand of uninterrupted birch.

"Let's stash the canoe."

Angie nodded and pulled toward the right bank. I steadied us with my paddle while she climbed out and held the canoe for me. We dragged it twenty feet up into blueberry bushes and high bush cranberries, the berries long gone, leaves turned to crimson. I wedged the shotgun under the rear seat and we turned the canoe over. If someone lifted one edge and looked, they'd see the paddles, but maybe not the shotgun. Still, I had the feeling I'd seen the last of the gun, and probably the canoe as well.

Angie looked at me and wrinkled her nose. "If you're planning to hitchhike, you'd better wash your face. You look like the *Night of the Living Dead*."

I knelt on the bank and scooped handsful of cold water onto my face, but still had that sunburned feeling. I blotted rather than rubbed, and noticed it was about time for a shave. Angie reached for my handkerchief and cleaned around the cut on my forehead.

"Okay, you look sick, but not frightening. You do carry a pocket comb?" She accepted the comb and worked the twigs out of her hair. That was an amazing process with pulling that would have snatched me bald. Her hair hangs well past her shoulders and she was holding strands in front of her to untangle the ends. Finally she shrugged it all back in place, ran the comb through it one more time, then worked on me. I had a terrible case of split ends, or maybe frizzies, where I'd been singed. We brushed down clothes, pronounced each other acceptable, and climbed through the bushes. Badger Loop Road was just over the hill.

Angie surveyed the empty gravel road with a skeptical scowl. "Which way shall we walk?"

"Doesn't matter much, either way leads to Richardson Highway so we can hitchhike in either direction, but let's head toward town. When we snag a ride, I'd rather it was headed for Fairbanks than Eielson. Fact is, I'm ready for some breakfast, or the dinner we didn't have last night."

"Yeah, I know what you mean. I'd sell my soul for a cup of coffee." We turned right and trudged down the center of the road.

"You're selling your soul too cheap. How about a big stack of blueberry pancakes, plenty of melted butter, with a couple of poached eggs and link sausage on the side?" We were leaving trees behind with the slough, passing scrub alders and willows. Thirty feet on each side of the road were dust covered. Beyond the gray dusting, tufts of grass looked brown and dead, leaves scraggly and dying.

Angie seemed to be considering. "How about a big order of eggs Benedict, really good hollandaise with lots of lemon juice, black olives on top and no turkey slice?"

"Good, toss in a couple of glasses of orange juice and our own coffeepot."

We'd walked in silence for ten minutes when the sound of a motor turned us around in unison. We nipped to the side of the road and stuck out our thumbs. If it was our pursuers we were dead anyway, no place to run or hide. It was a big blue crew-cab pickup with only the driver, and he looked young. He was wearing civvies, but he was clean-shaven and his haircut looked military. He slid to a stop, covering us with dust, but unintentionally. He rolled down a window.

"Hi, you guys are a long ways from nowhere."

"Right," I said, "car trouble. Can you give us a lift toward Fairbanks?"

"Sure, hop in. I'm headed for Fort Wainright."

He unlocked the passenger door and pushed it open. Angie scrambled up with me right behind her. He'd stopped in the middle of the road, so no need to check mirrors. He dropped the big rig into drive and we were off with a surge of quiet power.

"You have a car accident?" he asked. He was looking at the cut on my forehead.

"Not really, had to take the ditch to miss a moose. Car's fine, we just need to grab our truck to pull it out."

He nodded. That's such a classic Alaskan story that it almost goes without saying.

"You live out here?" Angie asked.

"Yep, wife and I bought five acres from the Markey homestead. Right now we just have a trailer house, but we have electricity and we have a company coming next week to bore a well. We'll start building a real house next summer."

"It's a terrific area." Angie said, apparently not referring to the brush and swamp we were passing.

"Yeah, we like it. Real quiet. We're expecting our first baby early next spring, and this is the sort of place where we want to raise our family."

A stop sign announced the Richardson Highway. Traffic was rushing in both directions. The two lanes on the far side were probably people who lived in Fairbanks but worked at Eielson AFB. Our side was gushing with people who lived out on the highway but worked in Fairbanks. Our host picked a gap in the line of traffic that was actually longer than the pickup, turned right, and burned rubber to join the queue.

Chapter Five

He dropped us at the corner of Gaffney and Cushman and we hiked two blocks down the dusty sidewalk to the Fairbanks Inn. The stone front creates a medieval castle effect, but behind that is steel and glass. I stopped Angie outside the entrance.

"Do you mind if we share a room?"

"Are you kidding? You're not leaving me alone." She looked quizzical, wondering why I had asked. It was a sop to my culture, where single men and women who share rooms have ulterior motives. In her culture, whole families, both sexes, and sometimes three generations, share a one- or two-room cabin with no problems. The no-problems part was what I had in mind. We needed to keep an eye on each other and think together. Sharing a room solved a whole spectrum of potential problems.

The receptionist struck me as a Filipina, dark, wavy hair surrounding a pretty moon face. She was too young but striving to make up for that with an air of ultra sophistication. She'd noticed that we weren't carrying luggage, and we probably did look as if we'd spent the night barhopping. I would have liked to register under a phony name, but was going to have to use a credit card, so the card and the register should match. I settled for Mr. and Mrs. Alex Price. The receptionist was doing fine until I suggested that we preferred twin beds. That destroyed her view of the world. She flipped a page in her ledger, found a room on the second floor, and handed me a key.

"We need two keys."

She produced a second one. I handed one to Angie. "Food or shower?"

"Shower, thirty seconds, then that soul's worth of breakfast you tortured me with." Stairs led up from the lobby. Our room was halfway down a long, carpeted hall and had a sealed plate glass window overlooking Cushman Street. I don't know why they call those twin beds. Each was the size of a queen, but with a four-foot aisle between them. We had two chairs, a dresser with a TV bolted on top, a nightstand between the beds with two reading lights and a telephone. A door led to a bathroom where Angie was already running the shower.

She was out in minutes, wearing towels and carrying her clothes. "Your turn."

A hot shower and clean-smelling soap can be life's greatest pleasures under some circumstances. However, the restaurant was calling. Angie had left me a towel. I dried, flapped my clothes to shake the dust out, and dressed. I took one more swipe at my strange new hairline, and tapped on the door before I opened it. She was dressed, fussing at her hair, and extended a now clean hand. I put my comb in it. She went back into the bathroom for one more minute, and we almost ran to the coffee shop.

Breakfast was still in progress. I was surprised to notice that it was only eight in the morning. It seemed like the end of a very long day. We must have looked desperate because in two minutes we were served coffee and orange juice, and in five more we were on refills and tucking into our dream breakfasts.

Angie demolished half an English muffin and seemed to approve of the hollandaise. She blotted her lips and sipped coffee. "What's the plan, Alex?"

"My pistol's in my flight bag at the airport. I'm going to feel a lot better when it's in my belt. After that?" I shrugged. "Stan mentioned that you're working at a TV station?"

"Yes, Channel Two, but not for a while. I just couldn't. Alex, I can't even think about normal things. If I let myself realize what's happened, I want to start screaming. I'll call in."

"Yeah, I guess I'd better call Bethel. Vicki will be wondering what I've done with the airplane."

"Alex, you won't go back to Bethel and leave me?"

"Angie, Stan was my brother in every way that matters, and you're my sister. No, I won't leave you. I don't believe in blood feuds, eye for an eye and all that, but we have to find his killers so he can rest easy, and neither of us will be safe until we do."

"Won't the police find them?"

"Maybe. Let's hope so, but we're a lot more motivated. Besides, the guys who came to the house were wearing police uniforms. I really think they were phony, but maybe we shouldn't rush to find out."

We finished and signaled for the bill. I added a twenty-percent tip, signed the tab, and we strolled back up to the room considerably more comfortable. We sat on the beds on either side of the nightstand. Angie motioned for me to go first. I picked up the phone and dialed Bethel but left the handset in the cradle so it was a speakerphone.

"Bushmaster Air Alaska."

"Hi, Vickie, little problem here."

"Alex, you didn't wreck the 310?"

"No, no, airplane's fine. This is a personal problem, but I might be here a while."

"Alex, if you weren't a partner, you know I'd fire your sorry ass. You just met the most beautiful girl in the world, right?"

"As a matter of fact she's here right now, but it's Angie, Stan's wife. Vickie, Stan was killed last night."

"Oh no, oh damn. Alex, do what you have to do, and tell Angie I'm terribly sorry."

"Thanks Vic, I'll keep you posted." I punched the *End* button, shoved the phone over to Angie, and lay back on the bed. It did feel very good.

Angie punched buttons and the phone said, "KTUU."

"Hi, Lydia, it's Angie."

"Oh, my God, Angie, how *are* you? We got the police report about the accident, and we knew it was Stan's truck, but they said only one person in it. Are you all right?"

"Not yet, but maybe I will be. Lydia, I need a few days off."

"Of course, we've got you covered. Oh, honey, I'm just so glad you're okay."

The word *accident* had me sitting up in shock. I mouthed, "Accident?"

"Lydia, exactly what did the police say about Stan's truck?"

"I don't remember the exact words. Do you want me to read you the report? It's in the newsroom."

"No, just tell me what you heard."

"Well, it was a freak accident, one chance in billions. It was something to do with a gas line breaking and the spark igniting fumes. Angie, the whole station is broken up over this. Everyone sends their love."

"Thanks, Lydia, I'll stay in touch." Angie hung up slowly.

"Accident?" I think we said it together and sat staring at each other. I got up to pace, but there wasn't enough room, so I punched the wall with my fist. That hurt enough to get my brain back in gear.

"Alex, could it have been an accident?"

I paused to add two and two and two before I answered her. "No, it could not have been an accident. Things like that happen in boats sometimes, fumes in closed spaces. Cars can catch on fire, but no, they do not explode. Stan was scared, and it wasn't paranoia. The guys who came to your house were real, and they came to kill us. I did not imagine the .45 slugs through your front door. Those were not hunters on the river this morning, or rather, they were, and they were hunting for us. So, no, it was no accident. Now, are we dealing with a police cover-up or just the usual incompetence?"

"What do we do, Alex?"

"First, we rent a car and I get my pistol in my belt. Don't you need things from the house?"

"Desperately. My purse, a hair dryer, some clothes. Do we dare go back?"

"Let's find out."

Avis brought a green Dodge Dart to the hotel. We dropped the driver back at their office in the Polaris building and did the paperwork before we headed to the airport.

I walked around the airplane three times, looked up under the cowlings, climbed up on the wing and looked into the cabin, no apparent tampering. Still, I took a deep breath and turned my head away when I used the key to unlock the baggage compartment behind the wing.

The flight bag is a heavy canvas duffel, loaded with survival gear in case you put an airplane down in the tundra. It holds sleeping bags, space blankets, buddy burner, mess kit, chocolate, water purification tablets, beef jerky, and necessary tools. The implements on the bottom of the bag are hatchet and spade; the one on top is my .357 magnum revolver and a box of Speer copper clads.

There are lots of sexier James Bond-type pistols around, like Glocks and Walthers, but those are for making movies, not survival in the bush. In the unlikely event that Speer ever makes a dud, a revolver doesn't jam. You pull the trigger again and fire the next round. It's not meant to spray an area with lead. It just puts a whopping hundred-and-sixty-grain missile precisely where it's pointed with enough velocity to penetrate the first two or three things it hits.

Mine is the Smith and Wesson patrolman model with a six-inch barrel. It's not quite a rifle, but as far as I know, it's still the most powerful and accurate handgun ever made, and it felt very good jammed into my belt with the windbreaker covering it.

If you know Alaska's gun laws, you're wincing, and rightly so. You can carry any weapon you wish, so long as it's showing, but it requires a license to carry it concealed, and I do have that. It's almost a joke, but in Bethel my most faithful charter customers are Alaska State Troopers, and theoretically they travel alone in the legal sense, but with a charter pilot. If the trooper is a good friend, situations just naturally come up that are illegal. My getting a private detective license doesn't make the events legal, just a little less illegal. Anyhow, the troopers conned me into it. I sent eight hundred bucks to the Professional Career Development Institute, read two good books in the Private Investigator Course, took twenty open-book tests, and got a handsome diploma. The diploma and a twenty-dollar bill got me the license that made it legal to pull my windbreaker over the pistol.

I rejoined Angie in the Dart. "Up for a drive through the woods on this glorious fall morning?"

"If you say so. Stan said he'd trust you with his life, so I should do the same."

That stopped conversation. We were both thinking that Stan had trusted me one too many times, and I had let him down.

We approached the driveway slowly, scanning the woods on both sides for snipers, hidden vehicles, anything out of place. I parked the car at the entrance to the drive and walked down the lane, pistol in hand, looking for traps. I'd let Stan down; I was not going to do the same for Angie. The driveway was clean, with only my pickup parked in front. I went back for the Dart, feeling a little foolish or paranoid.

I parked ten feet behind the pickup. When Angie stepped out of the car, a streak burst from the woods with a banshee howl and a clatter of dragged chain. Turk jumped onto her, paws on her shoulders, and knocked her flat. I grabbed the chain and dug in my heels to pull him off. He was licking Angie's face with the apparent intention of drowning or smothering her.

She sat up and wrapped arms around the big animal's neck. He was still licking her, and she crooned and rocked him. He had a nasty gash across his head, the thick hair matted with dried blood, and Angie was carefully petting his forehead below the wound.

"Stay put," I said, but apparently they intended to. I walked around the pickup once, gun in hand again, and didn't see anything amiss, but I didn't touch it. I gave the house the same once-around. If a curtain had moved, or something stirred in the woods, I would have shot it.

The window I'd used to shoot Turk's tether was still up, the back door still open. I looked them over for wires, but common sense said they were safe. The phony cops had come to shoot whoever was in the house, not to plant bombs. I walked in through the back door, and through the house, checking the bedrooms and the bath. All were empty and still. The front door had two nickel-sized holes, so I had not imagined those. I opened the perforated door. Angie struggled up and unclipped the chain from Turk's collar. They came in together, Turk rubbing himself against her legs at every step. They headed to the kitchen and dishes rattled. I stationed myself in the front door and watched the drive.

With only one way in or out we were in a trap, but it was also, in a way, a fortress. No one was going to come up the river without the sound of an engine announcing it. Trees blocked the view of the road, but I figured I could hear any approaching traffic and I was straining ears. This far out, the only normal traffic would be headed for the hot springs, and that's maybe a couple of cars per week. I kept the pistol in my hand, and continued telling myself that the silence and isolation were good things.

A pair of camp robbers fluttered down from a big cottonwood tree and stalked around the Dodge, heads up, chests out, marching like Hitler's Gestapo, the picture of pompous dignity. They decided the Dodge wasn't edible and flew up into the trees. Angie was back in ten minutes, wearing slacks and sweater, a suit jacket and a tiny purse over her arm. She carried an overnight case in her hand. Turk was still trying to trip her at every step. I took the case and stashed it in the front seat while Angie and Turk climbed into the back.

With the key in the ignition, I paused to turn around. Turk was nestled down with his head in Angie's lap. I had to reach over the seat and stroke his forehead. "Looks like you could use a vet, big boy. Thanks for saving our lives, by the way."

"He really did, didn't he? There's a vet at Creamer's Dairy."

I set the pistol on the seat beside me for the trip into town, but the lonely road with no driveways seemed like protection.

No one was going to walk that far out, so as long as no cars were parked beside the road, an ambush seemed unlikely. Still, I breathed easier when we hit the Steese, and then College Road, where traffic was normal.

At Creamer's Dairy, the barn, or maybe it's the milking shed, is a concrete block edifice, and clean, clean, clean. Apparently the cows are housebroken, and the vet's walled-off corner looked to me like any normal operating room.

The vet was Ichabod Crane incarnate, hands, feet, and head too large for connection to his stickman frame, but he seemed to be communicating with Turk on a personal level.

"That's one nasty cut, Turk, but we'll fix you right up. Gonna have to shave some of your beautiful coat. You'll look like an inverse Mohawk for a while." He was running delicate fingers over Turk's skull, and Turk didn't seem to mind.

"Probably a mild concussion, but your eyes are alert, and your motor reflexes seem okay. Just hold steady while I relax you a bit." The vet was scratching behind Turk's ear with his right hand, but gave him a shot in the shoulder with a hypodermic that looked the size of a grease gun to me. I winced. Turk didn't.

The vet condescended to talk to us. "I should keep him for a few days' observation. He just might have a concussion, and we don't want any infection."

Angie was nodding. She knelt and gave Turk a hug. He licked her face, but in slow motion. He seemed to sag against the vet's leg.

I pulled Angie back to the car. Turk apparently understood that he wasn't being abandoned. His tail was wagging, but with a beat suitable for Brahms.

"Angie, have you noticed that we haven't slept in a while?"

"Yep, a bed sounds good, but now that I have my girl things I need about two hours in the bathroom."

"Whatever for? You're the most beautiful girl God ever made, just as is."

"Yeah, that's fine for you bushmen to say, but we're in the city now. Never mind why, just take me back to the room. The hairbrush alone will be thirty minutes."

We tooled back to town, no one following us, and no lurkers in the hotel parking lot. The stairway was clear. I carried the overnight case in my left hand, pistol casually in right hand beside my leg, but the upstairs hallway was vacant. We ducked into our room.

I put the chain on the door, but decided that sliding the dresser in front of it would be overkill. I kept telling myself that two deadly professionals were out to kill us, but they wouldn't know where we were. I set the magnum on the nightstand and stretched out on the big bed. It was like floating on cloud nine. Angie had run straight to the bathroom, and I could hear water rushing into the tub.

The TV remote was beside the phone so I punched the set to life and ratcheted through the cartoons to the Channel Two noon news. I was slapped in the face with a picture of Stan's truck, and was glad Angie hadn't seen it. Next, a long commercial for Friendly Ford, then a talking head pontificating about the upcoming Governor's race. I recognized both frontrunners. The incumbent has been a personal friend for years. Alaska is a very large place geographically, but thousands of unpopulated square miles don't count in elections. Population-wise, you could fit us all into Rhode Island and it would seem deserted. The population is small enough that almost everyone knows the gov, and most of us call him Bill.

The challenger had been in Bethel on the campaign trail and I'd flown him to a few of the larger villages. I vaguely registered that he was the owner of Interior Air Cargo, and somehow that seemed significant, then my eyes closed.

I awoke to twilight. The TV was off, the curtains open, and it was getting dark outside. Angie was sprawled out on the other bed, wearing a robe over pajamas, with little pink twists caught in her hair. She was breathing deeply, regularly, a comfortable homey sound. I thought it must be nice to wake up to a scene like that every day. Maybe when I get back to Bethel I should try again to weasel Connie into marriage. She seems to like me well enough, but she wants a man who's home at six every evening. That's understandable. Her ex-husband was a long-haul truck driver who turned out to have a girl in every town. She's still smarting from that, and my schedule is too erratic for her. Maybe it's best that I didn't have to explain why I'm absent without leave and sharing a hotel room with an extremely attractive young lady.

I made a backrest of the pillows and sat against the headboard. It seemed like there was something I should remember, but it wasn't coming to the surface.

I went back over the conversation with Stan, every word and nuance, but it seemed hopeless. Two guys, one he didn't know, one he didn't see, talking about something he didn't hear. Then the blast at the club. Clearly, someone was smart enough to listen to the CB radio, but channel nine is the Fairbanks calling frequency so that didn't require special knowledge of Stan. I was calling from two thousand feet up, so my half of the conversation would have been heard anywhere in the area, and I had mentioned the Rendezvous and the time frame. Still, getting to the club within an hour and with a bomb required some organization. A bomb that didn't leave evidence for the police must have been sophisticated, unless there was a cover up. Having police uniforms handy screamed *professional*.

"You awake?" Angie asked.

"I hope not. I hope I'm having the worst and most convoluted nightmare on record, but probably not."

"Is it against your religion to feed a girl twice in one day?"

"Not if she's a very good girl. Do you want room service? Your PJs are cute, but they might cause a stir in the restaurant."

"Give me thirty seconds."

"Want to go to the Wagon Wheel for barbecue?"

"No, not tonight. I don't want to hear music or see happy people dancing. I just want to eat something, have a glass or two of wine, and go right back to sleep."

"The perfect agenda—twenty-nine seconds left."

In five minutes we were seated in the restaurant downstairs, dark, intimate, but no music and no dancing. The pistol in my belt felt reassuring and the other patrons were mostly the dregs of the tourist trade, poised to head south and causing no trouble. I got a shock when I noticed it was nine o'clock, twenty-four hours since Stan's death. It didn't seem right that we were still alive, ordering dinner. How could we be doing normal things, looking like normal people? Angie's world had just been ripped apart, mine had a terrible hole in it, and yet I was calmly asking the sommelier the vintage of their Pouilly Fuissé. I decided not to think. I'm pretty good at that. Angie was obviously struggling, emotions flitting like a kaleidoscope show, but she bit her lower lip and studied her menu. Life must go on, food must be ordered and eaten. Stan was there at the table with us, we just didn't mention it.

The lamb chops béarnaise were perfectly done, spicy crisp crust around pink centers, but somehow I didn't seem to taste them. Angie was toying with her salmon steak. We were washing the food down with a bottle of the 1973, which should have been pure ecstasy, and Angie was surpassing her two-glass estimate, but she didn't appear to be enjoying the wine either.

I know, it's utterly gauche to drink white wine with red meat. I don't know who makes up those rules, but I suspect they've never tried it. I think it's one of those truisms with no truth to it, but perhaps I don't have a sufficiently educated palate. In any case, no wine police showed up to arrest me. It occurred to me that even though Angie appeared poised and sophisticated, she probably wouldn't know the finer nuances of wine.

Our little candle in its glass bowl made a soft flickering light across Angie's features. Large, Kahlua-colored eyes reflecting candlelight, long black lashes that had not come from her makeup kit, high cheekbones and overall symmetry and harmony—she was exquisite. That thought led to how much Stan had to live for, and then to our campfire on the riverbank, the slender strength of her leaning against me for warmth and comfort.

"Whatcha thinking about?" Angie was watching me over the rim of her wineglass, and I hoped she hadn't caught me staring.

"I'm thinking that we can't wait around for killers to find us. We need to find them. Our best clue must be at the freight office. Tomorrow, I'll try to wangle my way in, maybe ask for a job handling freight or something. If we knew who was picking up or dropping off freight at closing time last night, it might give us a starting point."

Chapter Six

At breakfast, I scanned the dining room and decided I was being paranoid. Threats never seem quite real on sunny mornings in happy crowds. Angie had wrinkled her nose and announced her intention of buying me some clean clothes. I handed her three twenties and she made that come-on gesture, like "hit me" in blackjack. I added another twenty. She kept waggling fingers. One more twenty. She nodded and folded the bills into a pocket.

I started down Cushman toward Second Avenue, but turned right after two blocks, circled a block, and came back to Cushman. We were definitely not being followed. Angie spurned my suggestion of the Alaska Commercial Company so I dropped her at Monty's upscale haberdashery. She waved and the store sucked her inside. I drove out to the airport.

I parked in front of Interior Air Cargo. An office with large windows and an entrance was on the right. The rest of the building appeared to be a warehouse with an overhead door that could admit a truck, and beside it a pedestrian door into the freight area. That was the door Stan had used. I turned away from it, and entered the office.

A gray Formica counter reached from wall to wall, with a hinged section at the left end for employees to go through. Two sharp, attractive young women sat at desks, a no-nonsense brunette at a computer, a breathtaking blonde working on a ledger. The back of the room had two doors, apparently to two private offices, and to the left of them was the fateful door into the freight area. The ledger lady gave me a smile and came to take my shipping order. Time to think fast.

"Hi, I'm in town for just a few days, but I'm running short of cash and wondered if you happen to have a temporary opening? I'm familiar with shipping, but I'm also good with a broom and a mop."

"No, I'm sorry, we're fully staffed, and we use Pierson's janitorial service. I really don't think...."

The door of the private office on the right popped open and the shout startled both of us.

"Hey, Alex, what's happening, man?" It was Freddy. We've known each other since he was dispatching for Hawley Evans at Fairbanks Air Service and both of us were flying for the Tanana Valley Air Search and Rescue. We were flying free, building up hours. That's not an FAA requirement. We both had our commercial licenses, and the required hours for those are laughable. In Alaska, it's the insurance companies that rule the charter business, and their mandate is two thousand hours before they'll even talk to you.

"Hi, Freddy, in town for a few days and looking to starch up the bankroll."

"Oh, oh, let me guess. Was the problem named Jody?" He'd come to the counter and plunked his elbows down to make a chin rest of his hands.

"A gentleman would never tell, but yeah, I do need to earn a few hundred bucks to support my lavish lifestyle."

"Alex, I never thought you were the type, but you must have been sent from heaven. Pipeline is running us ragged. How the devil did you get time off in the fall? Everyone here is trying to beat winter with last summer's projects."

"Yeah, well, you guys have a pipeline. All Bethel has is a pipe dream, but I really do have just a few days off. Do you have something?"

"Show me some paper." He pulled a big ledger-type logbook from under the counter. I handed him my license and medical.

He started copying numbers. "You're current on the turbo-twin Otter, of course."

"Well, not…."

"Good." He didn't want to hear me say no. What he was proposing isn't quite kosher, but it is standard procedure. In theory you have to stay current in each aircraft you fly, but in fact, it's sort of like renting a car from Avis. You don't care who made the car. Switches may be a little strange; it might take a minute to figure out the wipers and the AC. The gearshift may be different from the Masserati you drive at home, but you get in and drive with no lessons. With thirteen thousand hours in the air, and experience in at least twenty different aircraft, you can do the same with airplanes.

"There's a new turbo-twin out front with a load of pipe fittings that they're screaming for in Wiesman. I was going to send Tommy up when he gets back from Prudhoe, but if you'll run it up, it'll save a lot of arm twisting."

"It's already loaded?"

"Yep, actually about five hundred pounds overloaded, but I promise it's perfectly balanced." He closed the ledger and stuck it back under the counter. Apparently I was now employed. He handed me a ring with two keys. "Second key is to the office. It may take a while to connect with their people and get off-loaded. If the office is closed when you get back, just fill out a flight ticket and put it on Celeste's desk." He indicated the pretty blonde ledger lady who was still standing at the counter. We gave each other little waves to acknowledge our introduction, and I tried not to stare at her fetching dimples when she smiled.

I snapped Freddy a military salute, an old joke from the Air Search days, and took the keys. If I'd been writing the scenario, it couldn't have been better, and I was very sure the office would be closed when I got back.

"Alex, the Otter is a cinch. Like driving a baby buggy with rubber bumpers. If you have any questions, give me a shout on the Unicom."

"Yes, sir." I started for the door.

"Oh, and if you could drop by about noon tomorrow? Another load for Atigun Pass, but half of that won't be up from Anchorage until eleven."

"Why don't I remember an airstrip in Atigun Pass?"

"You land on Chandalar Shelf, no problem."

"Oh, you mean I'm using a helicopter tomorrow?"

"Just wait until you've tried that Otter." He gave me a wave, dismissive this time, and I strolled out to the flight line to see what I'd gotten into.

Geoffrey de Havilland was twenty years old when he started designing the aircraft that tipped the advantage to England during WWI, and he, or at least his company, has never stopped. He built a four-passenger airliner in 1919, an eight-passenger in 1921, and in 1925 he built the Hercules that carried mail and passengers throughout Europe and Africa. At the same time he built his Moth, then the Gypsy Moth and the Tiger Moth that set the standard for light aircraft.

It was de Havilland Aircraft of Canada Ltd. that built the Beaver, then the Otter, then the Twin Otter. They were built for bush work. They're slow, but consummate flying machines when strips are short and quarters tight. Equally at home on wheels, skis, or floats, they set the standard that others strive for. When they took the reciprocating engines off the Twin Otter and replaced them with turbines, they lightened it by three hundred pounds and almost doubled the horsepower.

Nine-Two Bravo was like new. It even had a hint of the new-plane smell in spite of the boxes that were netted down from the back of my seat to the rear bulkhead. The turbines started instantly. I taxied to the end of runway one-eight and was cleared for takeoff. It's a little disconcerting to wind up the engines and hear a whine instead of a roar, but she was chomping at the bit. I released the brakes, and we were gone. Overloaded or not, that sucker took off like an over-inflated dirigible.

The strip at Weisman is eighteen hundred feet long, but I was remembering Chandalar Shelf as half that, so I used the landing for practice. The flaps came down like barn doors, airspeed dropped to sixty, still no shudder of impending stall. Fifty-five, still solid. Fifty, slightest tremor. Touch of power, and solid again. It was like landing a parachute. When Bushmaster gets rich, we'll buy a turbine Otter.

Since getting home late was the agenda, I wandered over to the portable cook shack after the valves were offloaded. One thing you can always count on at remote camps is excellent food, lots of it, and always available. I helped myself to two pieces of apple pie that had just come from the oven. I figured an hour and a half back to Fairbanks. Stan had said the office was officially closed at six, but no reason to cut it close. I settled down on a green vinyl-upholstered love seat in the lounge with a cup of fresh Yuban coffee and watched videotapes of *I Love Lucy* until five. Television has turned colored and seems faster, but it isn't any better. It was hard to leave the lounge.

I drifted down over Farmer's Loop Road at six-thirty and was cleared for a straight-in approach to runway one-eight. The rented Dodge was the only car in the lot, and the office was dark. I tied the Otter to the cable, gave it a pat like the faithful horse it was, and opened the office door with my key.

The light switch was beside the door. Fluorescent tubes flickered on until I felt like I was in a spotlight. My problem was that there were no window shades, and once the lights were on, I couldn't see much outside, but I would sure be visible in the office. Freddy had left a flight ticket on the counter for me, numbers already filled in. All I had to do was note the arrival time and sign it. I carried it back to Celeste's desk, sat in her chair, and dug a pen out of her center drawer. A whiff of perfume reminded me of the dimples, altogether pleasant.

Two large drawers on the right side were labeled *In* and *Out*. I pulled the *In* drawer and finger-walked to the front. Several invoices were loose, then a folder, and the tab was dated yesterday. The next file was the day I wanted. I tried to look down and riffle pages without being terribly obvious. Pages were in reverse order, the earliest pickups at the back, latest in front. The final pickup of the day was the Nevada Kid grocery store, four hundred pounds of perishables at four-fifty. Before that was Fairbanks Building Supply, a thousand pounds of hardware picked up at four-twenty. Neither seemed likely to be hanging around after six. I moved down to the bottom drawer.

I had just opened the drawer when a pickup stopped outside and two doors slammed. *Conscience doth make cowards of us all.* I pretended to study the flight ticket while I shoved the drawer closed with my knee and cursed myself for leaving the pistol under the car seat.

The door burst open and two cops came in. One held a big, ugly .45 pointed right at my face, but this cop was wearing a badge and it said Airport Security.

"Keep your hands on the desk and don't breathe. What are you doing here?"

"Filling out my flight ticket." I tried for an innocent smile. "I just got in, you must have seen me land the Twin Otter."

"Maybe, but I haven't seen you around before."

"New hire, just started today."

The partner had picked up the phone from the counter and consulted a list from his pocket. He dialed, and turned away so I couldn't hear his conversation until he looked up and spoke to me. "What's your name?"

"Alex Price."

He nodded and waved his partner to put the gun down. That was a relief. Staring down the barrel of a .45 automatic is decidedly uncomfortable and sweat inducing.

"Thanks, Freddy, it's him alright. Big and ugly, brown hair nineteen fifties style and a cut from a barroom brawl on his forehead." He nodded. "Sorry to bother you at home."

They turned toward the door. The one who had been threatening my life said, "Have a nice day." Car doors slammed again and they were gone.

I took a couple of deep breaths, promised myself a drink shortly, and opened the bottom drawer.

The last outgoing shipment was Fairbanks Furniture Factory, eight hundred pounds at three in the afternoon. I checked the next folder, and the first shipment of the day was Stan's motor, listed at eight in the morning. There was his signature. I just stared at it, feeling that all this couldn't be real. I needed to wake up from this nightmare.

I noticed that the next shipment was charged to Alyeska Pipeline, five hours of Twin Otter time, and another for the pipeline in the afternoon. I glanced back at the previous day and that, too, had two charges for the pipeline. No wonder they could afford new aircraft.

I closed the drawer, signed the flight ticket claiming a six-fifteen arrival. I left it center desk with the keys on top of it, switched off the light and left. I should have known that when getting into the office late was so easy, it wouldn't do any good. Murphy's Law would never stand for a plan working that well.

Angie was sitting on her bed, propped up on pillows, white blouse, dark skirt, hair shining and shoes off. Seinfeld was bantering with Elaine on the tube.

I rinsed off the travel dust and made a nest on my bed to join her. Maybe television still has some redeeming qualities.

"Any luck?" she asked.

I gave her an appropriately doleful headshake.

The program ended and she switched off the set.

"New clothes in the bathroom, next to a hot shower and a disposable razor." I took that to be a hint. I did feel like a new man by the time I put on the dress slacks and shirt she had picked out. Nice threads: tan slacks, blue shirt with button down collar, and no little pictures of alligators or logos confirmed her good taste. She hadn't asked my size, and our mutual loss washed over me again. Stan and I wear, or wore, the same sizes and she knew it. I stepped back to the bedroom in all my sartorial splendor and was greeted with appropriate applause.

"Alex, I'm going crazy. I spent most of the afternoon crying. I know that won't bring Stan back. I've got to think about here and now, and you've got to help me. Do you happen to know who broils the best lobsters on the planet?"

"Matter of fact, I do. That would be The Broiler, if we can get a table."

"We probably can. We have reservations in twenty minutes."

I nodded and extended my left elbow, she took it and I led her out. The pistol was on my right. Angie was caught in a culture warp and struggling. The one thing that her Athabaskan Indian ancestors have in common with the Eskimos on the coast is that the men die violently and early. In the villages, it's hunting or fishing accidents. Angie and Stan had reached for an urban, or *Gussak* lifestyle, so she hadn't expected to be widowed in her twenties. Now it had happened to her, just as it had to her mother before her, and she was struggling for the Indian stoicism that should have been her heritage.

It was only eight blocks to the restaurant, but six stoplights, so we made it with three minutes to spare. A neat young man wearing a tuxedo greeted us with a friendly smile. He plucked two menus from his podium and led us past the gleaming cavern of the bar to a corner table in the dining room. We didn't bother with the menus. Naturally, we both ordered the broiled African lobster tails. That was the whole point of going to The Broiler.

"You know, Alex, they have a bottle of 1971 Pouilly Fuissé, and tonight you can drink white wine without having to keep looking over your shoulder."

I nodded to the waiter; he nodded back and went to fetch the bottle. So, Angie did know I was an unforgivable bumpkin for drinking the wrong wine, and she hadn't said a word. I really appreciated that. I once had a fling with an actress in New York who would have thrown a tantrum, caused a scene, and refused to eat with me. I was giving Angie points for being much more the sophisticate.

Our waiter poured a sample and I deferred it to Angie. She sipped and smiled. How could she not? The only wine in the world better than a 1973 Pouilly Fuissé is the 1971. He poured and left in search of our lobsters.

"Total bust getting into the freight records? You were gone so long I thought you must have made it. I pictured you as their new night janitor."

"Pretty close. I'm on the payroll, today and tomorrow, and I had the records all to myself, but there weren't any late shipments, going or coming. Someone was there late for some other reason. All we have to do is figure it out." We both sipped and both smiled. "By the way, I work again tomorrow, approximately noon until six. What say we decontaminate the pickup and retrieve your canoe, if it hasn't already been liberated?"

She nodded and scooped her glass out of the way. The waiter set down trays with our lobsters and local potatoes, baked and stuffed. If you know The Broiler's lobsters, then you know why there was no more conversation, and why we were miserably full but still smiling when we drove back to the hotel and crawled upstairs to our room.

Chapter Seven

I looked that pickup over like a Missouri farmer about to buy a mule. One advantage of machines from the Eighties is that you can look up from underneath and see past the engine. I opened the passenger door rather than the driver's and leaned over to pop the hood latch. The engine was clean. Angie was in the house packing more clothes because she had decided to go back to work. There was nothing we could think of that she could do, at least at the moment, and she didn't want to spend any more time sitting in a hotel room thinking.

There was no traffic on the road. The camp robbers were squawking and arguing, but not concerned with trespassers. I went inside, borrowed a flashlight and looked up under the dash, nothing strange. I shoved the key in the ignition, gritted my teeth, and turned it. It was anticlimactic. The rusty old engine just coughed to life.

To get to Badger Loop Road, we had to drive back through Fairbanks and out the Richardson, so Angie drove the Dodge back to town, parked it at the hotel, and joined me in the pickup.

The canoe sat right where we'd left it, paddles underneath, shotgun still wedged inside. We balanced the canoe on the cab, tied the ends to the front and rear bumpers, and delivered it back to the riverbank behind the cabin. I couldn't quite part with the shotgun. You just never know when you'll need to shoot a pheasant, or an assassin.

"How about an old towel or something to wrap it?" Angie seemed to concur. She went inside and came back with Turk's blanket and a box of number six shot.

"Alex, this is too weird. There isn't a safer or more peaceful spot on earth, and you're hoarding guns like it was Washington, D.C." By *hoarding*, she meant the pistol that was in my belt. "When is it going to end?"

"It's going to end when we find who killed Stan. We have to believe they still plan to kill us. The strange part is that we don't know who *they* are, they may not know who *we* are, or at least what we look like, and we're hunting each other. They do know this pickup, so let's get it stashed back at the airport."

We stopped in town, Angie followed me to the airport in the Dodge, and we put the pickup to bed in its nest beside the Sea Airmotive hangar. I transferred the shotgun to the Dodge trunk because it wouldn't fit under the seat. It wasn't handy, but it felt good to know it was there.

"You sure you want to go to work this afternoon?"

"Yeah, I think so. You're going to be flying late again tonight?"

"Probably about five-thirty or six. I'll be home in time for dinner."

"Good. I'll walk back to the hotel when I get off. I may not stay at the station too long, but I don't want to spend the afternoon alone."

"Okay, but do stay wide awake. I really don't think any bad guys know you by sight or where you work, but they will be trying to find out, so watch it. Check the street before you open the door, jaywalk across Second and cut through the drugstore to Third. If anyone seems the least bit interested, lose yourself in the biggest crowd you can find. Call the cops if you even get a premonition...."

"Been watching too much television? Aren't you going to lend me your pistol?"

"Do you want it?"

"No, I'm being facetious. Don't worry about me, Alex. I'll be careful, but I'm not hiding under beds just yet."

"Might not be a bad idea."

When I walked into the office at noon, Celeste gave me a friendly smile, flashing bright blue eyes and those fetching dimples under her platinum blonde pageboy. Apparently we were now old friends. She picked up her phone, punched two digits, and Freddy came from his office.

"So, what did you think of the Otter?"

"I'm taking it back to Bethel with me. I'll just leave the Cessna 310 parked in the spot and you probably won't notice the difference. Sorry about the cops last night."

"Hey, no problem. That's what I get for hiring criminal types. Come on back to the office a sec. Reginald wants to say hello." He raised the hinged section of counter for me to slip through. We passed the fateful warehouse door to the first office on the left. Freddy tapped on the door and opened it.

I finally remembered the connection that had eluded me when I went to sleep during the newscast. Reginald Parker was running for governor, and he was also the owner of Interior Air. His office was dark paneled opulence, thick blue carpet, leather-upholstered furniture arranged around an eight-foot mahogany desk. Reginald reigned with a multi-line phone on his left, a scrimshawed walrus tusk penholder on his right, and behind him a framed picture of him shaking hands with Richard Nixon. A rollaway near his left elbow held a computer with a twenty-one inch monitor and a pullout drawer for the keyboard.

"Hey, Alex, I heard you were in town for a couple of days. No problems, I hope?" He stood with amazing alacrity for a six-footer who weighed two hundred fifty pounds, and reached across the desk for a handshake. It's not that we're such good friends, we'd spent just three days flying together. The handshake was part of his gubernatorial persona. So were the dark blue pinstriped suit, his movie hunk profile, and the abundant razor-cut salt-and-pepper hairdo.

"Nah, just a little R&R, and stopped by for a busman's holiday."

"Busman?"

"Am I mixing metaphors? Don't bus drivers go for bus rides on their days off, or is it postmen who take walks? How is the campaign going?"

"Ask me the day after the election." He motioned Freddy and me toward two chairs and sank back into his own. He turned to impress Freddy with what good buddies he and I were.

"Freddy, you should have seen the way we blitzed the Bethel area. We hit eighteen villages in three days, and everyone loved me. Lot of the credit goes to Alex because he's some kind of hero down there and when we showed up together, they thought he was endorsing me. You *are* endorsing me, Alex?"

"It was my very great pleasure." That was true in a way. The blitz *was* a great pleasure. Twenty flying hours and ten hours standby in three days had me feeling so rich that I took Connie into Anchorage for the weekend. That was one of the times she might have considered marrying me if Vicki hadn't sent me off to Kodiak for three days, starting Monday morning.

"Well, we sure impressed the Eskimos. I'm really counting on the Bethel vote."

He impressed the Eskimos all right. He tossed out Athabaskan words from the interior Indian language in the heart of the Yupik-speaking Eskimo nation. If I'd been endorsing him, I would have told him to stay in Bethel and make his pitch to Chief Eddy Hoffman because Chief Eddy decides how the Yupik Nation votes.

Reginald's phone rang and he picked it up. Freddy and I stood while Reginald said "Hello? Just a minute." He stood for another handshake, complete with a clap on the elbow. "See you at the polls." He turned back to the phone and Freddy and I fled.

I ducked back through the counter. "Otter ready to travel?"

"Yep, she's loaded. Seven hundred pounds over, but the plane doesn't mind if you don't."

"Hey, beggars are remarkably compliant. Any special instructions?"

"Nope. Be sure to buzz the camp when you get there because it's three miles from the camp to the landing spot and no phones. I did put in a request for a check. I figured four and a half hours yesterday and six today, but the check won't be ready until day after tomorrow. It comes from the accountants in Anchorage. Can I loan you a couple of hundred to tide you over?"

"Nah, I'm okay for a couple of days. The crunch will come when I try to leave town."

"Okay, just remember, fly low and slow." He tossed me the key ring and turned back to his office.

If the Otter was overloaded, it not only didn't mind, it didn't notice. My route was over the White Mountains, which mostly top out around thirty-five hundred feet, then over a hundred miles of Yukon Flats to the Endicott Mountains. Atigun Pass is the entrance to the Endicotts, part of the Brooks Range where several peaks reach for eight thousand feet. I ran on up to ten thousand for engine efficiency and speed, and tuned in the non-directional beacon at Fort Yukon.

That was the proverbial "hours of boredom" part of flying, but it was spectacular. Snow was creeping down the mountains, valleys still blazing with fall colors, lakes and rivers sparkling silver in sunshine. The satin-smooth turbines could lull a chap to sleep. I noticed that the Hobbs meters for both engines read three hundred thirty hours, so that was the newest plane I'd ever flown. Bushmaster tends to pick up bargains from stateside companies that go broke. The low engine hours were impressive because I had put on four of them. Planes that size are normally flown up from the factory in Toronto, so that was another twenty hours.

I stayed at nine thousand feet, passed the patch of rocks and dirt that Freddy was calling the runway, and flew over the camp. I didn't want to turn a heavy airplane around in the narrow valley and I wanted to be going downhill toward the runway when I buzzed the camp, not uphill with a need to climb. I pretty nearly took the roof off the bunkhouse, but it wasn't a satisfying buzz. With reciprocating engines, you drift down over your target and gun the engines to rattle the windows. The turbines just whined a little louder.

The Otter bumped and squatted over the rocks and rubble, but stopped halfway down the strip, where the road from camp abutted. I got out to stretch and stroll, but the air was bracing. It was pristine though, crystal clear, and utterly silent. There's something about the massive mountains that puts men and their little concerns in perspective. If there was an odor, it was new snow. The white line was working its way down the peaks toward the pass, and I spotted several Dahl sheep at the edge. Sheep are supposed to be camouflaged white, but actually next to the new snow, they had a yellow tinge. Perhaps they'll blend better in a few weeks.

Two pickups and a two-ton flatbed rattled over the rocky road, and half a dozen men had the plane unloaded in ten minutes. I stood close enough to supervise because I didn't want them knocking off any doors or railings, but they were good. A foreman signed my sheet and the trucks trundled away. I fired the engines to shatter the stillness but only produced the buzz of those incredibly quiet turbines.

I tied the plane down at ten after six, but the lot was almost deserted. Just one long black Cadillac sedan, a maroon Mercedes almost as long, and my little green rented Dodge were left in the lot. The office door was locked, so I used my key and snapped on the lights in the main room, but the light was on in Reginald's office and his door was open.

Freddy had left a filled-out flight ticket on the counter again. I entered my six o'clock arrival, signed it, and slipped through the drawbridge to put it on Celeste's desk.

"Hey, Alex, I want you to meet my campaign manager."

Reginald came out of his office, followed by an even more Italianate figure. He wasn't as large as Reginald, but he was a hefty specimen, the type who must spend all the time when you're not watching him in the gymnasium.

This guy was smooth, suit and haircut just a little better than Reginald's, black hair slicked back, olive complexion.

"Dave, this is Alex Price. Alex, Dave Marino is my campaign manager."

We shook hands. He had a grip like a steel claw, no warmth, but I was watching his eyes. He was good, no flinch if the name Alex meant something to him, but his irises snapped up one notch. Those eyes were cold, impenetrable, and I wondered if I was seeing the wolverine Stan had described. I couldn't decide if he recognized the name Alex from the CB conversation. Reginald was prattling on.

"Alex is our ambassador to the Eskimos. I'm sure we can count on their vote."

Didn't this guy know anything about Alaska? Sure, the Yupik Nation around Bethel may be over half the Eskimos, but they do not socialize with the Inuit to the north or the Aleuts south of them. It's only been a hundred years since the borders were armed and raiding parties hunted each other like wild animals.

I tried a more acceptable response than my thought. "Yeah, Reginald really impressed the Eskimos. I'm sure they're in the bag."

"You're just visiting for a few days?" Dave asked.

"Yep, our busy season starts in a couple of weeks when the Kuskokwim starts to freeze. We get swamped from the time villagers can't use boats until they can use snow machines. Meantime, it's a nice change to see mountains and trees instead of flat tundra, and it's a chance to visit old friends."

Dave was inscrutable. I couldn't tell if the *old friends* remark registered or not, but I had the feeling that I was playing poker with a pro. Tension was in the air, and the more I studied Dave's eyes, the more they looked like wolverine.

"Care to join us for an aperitif?" Reginald invited.

"I'd love to, but I have dinner plans with friends." I checked my watch and winced. "In fact, I'm late. Nice to have met you." I aimed that remark at Dave. He nodded.

"See you at the polls." Reginald dismissed me with a casual gesture and I hiked for the Dodge.

Chapter Eight

The airport provides a couple of pay phones on a post at the exit from the general aviation area. Itinerant pilots can call taxis without having to hoof a half-mile to the terminal. That's a little old fashioned by most standards, and if you live in Anchorage or Fairbanks, you might have a cell phone, but those don't work in the bush. In the villages everyone has a CB radio, and there's one in every airplane, but when you visit a city, it's good old-fashioned pay phones. I hid the Dodge between two hangers and jogged to the phones to call Angie.

"Hi, Alex, what's up?" I could hear Seinfeld in the background, George Costanza whining about something.

"Probably nothing, but I may be late. You go ahead and have dinner. Be a good girl, order room service, and be damned sure the waiter is from the restaurant before you open the door."

"Yes, mother, I'll be fine. Are you in danger?"

"No, or not yet. Don't worry, pistol in belt, keen insights and lightning reflexes honed. I'll either join you at dinner or be a little late. Give my love to Elaine."

"Huh? Oh, sure. Be careful, Alex."

"That's my middle name." I hung up the phone and ducked back to the Dodge.

The first car to leave Interior was the Cadillac, and the driver was Dave, the campaign manager. I let him go three blocks down Airport Road and followed him.

We turned left down Cushman Street into town, but kept going across the river on the Cushman Street Bridge. He turned right on College Road, then left on the Steese Highway. I pulled into the service station at the corner and waited. When you're following a car you don't want too much traffic, but you also don't want too little, and his was the only car on the Steese.

Just before I was going to have to pull out and follow, he turned left into the parking lot at the Rendezvous. I gave him three minutes and raced to the club, but drove the Dodge around back and parked beside the bartender's Lincoln. Five minutes later, four guys jammed into the cab of a pickup came weaving down the highway. They slued into the lot and staggered toward the door. I was right behind them when they entered. They trooped toward the bar. I turned right, followed the wall past tables, and sat down in the darkest corner.

Several tables around me were occupied, most with a B-girl and a victim. Laughter, giggles, a general hubbub of horseplay and ice tinkling in glasses almost drowned out Jack's piano. Hunkered down behind my table I felt inconspicuous enough.

Dave was at the bar with his back to me, and earnestly discussing something with two men. The two were dressed typical Fairbanks roughneck in jeans and work shirts. One was taller, one was wider, but that's true of any two guys. I couldn't pick out anything from their backs in the dark that might or might not resemble the phony cops who had come to Stan and Angie's place. When they attacked at the house, they'd been wearing hats, so I hadn't seen the features that could have identified them. I hadn't had time to form a plan when Jody descended on my table.

"Hi, handsome, you came back for me."

"Yeah, I got a little distracted the other night with all of the excitement."

"Gawd, wasn't that awful? Are you going to buy a thirty-dollar bottle?"

"Sure thing." I peeled a twenty and a ten off the roll. She skipped to the bar and was back in a flash with a bottle and two glasses. She started to scoot her chair next to me, but I caught her shoulders and guided her down onto the chair opposite so she was between me and David.

"What's the matter? Afraid I might bite? I do use teeth, but never draw blood."

"See those three guys at the bar? The suit and the two scruffs?"

She tossed her mane to glance over her shoulder. "Yeah, what about them?" She popped the cork like the expert she was and poured the champagne. Don't be impressed by the price. That bottle would cost four bucks at a grocery store, and fifteen of the thirty goes into Jody's garter.

"Do you know them?"

"Hey, I don't rat on my friends, but no, not really. Those guys are tighter than a fifty-cent condom. They want to feel the merchandise, but for free."

"Do they come in often?"

"Well, the scruffs are pretty regular in the last couple of weeks. Not sure about the suit. Maybe I seen him, maybe not. Nice threads, I should check him out. Aren't you going to drink your champagne?"

"Jody, I can't drink that stuff. It would give me the trots if I didn't actually upchuck it."

"Yeah, me neither. I just wait until the customer is occupied and pour it on the floor. Problem is we've got to get rid of it. I plan on another bottle every ten minutes."

"Okay, we've got eight minutes to go. Try not to breathe the fumes." Actually, the fumes I was trying to avoid were Jody's perfume, but they did seem to mix with the noxious emanations from the champagne.

Dave got up and strode out the door. No empty glass on the counter where he'd sat, so he hadn't even had a drink. He'd come for a conference, and I did not like that at all.

"Jody, if I was to buy the next bottle ahead of schedule, do you think you could get one or both of the glasses the scruffs are using?"

"Probably. I can likely get everything except their wallets. Why, you some kind of cop or something now?"

"Or something. If you can get them, pick them up by the rim, don't touch the sides, and be careful not to smudge or wipe them."

"How much?"

"Twenty dollars a glass?"

"I like nice round figures. How about thirty?"

"Okay, but Jody, I will be checking fingerprints so you damn well better have the right glasses."

"Hey, honor among thieves, right? You and me, baby." She reached under the table to squeeze my knee. "Time's up, need another bottle."

"Right." I handed her two more bills. "It would be a good thing if you can keep them here for a while, if you want me to live to buy the glasses."

"Indubitably." She swayed toward the bar, skirt raised for garter stuffing. She straightened the skirt, did a full body check that everything was in place, walked up behind the two scruffs and draped arms around their shoulders. I split.

"Angie, grab your stuff, we're moving."

"Where to, and how about dinner?"

"No, I mean we're moving now, like this instant. Pretend the building is on fire, and it just might be." She caught the urgency in my voice and ran for the bathroom.

"I'll just put your stuff in with mine. What's the matter?"

"Usual drill. I don't know, maybe nothing, but I think some very bad people just learned my full name, and that's the name on the hotel register."

She zipped out of the bathroom carrying her overnight case and swept the room fast with frightened eyes. I picked up her suitcase from the folding stand, and we were out the door.

We did a fast walk the length of the hall and down the stairs. The lobby was empty so I dinged the bell and a receptionist came from the office, wiping sleep out of her eyes. It took thirty seconds to check out. The Dodge was six spaces down the row. This time I'd gotten smart. I'd found an empty cigarette pack in the gutter, ripped the cellophane off, and stuck a sliver in each door. When I opened the passenger door for Angie, the cellophane fluttered out, so I tossed the bags in back and let her get in. Cellophane was in place on my door too, and one can't open the hood without getting inside. I jumped in, engine started, and we raced for the Polaris building.

"Where are we going?"

"To change cars. Too many people who might be bad may have seen this one."

"Don't you ever make a positive statement?"

"I will, if anything positive happens." We parked the car in the lot and the attendant took the keys. I popped the trunk and collected the shotgun. It was wrapped in Turk's blanket, but was still pretty obvious and the attendant was staring. There's nothing illegal about carrying a shotgun, and it wouldn't even be unusual in your own car, but it did seem a little out of place in a rental. We ran across First Avenue toward the office, Angie leading, me carrying cases and the shotgun.

"Alex, they must know it's a rented car, so if they know your name and you rent another, they can check on that."

"Got a better idea?"

"Yeah, let's use Mary Angela Demoski. They won't recognize that name."

"Mary? Even I don't recognize it."

"Yep, on my birth certificate, driver's license, and credit card. I kept my maiden name when I married Stan. Not disloyalty, it just seemed right."

Angie took charge, stepped up to the counter, and rented a white Buick Regal. I hovered outside the door, trying not to look like a desperado who might want a rental car to rob a bank. Angie came out dangling a key ring. We walked back across the street to the lot and she opened the trunk. I stashed luggage and shotgun in the trunk. Angie nodded her approval and tossed me the keys. "Now where to?"

"Well, you mentioned dinner, and we are homeless."

"How about the Maranatha Inn on South Cushman?"

"Never heard of it."

Angie was nodding. "That's precisely the point. Neither has anyone else, but the food is excellent. No wine though, it's run by a religious group of some kind."

"No sermons?"

"No, but there are bibles in the rooms. The drinks are really funny because the menu lists all the usual stuff, piña coladas, mai tais, whatever, and they're really cheap. You should have seen Stan's face when we figured it out. See, we'd been whiffing down hurricanes, really good, and we'd had three or four when Stan realized we weren't getting drunk. Gimmick is there's no alcohol in them."

"Not sure I'm up for being stranded in the desert."

"No problem, the Squadron Club's right next door."

The young man behind the counter at the Maranatha had that clean-cut innocent look you associate with Mormon missionaries. Angie's request for twin beds was what he expected, and this time we were carrying suitcases.

Our room had seen better days, quite a few of them, but it was clean. The beds really were twin size, and sure enough, there was a bible on the dresser where the TV usually sits. I dumped the bags. Angie inspected the bathroom. I opened the curtains and checked out the view. A courtyard had a couple of straggly trees, but they were likely very nice in spring and summer. Fifty feet away, beyond the trees, South Cushman Street was gushing cars and flashing neon signs. The offer of booze and sex was pretty clear just from the lights. The devil was held at bay by our courtyard.

Angie came out of the bathroom. "Ready?"

"More than."

We retraced our steps down the walkway and stairs in search of sustenance. The walkway was alfresco, two-by-four railing over a two-by-four grate, everything coated with layers of green paint.

Gaps between the two-by-fours were wide enough to let rain through, so apparently their guests didn't wear stiletto heels.

The restaurant appeared normal. Maybe the crowd was younger than usual, but they were quiet and studiously feeding their faces. The room was bright, meant for eating, not seduction, and there wasn't a candle in sight. Our waitress was obviously working her way through college, or maybe high school. I momentarily spaced out where we were and ordered the scallops. Angie went for salmon again, and we ordered a bottle of sparkling apple juice without discussing the vintage.

"How was your day at work?" I asked.

Angie was inspecting the silverware with obvious approval. It was super clean; probably not real silver, but it could pass. "It was okay, and it sort of worked. We have a big special live show coming up tomorrow night, so we were busy and that helped. What the heck disturbed the bee in your bonnet?"

"I met Reginald's campaign manager. Nothing overt, but he and Reginald were hanging around the office after closing, and he could have been the man Stan described. He's the unstoppable executive type and I would not want to lie down in the street in front of his car. He might have recognized my name, and if he did, it was from listening to Stan and me on the CB radio, but he might not have. All I know for sure is that I got a very creepy feeling."

Our salads arrived, local produce, vinaigrette dressing, tasty and crisp.

"Right, Reginald Parker is running for governor, isn't he? That's the big crunch at the station. I know the guy you mean, the campaign manager. His name's Dave Marino and he's insisting on deals for advertising. The big doing tomorrow is that Governor Bill is coming up for a State of the North address. It's like the State of the State address, but local. It's pure campaigning, but it is newsworthy. That's the perk of being the incumbent."

A teenaged busboy removed our salad plates to make room for entrees. Too late, I remembered we were in Fairbanks. Scallops in

Seward, Valdez, Cordova, Kodiak, or Homer were a pure delight to rival lobsters. In Fairbanks they had been frozen, so they were the same rubber pucks that wrinkle your nose in Kansas City. Angie was obviously relishing the salmon.

"You're broadcasting the governor's speech live?"

"Yep, right after Seinfeld. He's speaking in the Lacey Street Theater, almost underneath the station, so we just drop cables out the fourth floor window and into the theater balcony."

"And you'll be working the broadcast?"

"Yeah, I'm not really the producer, more like a gofer, but we'll have announcers and scripts, so someone has to keep everything straight."

"Good Lord, Angie, you don't suppose they thought Stan overheard a plot to assassinate the gov?" I was so shocked by that thought that I forgot and ate a scallop. I killed the taste and texture with apple juice. It was tough, but the flavor was really not too bad. It was just a pale imitation of fresh scallops. The locally grown baked potato was wonderful and loaded with all the good stuff, so at least I was filling the void.

Chapter Nine

We lay on our respective beds in the dark and chewed over the assassination idea. It was tougher than the scallops and seemed pretty far out. Fairbanks has some of the earmarks, but it really isn't the third world. Still, we'd been in the Twilight Zone for the last few days, so anything seemed possible.

"Shouldn't we be reporting this? Tell the cops or something?" Enough light came in through the window to show Angie propped up on her elbow, looking my way. The hotel was silent except for the muted hum of traffic and sounds of people having fun on Cushman Street.

"Report what, Angie? Tell the cops that I have a bad feeling about Reginald's campaign manager? Anyhow, there'll be plenty of security. State troopers will be traveling with the gov, and even the local cops probably won't let people into the theater with rifles."

"Alex, we've got to do something."

"Right. Do you suppose you could get me on the TV crew, help set up maybe?"

"Not officially, but I could get you a cap and jacket so you'd blend in. What are you planning?"

"I'll just keep an eye on things. If the phony cop from your driveway shows up assembling a submachine gun, I could set off the fire alarm or something. You know, in movies, assassins always carry high-powered rifles in clarinet cases and assemble them on site. I could watch for that."

"Ready for some sleep? I've got all my mattress lumps in comfortable positions."

"Let's give it a shot. I'm trying to think and that always knocks me out."

Angie lay down and pulled up the blankets. I squirmed around and watched the lights from Cushman Street sweep across the ceiling. I would have slit my throat long before I made a move on Angie. Loyalty to Stan would have made it unthinkable, and our brother/sister relationship was taking on a sacred aspect. Still, I couldn't quite forget that she was there.

I did question the hotel's sanctimonious propriety in not providing television. Normally the boob tube would have put me right to sleep. Its absence reminded me of an episode in my teens when a buddy and I had dated a couple of Pentecostal girls. They weren't allowed to go to movies or go bowling, or attend any worldly activities. It turned out the only thing we could do was park, which was fine with us. It is a fact that both the birthrate and domestic violence declined in the bush when TV encroached.

I must have slept because I awoke to daylight and Angie was running a shower in the bathroom.

We took the elevator to the fourth floor of the Lathrop Building, but I waited in the hallway while Angie went into the station. In a couple of minutes she stuck her head out and handed me a jacket and cap. I faded down the stairway to don my disguise. The blue cap had KTUU emblazoned in gold, and the matching jacket had NBC on the back. I was no more conspicuous than a Volkswagen in the employee lot at a GM factory.

I was the only employee on the sidewalk, but a window opened on the fourth floor above me and a bundle of cables started snaking down. They descended in short jerks, three feet at a time, with ends swinging back and forth until they began to pile up on the sidewalk. A window opened on the second floor of the theater and a clothesline rope slid down. I caught the end of the rope, tied a timber hitch around the cable ends, and the rope went back up.

Cable ends went through the window, then the cables moved smoothly from one window to the other until the top stopped with a jerk. Cables flopped up and down a couple of times while someone in the theater tried to pull more and someone on top held them back. The guy on top won.

The lobby door of the Lathrop Building opened and a grip dressed like me shoved a cartload of cables out onto the sidewalk and into the theater. I followed him in and no one objected. The grip draped a roll of cables over each shoulder and climbed the balcony stairs. I picked up the next two rolls and followed him.

Two techies were busily connecting new cables to the end of the bundle and unrolling them down toward the auditorium. The grip dropped his cables beside the knitting project and trooped down the stairs for more. I dropped my cables and wandered across the balcony to inspect the projection booth. I was thinking that a sniper rifle in a crowded auditorium might attract attention and the booth would be a perfect place for a rifleman.

Four openings marked the location. Two were six inches square, obviously in front of the projectors. The others were two feet square with glass coverings. Light in the balcony was dim, the booth darker than midnight in a coalmine. Activity at the splice point tapered off. One coaxial cable ran to the balcony rail, turned left, and ended in the corner. The rest of the cables were rebundled and dropped over the railing to the main auditorium. The crew disappeared down the stairs and cables appeared fanning out to platforms that spanned seats. I took off my official cap and settled down in a comfortable loge seat where I could watch the door to the projection booth.

My watch crept slowly toward the seven o'clock show time. By six-thirty, tripods were set up, cameras mounted, and floodlights began to come on. Someone climbed up to the podium on the stage, caught a cable end and set up a microphone. He talked to it a while, but no sound came out, so the feed was going directly to the TV station. At six thirty-five, a wizened little guy wearing corduroy pants and a short-sleeved shirt opened the projection booth with a key. He was not carrying a rifle or a piccolo case. Lights came on in the projection booth, houselights brightened, footlights came on to form blue and gold scallops on the velvet curtain.

One of the glass windows into the booth opened. I wandered over to have a look. The same little guy was shoving a Klieg spotlight into position, looking bored. No one was holding a gun to his head. I went back to my seat. By six-forty people were streaming in and taking seats. The PA system came to life with subliminal elevator music. By that time, the front doors would be manned by troopers, and getting in with a pistol, like the one under my jacket, would be highly unlikely.

That ploy would not work in a presidential situation, or any time the Secret Service is involved. They mandate that all equipment be set up and everyone out of the building two hours before the potentates show up. They sweep the building and let the crews back in with more scrutiny than a high school chaperone at a dance.

The auditorium was packed. Governor Bill was very well liked, and if someone were to unseat him, it probably would take an assassination. At the stroke of seven the houselights dimmed, the spotlight snapped on, and Wee Willy Wally, the mayor of Fairbanks, appeared behind the podium.

Wee Willy got his nickname when he was a teenage announcer for KFAR radio, but that was thirty years ago. There's nothing wee about him anymore, but he still capitalized on the teddy bear image. He raised his arms and the audience rose to their feet as one. Alaska's flag song burst from the speakers, and we all belted it out.

"*Eight stars of gold on a field of blue, Alaska's flag, may it mean to you…*"

Five hundred people singing their hearts out were vibrating the balcony, and quite a few people around me had tears in their eyes. Alaska does that to you. If you aren't fiercely loyal, you aren't there anyway. I kept enough presence of mind to know if the door to the projection booth had opened.

"*The gold of the early sourdough's dreams, the precious gold of her hills and streams...*"

Most people were concentrating on Wally but a few had their eyes closed, lost in introspection and reminiscences of what Alaska and its flag meant to them. I have to admit to emotions that don't fit my macho image of myself.

"*...the simple flag of the last frontier.*" Wee Willy lowered his arms, the crowd sat.

"Ladies and gentlemen, the Governor of Alaska." Bill stepped into the spotlight with Wally, but if anything was said, no one heard it. The crowd was on its feet, clapping and cheering. That would have been a perfect moment for a shot; a silencer wouldn't have been needed. I gripped my pistol and scanned the booth and the back row seats. No blue steel tubes came out of the booth. Everyone in the balcony was using both hands to clap, so not drawing weapons. Wee Willy disappeared, the governor raised his arms and made a sit-down gesture. He repeated it three times before the din tapered off and his standard greeting rang out in the clear tones of the master orator that he was.

"My fellow Alaskans...."

It was dark inside the projection booth, but nothing moved near the windows. An old-timer in the back row reached inside his jacket to pull something out. I figured it would take him a second to aim and me less than half a second to shoot him, but he pulled out a handkerchief and wiped his eyes.

Funny, Alaska is supposed to have the youngest average age of the states, but I was guessing the average age on that balcony to be a least seventy. A woman next to the railing pulled a dark metal object out of her purse and raised it. She looked to be ninety and I was so surprised I could have missed her if I'd shot, but she raised opera glasses.

One of the best things about Governor Bill is his brevity. He spoke clearly, sincerely, but fast, for precisely fifteen minutes. He raised his arm in a farewell salute. The spotlight snapped off, the crowd went wild, and when the houselights came on, the governor was gone. No doubt he was in the protective arms of his special detail of state troopers. I rolled my disguise into a bundle; I did not want to join the crew that was rolling cables. My windbreaker still covered the pistol and no one was checking the departees. I joined the crowd streaming out of the theater, then took the stairs in the Lathrop Building. I'd waited five minutes when the elevator opened and Angie came out accompanied by Barbie and Ken look-alikes. The handsome pair were dressed in formal business suits, proclaiming them the talent. Angie was carrying two clipboards. I shoved the bundle of disguise into her fingers, and the trio disappeared into the inner sanctum.

Angie was back in another five minutes and punched the button for the elevator.

"Congratulations. You certainly foiled the assassination attempt. What's your next brilliant plan?"

"You're not going to believe this one. We're going barhopping, then some ribs at the Wagon Wheel?" I made it a question. Angie looked doubtful.

"I don't know, Alex, I'm functioning, but I don't think I can handle a party."

"Angie, some music and dancing are exactly what you need. Sweetheart, it's going to take years to get over Stan's death. I'm not suggesting we forget about it. I'm suggesting we grit our teeth and plow into the world we're going to have to face sometime. If it gets too rough, I'll take you straight home."

"Okay, Doctor Price, I'll give it a try."

The elevator came and with it a grip pushing a cartload of cables. Angie held the office door for him, I held the elevator door for her, and we escaped. The street door was glass with chicken wire mesh embedded to make it unbreakable. A lot of traffic was plying the street and a solid line of parked cars fronted the sidewalk. One car, two parking spaces to the left, had two men sitting in the front seat and they might have been watching our door. No weapons were apparent, but of course there wouldn't be until we stepped outside. The interior of the car was too dark for identification of the cops at the cabin or the two scruffs Dave Marino had conferred with at the club.

I gripped the pistol with my right hand, holding Angie behind me with my left. One option was to leave Angie inside, step out and approach the car. If they raised weapons, I could probably shoot them both. The cowardly way was to sneak out another exit.

"Angie, isn't there a connecting hallway between the Lathrop building and Monte's Department store?"

"Yeah, fifth floor. You can cross over and come down the other elevator. What's the matter?"

"Just more of my indecisiveness. I have a sudden urge to do something unexpected." I shoved her back toward the elevator, endured her exasperated grimace, and she punched *Five* on the elevator console. The fifth floor of the Lathrop Building was all apartments with electronic noises behind doors, and cooking smells in the hallway. We threaded through dark hallways, came to another elevator. The fifth floor above Monte's housed offices, dark, silent, deserted, and ominous. The only lights were exit signs on both ends of the hall, and the elevator buttons. Angie punched a button, a mechanical rumble replaced the silence, and a door slid open into an empty car. Angie stepped in and punched *Lobby.* I was right behind her. That brought us to another glass door to the street, but this time behind the suspicious sedan.

"Angie, wait here for a minute while I check out the coast."

"You are one sexist S.O.B., aren't you? If there's a problem, let me help."

"Sweetheart, I'm counting on your help. Hold this door open in case I make a hasty and ignominious retreat, because if the door closes, we'll be locked out and that could be a bad thing."

"Aye, aye, my fearless if sexist protector. You go out and get shot. I'll wait here like a good little girl."

"Damn it, Angie. Me Tarzan, you Jane. We both have roles to fulfill. It was foreordained by the primal drive for the survival of the species. As the female, you must be protected at all costs; as the male, I'm highly expendable. You hold the door. I'll go out and get shot. There might be enough trouble outside without you giving me any in here. Men have all the fun, so shut up, like it, and hold the door."

"Yes, master."

She did hold the door open a crack. I gripped the pistol and walked up behind the sedan. I could see through their windows, no weapons apparent. Two women came burbling and giggling out of the theater, opened a back door and slid into the sedan. The engine started, the sedan pulled out into traffic, and I beckoned to Angie to join me.

The Buick was parked on Second Avenue, but short of the din that was coming from the native bars. My cellophane fluttered out of the doors again. We tucked ourselves in and found a hole in the traffic. We turned right on Cushman, over the bridge, and thence to the Rendezvous Club. No Cadillacs, no Mercedes, so I parked in the lot, and was surprised when Angie climbed out of the car with me.

"Sure you want to go inside?"

"Yeah, I've always been curious. You will protect me? I mean, you are still carrying your gun?"

"Not much protection against Jody, but come on in. The club is a little scary but it actually is legal."

Angie stopped just inside the door and stared. Romey was on the stage, wearing very little more than a smile, and making suggestive gyrations around a fire pole. The stage was ringed with shouting admirers, most waving bills to be stuffed into the few strings Romey was wearing. I scanned the bar, saw no familiar backs, so turned a sharp right to the dark corner table, and Jody beat me to it. She was carrying a paper grocery bag.

"Here's your glasses, handsome. Cash on delivery, of course, and no more assignments. I was mauled worse than when the sourdoughs come in from the creeks."

"Thanks a bunch, Jody. I really appreciate this." I handed her three twenties which went straight into her garter.

"And I appreciate this." She meant the cash. "Care to buy me a thirty-dollar bottle?"

"Some other time, okay? I'm with a friend."

"I thought you came in with that sweet pea who's cowering by the door. If she's looking for work, I'll bet Satch could use her." She didn't catch the double entendre of *use*.

"Thanks again, Jody. Always a pleasure doing business with a pro." She didn't catch the implications of *pro* either. I left Jody adjusting the bills in her garter, caught Angie's elbow, and steered her outside.

"My God, I didn't realize men are so desperate. Alex, you didn't, you *couldn't*."

"Of course not. I told you she tried to glom onto me and I had to brush her off. Ever try to clean molasses out of velvet?"

"So, what's in the bag? If it's souvenir lingerie, I'll kill you on the spot."

"What I have here, my doubting and possibly jealous Thomasina, might be the evidence that's going to break the case. Now, how about barbecued ribs at the Wagon Wheel?"

"Lead on, my stalwart and sterling-charactered protector."

Cellophane was in place on both doors. I drove fast into town, crossing the Lacey Street Bridge, then circled a block and came back to the river at Wendell Street. We were not being followed. I decided to give paranoia the night off.

The Wagon Wheel is a long low structure with appropriate bits of memorabilia from the horse-drawn era hung on rough-hewn log walls. Its two claims to fame are superb pork ribs slow barbecued over a birch wood fire, and Steve Hahn playing an electric organ that can make you cry, laugh, or sing at his command.

We were ensconced at a table in a dark corner beside the dance floor, enjoying both the ribs and the music. We'd started with rum and Coke, and when the ribs were delivered, we didn't bother to change. The atmosphere was too rugged for wine, and the rum too good.

Maybe thirty couples occupied tables that were scattered around the edge of the dance floor, most of them gnawing ribs, all of them seemed to be enjoying themselves. The thing is, you can't be stuffy or formal because you have to eat the ribs with your hands, and are going to get barbecue sauce on your fingers and your cheeks. You keep mopping cheeks and licking fingers, but you still have to laugh at yourselves. A perky little waitress in a cowgirl outfit kept us supplied with towelettes and kept the rum and Coke flowing.

"Kinda gives new meaning to *informal dining*, doesn't it?" Angie asked.

"I think it gets back to the basic human condition. Ever see the movie *Tom Jones?*"

"Yep, and I know the scene you mean. They're gnawing on bones, grease to the elbows, and it was the sexiest scene that's ever been filmed." She reached across the table with a towelette and took a swipe at my cheek.

"Trying to keep me from getting too sexy?"

"No, that was the maternal instinct. Ever watched a two-year-old eating cereal?"

A few couples had finished dining and moved to the dance floor. I noticed a familiar back, and when he turned, it was Freddy, wrapped around a fragile-looking redhead. They were half tripping, half gliding, and headed our way.

"Look out, Angie, I think that couple is about to join us."

"Quick, finish that last rib and clean yourself up. This could be embarrassing."

"Yeah, well you've got a dab of sauce on your nose, but it's kind of cute, and I'm too polite to mention it."

We dived in, finished the last ribs. Leaving even one bite was not an option, and we both applied towelettes. We made it just in time; Freddy spotted us and dragged the redhead over.

"Hi, Alex, this is Jeannine. She just got off the jet from Arkansas this afternoon. She's the new schoolteacher for Stevens Village and I'm teaching her some survival skills."

"Hi, Freddy, hi, Jeannine. This is Angie, born and raised on the Kuskokwim, and she's just been giving me a few pointers. Care to join us?"

Jeannine peeled herself loose and sank into a chair. I got the distinct impression that her first priority was surviving Freddy. Freddy grabbed the other chair, just a little too close to Angie, and rubbed shoulders with her while he sat. Angie adjusted her chair a couple of inches my way.

"Where in Arkansas?" I asked.

"Fort Smith, and it is pretty different. Ever been to Arkansas?"

I nodded. "Yep. I was in Fort Smith on New Year's Day once. Comfortable in shirtsleeves and fall-colored leaves still on the trees. You are so right, this is very different, and it's going to get a lot more different in the next few weeks."

Freddy flagged down our waitress and ordered two gin and tonics, so apparently he intended to stay a while. I pointed to the two glasses Angie and I had nearly emptied. The waitress nodded and went to fetch a round.

Angie was shaking her head, and reached to squeeze Jeannine's hand. "Arkansas to Stevens Village? What have they told you?"

"Well, it's a one-room school with eight grades, but only twelve students. What else do I need to know?"

I jumped in. "One thing you need to know is the school is heated with a wood stove, and your contract better specify that someone in the village will cut the wood and light the fire every morning. Where are you going to stay?"

"I have my own room in the storekeeper's house. His wife does the cooking, so it will be like boarding."

"That's appropriate. Six of the kids belong to them, but having your own room may mean you're only sharing with the girls. Anyhow, they're good people."

"Freddy has just been telling me that I need to wear a wedding ring, and he's volunteered to pretend to be my husband." Jeannine looked up at Angie, then me. She was hoping we'd contradict that bit of advice, and I was sorry to disappoint her.

"Well, the wedding ring is a must. If you show up as single, the men in the village will not understand why you don't pick one of them. You'll be the most beautiful girl they've ever seen, so the competition could get ugly and the women won't like it much, either. You pretend to have a husband and talk about him all the time. A single woman who wants to stay that way simply won't make sense to them."

Jeannine blushed, but I hadn't intended a compliment; I was telling her the unvarnished truth. "You're scaring me. Am I really in for an ordeal?"

Angie took over. "That depends on your attitude. If you came for an adventure, you'll love it. Watching the Yukon freeze up, stop, and become a highway is fascinating. I promise you, if you make it to spring breakup, you'll never want to leave. The power and grandeur of the Yukon waking up in the spring might be the most exciting thing on the planet. If you just came here for the money, you're in trouble."

Jeannine seemed to be considering. She picked up a fresh towelette and shredded it, stacking the strips on my plate of bones. "I've read Robert Service and Jack London, and all of that, and I've always dreamed of coming to Alaska, but they *are* paying me over twice what I was earning in Arkansas."

Freddy piped up. "They darn sure should, and believe me, you're going to earn every penny of it."

Angie stood and reached for Jeannine's hand. "Come on, you and I need to powder our noses." She led Jeannine past the dance floor toward the facilities.

Freddy leaned back and got comfortable. "Well, you old dog, where have you been hiding Angie, and how much am I bid not to tell Celeste about her?"

"Sorry, not up for blackmail. Why do you think I care what you tell Celeste?" I thought Freddy frowned when I said *blackmail,* but it was his idea.

"You think I'm blind? I'm surprised the two of you haven't got it on right on the counter."

"Okay, I guess I did notice Celeste, but Angie's my sister-in-law, and our relationship is as pure as the driven snow. Tell you what. I'll buy the next round, just on general principles, and you keep your mouth shut to save me some explaining. Fair enough?" He nodded. The waitress appeared and dealt out the drinks. I dropped a twenty and a five on her tray. The five was a tip, and it did earn me a half smile, but the poor kid appeared almost too tired to smile. She squared her shoulders and dove back into the fray.

Freddy sampled his drink. "Sister-in-law, huh? Funny, I disremember you having a brother."

"Don't get too technical, I'm telling you the truth. In the Yupik Eskimo Nation where her husband and I worked together, we were called *Eelooks*, partners to the death. You don't have to share genes to be brothers. It was my partner, Angie's husband, who was killed when that pickup exploded at the Rendezvous Club."

"Aw, Jeeze, Alex, I'm really sorry." Freddy did look stricken and subdued. Either there was more human compassion in him than I had supposed, or else the gin had finally caught up with him.

The ladies seemed to be taking a long time in the powder room. Freddy and I sipped politely for a while, then just gave up and finished our drinks. I waved down the waitress again and she brought two more. That time I dropped a ten and a five on her tray and she smiled again.

"So, you're flying Jeannine out to Stevens in the morning?"

"Yep, got to get my new wife properly settled."

"Anyone ever tell you you're a despicable scumbag?"

"Oh yeah, the subject comes up now and then, but it's worth it. Look, I'm not going to rape the girl. I just happen to know how lonely she'll be in a couple of months. Hey, giving her a shoulder to cry on is practically a public service."

Angie and Jeannine threaded their way back across the dance floor. Jeannine seemed to be taller and happier than when they left. Angie sat down, but Jeannine stood by her chair.

"Freddy, would you take me back to the hotel, please? I'm really jet-lagged and tomorrow's a big day." She didn't wait for an answer, she turned and started for the door. Freddy scowled, drained his drink, and got up. Then he reached for Jeannine's untouched glass and carried it with him, sipping as he went.

"Good Lord, Angie, what did you tell that girl?"

"Oh, I just mentioned the birds and the bees, Alaskan style. She may have a new idea about who's boss, and she does know to call me if she gets lonely. Just the usual girl talk. Alex, do you think Freddy is a friend of yours?"

"Well, he used to be, but after tonight I'm not so sure."

"Damn, men are so blind. He can't blame you for Jeannine's rescue, I mean in general."

"Aw, come on, Angie. I've known Freddy for fifteen years. We flew together when we were trying to figure out which end of the airplane goes first."

Angie shook her head, obviously disgusted with me, and downed half her drink. The ice was almost melted. She wrinkled her nose and reached for my glass. "Alex, all I can tell you is to just look in his eyes sometime. Did you bring me here to dance, or to argue?"

We danced. Swede was on a nostalgia kick. We did foxtrots from the Fifties, the Swing a couple of times, even some disco. The mood was just right for us. If you're dancing for fun, not trying to smother your partner or using the dance as foreplay, you give your partner some room and go with the music.

The waitress brought fresh drinks. I tipped her again, we danced again, and again. Around two, Swede played his theme song.

The theme song, of course, is "Wagon Wheels." I hope you know that song, and if not, your parents and grandparents do. *Wagon wheels, wagon wheels, keep on a turnin' wagon wheels....* It evokes endless prairies, loneliness, but bravery and determination. That song has always struck me as appropriate for Fairbanks because if there weren't people with more bravery, guts, and determination than good sense, Fairbanks wouldn't exist. *Wagon wheels, carry me ho-oo-ome,* then, very softly, *wagon wheels, carry me home.* Swede shut down the organ.

House lights came up full and people scrambled out as if the lights were a cold shower. We sank down at the table and drained our glasses.

"Want to take me back to the hotel, Alex? I may be catching jet lag."

"Nonsense, the party is just starting. Help me stand up and I'll show you some real music and dancing."

Chapter Ten

Come what may, time and the hour run through the roughest night.
We gave up trying to appease hangovers with decaffeinated coffee
at the Maranatha, and I braved the morning sunlight in search of
a phone. No telephone in the room, of course, no doubt because
it might disturb our meditation. I found a pay phone in the lobby
and fed it quarters until Trooper Tim came on the line.

Tim is the special trooper who serves the villages around Bethel
so he's a steady charter customer. He's also a very good friend.

"Alex, when are you coming home? My hair's turning gray."

"What, you want me to pick up some hair dye in Fairbanks?"

"No, I want you to come back to work. Vickie has been
sending me out with Pat."

"Hey, Pat's a fine pilot. One of these days he'll be driving the
jet when you go into Anchorage."

"Yeah, the sooner the better. You know that sand spit where
we land across the river from Sheldon Point?"

"So?"

"So, Pat and I landed there yesterday and we were both terrified."

"Tim, Pat is a good pilot, what can I tell you?"

"Maybe he is, but I wish he wouldn't turn pale when I show
him where to land. What's up?"

"If I send you a couple of drinking glasses counter-to-counter
can you get them fingerprinted and cross checked?"

"If it will bring you home sooner. Prints belong to Saddam Hussein?"

"I have no idea, but I need to know. The glasses will be on the next jet." The phone dinged for more quarters, but I was tapped out. It went dead, so I hung it up.

Angie was hovering by the coffee shop door. "Alex, I'm hurting, and I should go to work in a few hours."

"Want to hit the Model Café for some real coffee?"

"That would help, and a Bloody Mary wouldn't be bad either."

"Check and cheque. The coffee shop at the Traveler's Inn."

We drove across town, and I was pleased to note there were no dents in the Buick. When you wake up with a fuzzy memory of the night before, there's always some concern for the car. Venturing out on the highway in that condition would be tantamount to suicide or murder, but a few blocks in town are usually survivable. Not smart, just survivable. Most cars in Fairbanks have a crumpled fender or two, and no one seems to mind.

"How much rum did we drink last night?" Angie did look a little pale, which was alarming, considering her ancestry.

"I never count while the party is raging. It spoils the mystique, you know. Maybe six before they closed the Wagon Wheel Club. After that I have no idea."

"We went to the Squadron Club so we could park at the hotel. You were driving mostly in the right lane and gave me a lecture about the drunk drivers on the road. Traveling with you certainly is educational. I'm amazed at how many occupations are open to women in this town."

We parked at the Traveler's, had Bloody Marys and a pot of real coffee, and the world did settle down. Normally I want nothing to do with vodka, but on the morning after, when it's suitably mixed with tomato juice and Tabasco, it is prescribed by nine out of ten drunks.

Angie had returned to her normal hue and was even getting some sparkle back in her eyes. "Orders of the day?"

"I need to nip out to the airport. I want to get Jody's under-wear on the morning flight. Then, I guess I'll stop by Interior and pick up my paycheck in case you want to lead me astray again tonight. Can I drop you at the station? It *is* your car."

"No thanks, and I'm never touching alcohol again. Take me back to the room for two hours repair work and I'll grab a cab to the station."

"Your slightest whim is my edict. Do you need help standing up?"

I stopped at the strip mall on the way to the airport and scrounged a cardboard box and a pile of Styrofoam peanuts to pack the glasses. The airline obliged with the morning jet, but it doesn't go to Bethel. Jets from Fairbanks to Bethel go by way of Anchorage, and with only two flights per day to Bethel, the glasses would arrive on the evening plane. I can't complain about that schedule because it is good for the charter business, including my current residency in Fairbanks. Sending the glasses counter-to-counter costs a few extra bucks, but it's the fastest way. I delivered the package to the ticket counter in Fairbanks. Tim could pick it up at the ticket counter in Bethel two minutes after the jet landed.

Celeste was bright and bubbly. "Hi, Alex. I have your check here. Does this mean you're leaving our fair city?" She brought an envelope to the counter and splayed her left hand out on the Formica, no wedding or engagement rings.

"Probably soon, but never know when I'll be back. You know how the charter business is. Maybe next trip I can give you a call?"

"Sure, you can do that. My phone number's on the envelope."

I was returning her smile when Freddy came out of his office.

"Hi, Alex, what the hell happened to you? Run over by a truck?"

"Sort of, a brewery wagon." Celeste was listening so I added, "It gets lonely on long nights away from home."

Her smile definitely turned to smug and she went back to her desk. Freddy was leaning on the counter again. He gave me an I-told-you-so smirk.

"I thought you had a charter to Stevens Village this morning."

"Eleven o'clock. My passenger has to do some shopping."

"Sure I can't help you out with the trip?"

"No thanks, you've already helped more than enough with that one, but you did say you're driving a Cessna 310?"

"Yeah, Bushmaster's executive choice."

"Perfect. I need a charter tonight. You know how the charter business is. If you have a pilot and a plane standing by, then you're losing money, but if a customer calls and you don't have a plane available, they'll call someone else and you still lose out."

"This isn't a job for the Otter?"

"No, four executives from British Petroleum. Evening meeting in Valdez, stand by an hour and bring them back. They'll appreciate a fast comfortable trip in the 310."

"Sure, Vicki will like that. Our normal charter rate for the 310 is three hundred per hour, but you probably can negotiate a wholesale price."

"No need. I'll charge BP three-fifty. Be here at five o'clock?"

"Can do."

"And Alex, see if you can shave and finish sobering up in the meantime?"

"Aye, aye, sir." I slunk back to the rental. It struck me that the Otter wasn't being loaded, and from the steady stream of flight tickets I'd seen in Celeste's file, that must be unusual.

By four-thirty I was looking pretty good, had the 310 cleaned out and fueled. I'd left a note in the room for Angie, but was pretty sure she wouldn't want to party. I figured she was safe at the Maranatha under a name that even her mother had probably forgotten. I taxied the 310 up to the flight line at Interior, but waited in the airplane. Somehow I didn't want to bump into Celeste just then, and I wondered why. I was remarkably single, or would be if or when Angie and I got out from under the cloud, and there was no romantic attachment there. Connie had made it quite clear that we were not an item, although we did seem to be seeing each other exclusively. Still, maybe that was masochism on my part.

The Otter was still parked, and apparently hadn't been out all day, so they must have caught up with the pipeline demand. At five to five, Freddy came out escorting four suits. He introduced them so fast that I didn't catch any names. Freddy handed me the office key and I pocketed it; clearly I'd be back long after the office closed. Passengers settled down in the back seats, strapped themselves in and immediately opened briefcases. I called the tower for permission to taxi.

The flight from Fairbanks to Valdez is almost straight south, two hundred sixty miles, which is why Freddy wanted the 310. I trimmed us out at ten thousand feet, indicating a hundred seventy knots, which equals one hundred ninety-three statute miles per hour. We were an hour and a half from tarmac to tarmac, and that was all my passengers cared about. I hope I never get that jaded. Our route took us between Mt. Deborah and Mt. Hayes in the Alaska Range, across the Glennallen Flats with Mt. Denali and its buttresses clearly visible on the right, then into the Chugach Mountains and finally screaming down into Prince William Sound.

I don't know any more spectacular flight on the planet, and my passengers were back there shuffling papers. Prior to the 1964 earthquake, I would have gone into town with them, but after the tidal wave wiped out the old town I wasn't much interested, and these were not types I cared to cultivate. I stayed with the airplane while they took a taxi into town.

I strolled, stretched my legs, marveled at the jagged rock mountains with snow halfway down, then went back to the plane and took a nap. The copilot seat slides back and reclines, so it was more comfortable than the cot at the Maranatha.

Taxi lights wiped across the cabin and woke me. I slammed the seat upright, slapped my cheeks, rubbed my eyes, and jumped out to hold the door. My passengers seemed to be fumbling out of the taxi and had a little trouble climbing the steps onto the wing. As each one passed, I was treated to fumes reminiscent of the previous night. I checked that they did manage to get their belts buckled. One was already snoring, and the others had their eyes closed.

My watch said eleven-thirty, so Freddy's hour of standby was off by five hundred percent, but that was fine with me. Standby time is at half charter rate and half pay for the pilot, but if you're sound asleep, the more the better. I snapped on the master switch to light the panel before I closed and locked the door, which turned out the interior lights. It was darker than a lawyer's heart, so an overcast must have moved in. I cranked engines, turned on taxi lights, and we rumbled to the end of the runway facing east. That made our departure over flats, then water.

The engines passed their checks individually, and those Lycoming gasoline burners made a healthy growl. I set flaps, released brakes, and when we broke ground, snapped off the landing lights. The lights of town fell behind us, and only the soft glow of instruments lit the universe. We ran up to five thousand feet, well above the local mountains, at ninety miles per and eighty percent power, and turned north.

At ten thousand I set up a cruise and tuned in the non-directional beacon at Glennallen. Flying on instruments is probably the most relaxing thing you can do. It's like playing the world's slowest video game. Tiny corrections of rudder keep the needle centered, once in a while a little pressure on the yoke maintains altitude, and you just sit back and let the airplane do its thing. Alcohol fumes in the cabin were approaching an explosive level, so I opened the cabin vent and turned the heater up a notch.

When we passed over Glennallen, I tuned the automatic direction finder radio to 660 kilohertz, which is KFAR radio on Farmer's Loop Road in Fairbanks. That ten-thousand-watt beacon has been guiding aircraft over the pole since the 1940s, and it's a clear channel so there are no false readings. When the VOR came alive we were sixty miles out with a heading of three hundred fifty degrees to Fairbanks, solidly over the Tanana. I reduced power, drifted down. Fairbanks Radio reported a five-thousand-foot ceiling and twenty miles visibility. They were right on in both cases. I parked at the passenger terminal and opened the door.

The sudden light and cold air threw my passengers into a tizzy, and I had some sympathy for them. They struggled for dignity, adjusted their neckties, buttoned jackets, and retrieved briefcases. I climbed down ahead of them and met each at the stair, making sure their feet hit the steps, and that each had his case. Once again, my passengers turned toward the restroom and I taxied down to the general aviation area.

At Interior some light flickered inside, maybe one of the offices with the door not quite closed. I spotted a car in the lot, but it was parked in shadow, possibly hidden on purpose. The rented Buick wasn't in the lot because I had left it in the tie-down space when I moved the 310. That saves your spot and can be important if you're coming home late. I went right on by Interior, moved the Buick ahead one length, and tied down the plane.

The lot suddenly seemed too well lit, but I slipped from plane to plane until I could see the parking lot behind Interior. Two cars that I didn't recognize were parked in shadow. The flickering light was coming from Reginald's office, the door not quite closed, and at least two or three people were moving around in there. I sneaked back to the Buick and headed for town with the office key still in my pocket. Whatever was going on in the office after midnight seemed like something I needed to check into, but opening the office door might be a quick way to get shot. I told myself I wasn't being a coward. I just preferred a more oblique approach.

The hotel room was dark. I slipped in, closed the door silently, and tiptoed for the bathroom. Angie was breathing softly, apparently sleeping the sleep of the innocent. I closed the bathroom door before turning on the light, performed ablutions quietly and turned off the light before I opened the door. I was halfway to my bed when Angie snapped on her reading light.

"Hi, Alex. Do you always sneak in so quietly?"

"Shhh, don't wake Angie. The poor girl's exhausted."

"You got that right. So what daring adventure kept you out half the night?"

"Not much of anything. I hauled some executives to Valdez, brought back some drunks, but something is going on at Interior. Someone is burning midnight oil."

"You didn't creep through the night and beard them in their den?"

"No, I slunk home, tail between my legs, but I do have a key to the office. I'll sneak back when the coast is much clearer."

"My hero. Good night, Alex." She snapped off her light.

Chapter Eleven

We woke up slowly to bright sunshine outside. We lazed around, took turns in the bathroom, and sauntered down to the restaurant.

I had a hankering for potato pancakes and little pig sausages, but Angie went for the eggs Benedict again. The orange juice was fresh, and the decaffeinated coffee was good enough at the moment. It began to dawn on me that Angie was wearing jeans.

"Hey, don't you have to go to work or something?"

"Well, Alex, it is Saturday, you know?"

"No, actually, I didn't know. You mean people with real jobs have the day off?"

"That we do, and the vet called the station yesterday while you were out partying. We can pick up Turk today."

"That might be a little awkward. Did you notice there's a No Pets sign by the front desk? Maybe you could get some dark glasses and pretend he's a seeing-eye dog?"

"We could do that, but we also could take him out to the house."

"Won't that be a problem, feeding him and such by remote control?"

"Not too bad. We'd need to check on him every couple of days, not a big deal."

"Okay, let's do it. I need to return an office key to Interior, then make a call to Bethel, and we're good to go."

I stayed on Cushman down to First Avenue and turned left into the Alaska Commercial Company lot. The gnome in the key booth cut me a duplicate office key in two minutes for three dollars. Naturally the key was stamped *Do Not Duplicate*, but most keys are, and it's never stopped anyone yet. I didn't have a good idea of why I needed it, but having my own key to the office felt like an ace in the hole. We drove out to the airport, but I parked Angie and the Buick at the Sea Airmotive hangar.

"Oh, oh, a new girlfriend at Interior and you don't want her to see me?"

How the heck do women know things like that?

"Certainly not, but no one there has seen the Buick, and I want to keep it that way. You be a good girl, sit here and contemplate your sins, and I'll be right back."

"Okay, but if you take off for Valdez, I will be mildly irritated."

"Hey, I left the keys in the ignition. If I'm not back in eight hours, you can go get Turk without me."

I drove the company pickup down the flight line to Interior. Celeste wasn't there, and Freddy didn't spill out of his office. The sole occupant was the brunette who commanded the second desk, and when I came in she jumped as if she'd been shot and shoved papers under a notebook. I didn't really see what she was hiding but it seemed to be just billing, not the slick cover of *Playgirl Magazine*.

"Hi, I'm Alex. Just stopped by to drop off the office keys and a billing from Bushmaster for the Valdez charter. We got in pretty late last night."

She got up and came over to the counter, no smile, no expression at all, but she did have a face that belonged on a cameo and a remarkable figure that put me in mind of a tiger when she moved. I remembered my first impression when she and Celeste were both sitting at desks, and wondered why I had swayed so easily toward Celeste. I hoped I wasn't guilty of the old *Blondes have more fun* cliché.

"Thanks." She took the bill and the key, tossed the key on Celeste's desk and carried the bill back to her own. I was dismissed, but I had the impression that this girl might be the cake and Celeste only the frosting. She opened a ledger exactly like Celeste's and entered the Bushmaster billing. That seemed strange. Why two ledgers? I concluded that my knowledge of bookkeeping is no better than my judgment of women.

Thank heaven Angie was still waiting in the car and confirmed my latest impression that brunettes are to be sought after. We stopped at the strip mall. Angie bought a few things, mostly for Turk, and conned the cashier out of three dollars in quarters. I hit the booth outside and called the troopers' office in Bethel. Tim came on the line, of course. He's no more hip to weekends and their meaning than I am.

"Alex, I thought you were calling from Fairbanks."

"I am, who says different?"

"The fingerprints. One glass was a bust, smudges and some horrible cheap lipstick, but the other had nice clear prints from a guy who's known to be in Motown."

"Motown?"

"Detroit City. He's a soldier of fortune, alleged to be an assassin for hire."

"What do you mean, *alleged?*"

"That means the FBI knows damn well who he is and what he does, but he hasn't been caught and convicted, so he's innocent until a jury of his peers…if they can arrest twelve of his peers. My advice is to find a new playmate, fast."

"You mean he's on a most-wanted list?"

"Not yet, but you should read his ads in the magazine. He will be."

"So, the police do officially know him?"

"Not officially, but even cops can read magazines, and he was interesting enough to be checked out. He was discharged from the Marine Reconnaissance program as being undesirable, and that's pretty darn undesirable."

"Reconnaissance, like intelligence gathering?"

"Theoretically, but think Navy Seals or Army Rangers, trained in every nasty skill that the services pay people for and we arrest them for."

"Thanks, Tim. I really appreciate this."

"My pleasure. If one of you gets shot, which seems highly likely, be sure it's him, unless he knows how to land on sandbars."

"I'll do my best. The secret to landing on sandbars is my St. Christopher medallion. It's in the jockey box of Eight-Three Fox. Out of quarters, got to run."

I walked back to the car and met Angie.

"Any luck?"

"Yep, Jody's underwear is the real McCoy." I unconsciously touched the pistol in my belt and Angie caught the gesture.

"Here we go again, damn stupid macho males protecting the poor helpless little woman. What the hell is going on?"

"Okay, okay, don't shoot. Let's go get Turk and I'll spill my guts."

We headed across the Chena on a new bridge. I hadn't known it was there, but the sign said *College* with an arrow, and it worked.

"Going to tell me that poor Jody is wasting away from incurable avarice and needs our sympathy?"

"No, I'm going to tell you that a state trooper in Bethel got an ID on one of the phony cops who came to your house."

"And?"

"And, he's a known assassin for hire. Now, do you feel better?"

"Damn right I do. Don't drive past the dairy."

I turned in. Angie and Turk had a joyous reunion, and I made the vet joyous with my credit card. Turk had a two-inch-wide white plaster stripe across his scalp, but otherwise he looked fine. Angie and Turk snuggled in the back seat while I drove us out the hot springs road. A black sedan with two male occupants was parked in the Rendezvous lot, but they had their heads down studying a map and showed no interest in us. I was wondering just how professional *professional* killers are, and what sort of resources they had. No cars were parked along the road or in the driveway.

The sun was almost warm. Fall had moved up a notch with most leaves yellow and reflecting back the sunlight. All was peace and beauty, including the special musty smell of autumn. I parked in front of the house. Angie and Turk went inside, and I leaned across the car top to keep a lookout and enjoy the warmth. I'd just been thinking how profound the silence was when I heard gravel crunch. A car had coasted to a stop on the road. In any other setting I wouldn't have heard a thing, but in the silence of the woods there was no mistaking that sound, and my hackles went straight up.

I was thinking that Turk saved our lives the first time, but was probably the Judas if that crunch on the road meant what I was afraid it did. Someone had stopped without driving by to see if we were home. Either they had staked·out the highway for a week or had just called the vet to ask about that beautiful husky. The vet wouldn't have ratted us out intentionally, but would have had no qualms about telling an interested party that Turk was on his way home.

I popped the trunk, grabbed the shotgun and the box of shells and burst into the house.

"What's the matter?" Angie came from the kitchen and I shoved the shotgun into her hands.

"Do you know how to use this?"

"Are you kidding? Did you reload it?"

"No."

She grabbed the gun, dumped two shells out of the box, jacked a shell into the chamber and refilled the magazine.

"Good, close the doors and windows, and do not let Turk out of the house. Keep a watch on the woods, mostly on the downriver side, and if anyone comes out of the woods except me, blow them away."

"What are you going to do?"

"I'm going to do the damn stupid macho male thing, what else?"

I stepped out, closed the door, got the pistol in my hand, and crept into the woods.

The car I'd heard had seemed to be about fifty yards to the left so I angled that direction but kept the driveway in sight. I found a big spruce in a spot where I could make out the house and the driveway through the trees, and crawled under the branches. That's an old moose-hunting technique. You do not go looking for moose because when they're grazing they cover twenty miles per day. You stay quiet, and let the moose come to you. I didn't even breathe.

It was five minutes before I detected movement. It wasn't noise, just a subliminal sense of something changing. They hadn't headed directly for the house. They were apparently headed for the river, planning to come at the house from behind. I left my spruce and crawled on a course to intercept them. They were moving slowly, and I was moving slower, but the vector was in my favor.

I started getting glimpses through the trees, definitely two men, both carrying rifles. They were fifty yards away, not a difficult shot for the .357, but I did want a positive ID, and I wasn't seeing faces. Shooting a man is a nasty business, and I hope I never get to like it, but sometimes it has to be done. Both Trooper Tim and I would be dead now if I hadn't shot men in the past.

I also hate the thought of slaughter yards, but I love beefsteak. Someone has to kill the steers, ultimately for my enjoyment, so I can hardly claim not to be in favor. When a man with a gun is intent on killing, particularly me or mine, and assuming, as I was, that these were the guys who killed Stan, I didn't mind very much. It was an unpleasant job that needed to be done. I just wanted to be sure. They stepped into a relatively clear spot between birch trees. I picked up a baseball-sized rock and tossed it into a bush on my left. They spun around and there was the phony cop. No more thought, and no compunction. I put a bullet in the center of his forehead.

His partner dropped instantly. For a few seconds I couldn't see him, then something moved several yards closer to the road.

I put a bullet in the movement, but too late. It was a rifle and his bullet ripped a chunk out of my cheek. I didn't feel it for a second, but had already dropped to the ground when the next bullet slammed into a tree above me.

Bushes moved. He was crawling toward the road, and I couldn't see him. I crawled too, paralleling him, ready to fire if I saw anything but bushes. My cheek didn't hurt as badly as I thought it should. I hoped it was adrenalin, not shock setting in. He was getting close to the road, apparently crawling in a depression. I took a chance, tried a hunkered-down run toward the road. A bullet slammed a tree three inches from my nose. I dropped again and crawled, thank you.

He got to the road and rolled right under the car. I could see bits of him, but a shot would have been through bushes and probably deflected. The car door on the far side slammed, the car started and threw gravel. I stood up, put a bullet in each near side tire, and ran for the road.

The car swerved, skidded back and forth across the road, and slammed into the ditch on the far side. He came out, leading with his rifle, and we were both in the open. I had two bullets left, and I put the first one in his heart. His shot went wild. He dropped the rifle and crumpled. I kept him covered, and walked over. He was not going to be a problem anymore. I eased the hammer down on the final chamber and backtracked through the woods to check on his partner. I was sure, but you can never be too sure. I let the pistol lead, ready to fire, until I spotted the body and stalked up to it. Never mind, you do not want a description of his head. I stuck the gun in my belt and stumbled toward the house. Suddenly I was feeling queasy and light-headed.

"Hey, Angie, it's me. Don't shoot. I'm through playing damn stupid macho games for a while. Just come help me into the house."

She came out, carrying the shotgun and holding Turk on a very short, very stout leash.

I waved her back. "Better get Turk inside."

"Are they still out there, Alex?"

"In a manner of speaking, yes they are, and I don't want Turk investigating right now. Will that radio of yours reach the state troopers?"

"Not directly, but through relays. Alex, what's the matter with your face?"

"Nothing that Turk's vet can't fix. I think it's what they'd call just a flesh wound."

"Yeah, quite a lot of flesh, and you won't be wearing an earring on that side anymore." She ran for the first aid kit, swabbed me with something that hurt a hell of a lot worse than the shot, and slapped on a bandage. "Sit down, and keep quiet for a change. Don't let your male ego get in an uproar. Just trust little old me to call the cops."

I leaned back on the couch and closed my eyes for a minute. Something tickled my nose and I looked up. Angie was waving a brandy snifter. She smiled and handed it to me.

"Cops will be here in a few minutes. I thought you'd like to be awake to talk to them."

"Thanks." I sampled the brandy. It was Rémy Martin, delicious, satisfying fire. It burned all the way down, waking up organs as it passed. I sipped again, savored it, and I was glad to be alive.

"Did you say a few minutes?"

"Yeah, that's what I said. You've been out for almost half an hour."

"Damn, there goes my stupid macho male image, for sure. Can I beat my chest and make it up to you?"

"You can shut your stupid macho male mouth, and just try to wake up."

I sipped the brandy again, then just cupped the snifter and breathed the fumes. If doctors don't prescribe that, they should. Sirens came screaming down the road, and sorted themselves into two cop cars. They stopped by the wreck in the road, sirens still blaring, then one came down the drive, his siren winding down the scale and ending with a burp.

Angie opened the door. The state trooper came in, so big he almost filled the doorway. Neat uniform, Irish face, black hair regulation cut under his trooper hat, and his hand on his service revolver. "What happened here?"

I was glad to be awake. "Two guys came through the woods and attacked us with rifles."

"Two guys? There's only one by the car."

"The other is in the trees. Come on, I'll show you."

Angie had both hands on Turk's leash and was braced in the bedroom doorway, but Turk wasn't in attack mode. The poor dog was confused. I led the cop outside and we tromped back to the scene of my crime. He winced at the bloody mess.

"Want to tell me what's really going on? There's two bullet holes in the door, but they weren't made by that rifle."

"Right. Contact Trooper Timothy Literra in Bethel. He has an ID on one of these guys from fingerprints. He's a hit man from Detroit and this is their second pass at us. We just don't know why we're targets."

We walked back to his car and he stood outside to talk to his radio for a while. His partner drove down the lane for a conference, then backed up onto the road, apparently to stand guard. More radio talk, then the trooper walked over to the doorway where I was leaning.

"Okay, you're clean. Trooper Literra swears by you and says he made you a special deputy. Horse pucky, of course, but good enough for now. Unless you're an albino, you'd better go in and sit down."

Judging by the scratching on the door, Angie had locked Turk in the bedroom. I sat down on the couch and Angie handed me the brandy snifter. I resumed my therapy.

The trooper was looking at me, but talking to Angie. "How much blood has he lost?"

"Oh, very little. He's a real sissy, you know, a regular pansy. There isn't a macho bone in his body, and he always faints at the sight of blood."

"Is he your husband?"

"No, my husband was killed a few days ago in an accident. It was his pickup that exploded in the parking lot at the Rendezvous."

"Accident?"

"That's what the police report said."

"Yes, that's what the news report said. No point in scaring the public, and no point in alerting the bomber that we were looking for him. Actually it was a very sophisticated bomb that screamed Marine Reconnaissance, and the dead guy out on the road is almost certainly the bomber, but you knew that, didn't you?"

Angie nodded, a kind of a deep, almost sarcastic nod that told the whole story. The trooper matched her nod. I concentrated on breathing brandy fumes.

Chapter Twelve

The ambulance was one of those big, square, boxy vans that look as if they should be delivering bread. A wrecker came, snorted and squealed cables for a while, and left with the car on a trailer. One trooper had followed the wrecker but ours stayed to supervise the environmental restoration. He came in carrying a notebook.

"Coffee?" Angie asked.

"Wonderful. I just need to take your statements. May as well level with me and tell me the whole story. I've got plenty of time, and I'm not going anywhere just yet. By the way, I'm Jim Stella. Here's my card, office and home phone." I was sitting on the couch, and the trooper had sunk down into an easy chair, so we both had to reach to transfer the card.

"Thanks," I said. "Alex Price and Angie Demoski. I didn't realize troopers gave out home phones. Oops, lieutenant, I should have recognized the bar."

"We don't give out cards, and never mind the rank, it's embarrassing. The card is because I have a feeling this isn't over yet. Trooper Literra tells me you can hit anything you can see with your pistol. That mess in the woods confirms it and today it was a good thing, but as a general rule, we'd rather you didn't do that."

Angie brought coffees and offered sugar and cream. Stella and I both turned down the embellishments, so she put her tray on the table and came to sit beside me on the couch facing the trooper.

Stella took a grateful sip of his coffee. "So, if you see another situation coming up where you might be tempted to shoot people, I'd like a call. The point of calling me personally is that I'll know who is calling and why, so you won't waste a lot of time answering questions."

"Thanks, I really appreciate that."

Angie frowned. "So it's really not over?"

The trooper and I both shook our heads, but I answered, "Angie, all we did today was cut an arm off an octopus. Those guys were hired guns, easily replaceable. Our problem is whoever hired them."

Stella nodded that time. "Okay, we all understand each other. Now, about those statements. Skip the car bomb and start with the bullet holes in the front door."

I filled him in with what we knew, which actually wasn't much. What we suspected and wondered about was way too sketchy for a police report. For instance, I did not tell him about my stint as bodyguard for the governor, nor mention men with hard eyes.

He finished his notes and his coffee and stood. "Please call me Jim, because I'm going to call you Angie and Alex." We shook hands, Angie held the door for him and we stood on the step while he backed down the drive.

"Shall we trust him, Angie? He seemed sincere and he didn't confiscate my pistol, although he probably should have."

"Yep, trust him. It's his eyes, same as Stan and you. He's tougher than walrus hide, has seen it all and is ready for anything, but there is nothing hidden in him."

"You read all that?"

"Hey, me heap big Indian medicine woman, but it's true. In the old days when shamen were judge and jury, they didn't bother with testimony and such. They just sat with the accused and stared into each other's eyes, and it always worked."

"Remind me to pick up some sunglasses. What do we do with Turk?"

"First, I let him out of the bedroom, then we set out food and water, then I tell him to stay here."

"No chains?"

"Nah, he may get into some mischief but he won't wander off, and he does know better than to attack porcupines."

"He learned by trial and error?"

"Yep, had so many quills in his feet that he was trying to walk on his wrists. Do dogs have wrists? It took the vet two hours to dig all of the quills out of Turk's nose and mouth."

Angie was driving because she said I still looked pale. I felt fine, but the road did seem to be undulating in a way I didn't remember. It seemed like taking a nap would be a good idea, but the cot at the Maranatha wasn't inviting.

"You know, Mary Angela, I'm about as healthy and tranquil as I care to get for a while. Do you suppose that credit card of yours would go for a room with a phone?"

"With the greatest of pleasure. My mouth is still watering for the lamb béarnaise you had the other night, and I need to teach you about Côtes du Rhône. How about a cottage at the River's Edge Resort? Mary can afford those from September first through April. The bungalows have two queen-sized beds and the restaurant is wonderful."

"Great, sooner the better. There's one bullet left in the .357 and the box is back at the hotel, so don't run into any ambushes."

When we checked out of the Maranatha, they loaded us up with tracts, various versions of the *Good News*. We took the material, thanked them, and fled.

The River's Edge Resort is on Boat Street, and it was better than good. Mary Angela checked us in and produced two keys with the satisfied smirk of a cat with a bowl of canaries and cream. Our new digs featured two queen-sized beds, every amenity that's ever been in a bungalow, and the Chena River gurgling along right outside our picture window.

Angie was right about the restaurant, too. Another picture window overlooked the Chena with a floodlight making a crescent on the water. It was good to be dining by candlelight again with a waitress who had finished college. We both ordered lamb, Angie dealt with the waitress, and a bottle of Côtes du Rhône appeared. Once again she sampled and smiled, once again I took a sip and I smiled, too. I've got to remember that: red wine, *Côtes du Rhône*.

A miniature loaf of sourdough bread showed up with the wine, then Caesar salads, and rare racks of lamb with béarnaise from heaven.

Angie swallowed, blotted, sipped, blotted and smiled, but she was thinking seriously beyond dinner. "What do we do next, Alex? Keep getting lucky and shoot a few assassins every day before lunch?"

"Could take a while. There are several million people in Detroit, and if the newspapers are correct, at least half of them are killers. We've got to get to the head of the octopus, and my money is still on Interior. Nowadays it's incumbent on all criminals to keep records and leave evidence in their computers, so perhaps we should have a look? Reginald is a Nixon fan, so he probably tapes all incriminating communications."

"Won't they notice you snooping around?"

"Maybe not. I do have a key to the office, but this time it's stealth and flashlights. Say around midnight?"

"You mean I get to come, too? Enfranchised at last?"

"Yep, you can sit on a cushion and sew a fine seam while keeping a lookout, and I'll toss the files and computers...doing a word search for *murder*, I guess."

In black slacks and turtleneck, Angie did look like Cat Woman. The lot was empty, office dark. We parked several spaces down the line and walked back to Interior. The tie-down area is nominally lighted for security by mercury lamps on poles, but we ducked from shadow to shadow. Not that it was practical, but it made us feel like commandos. I didn't see the security pickup cruising. Perhaps they take Sunday mornings off.

I unlocked the door with my copied key, we slipped inside and snapped on flashlights. Angie wrinkled her nose. "Cheap perfume. Is that your new girlfriend?"

"No, that's the smell of a successful business. Park yourself in front of the window and holler if anything moves."

"Don't I get a cushion?"

"Yep, union rules, fifteen minutes every two hours. Meantime, see that door on the left?" I flashed it with my light, then lighted the drawbridge in the counter. "If we're about to be assaulted by an army, duck under the counter and out that door. It leads to a freight shed big enough to hide in for a week or two. What I'm actually expecting is airport security in a pickup. Just holler in time so that I can switch off my light, and hit the deck under the window until they drive away. They won't come in unless they see lights flashing around."

"Gotcha. Go do something useful." Angie assumed a sentry stance, I ducked under the drawbridge and wondered what to do next. For want of something constructive, I plopped down at Celeste's desk and fingered through the flight tickets. The Otter was still flying, two trips almost every day. I checked the rest of the flight tickets. Some were pilots I didn't recognize, and Freddy himself had flown several.

That made perfect sense and I wondered why he needed me at all. Maybe it was just charity, or maybe he really was busy with office work. I noticed a slip signed by Tommy Olsen, and that was a surprise because I thought Tommy was flying out of Cordova, but then, pilots do get around, and he'd be equally surprised to find a ticket signed by me.

I noticed a flight ticket signed by Alvin Hopson. The name caught my eye because the Hopson Brothers are the big names in the North Slope Borough, but I didn't recognize the name Alvin. Probably he was the son of Steve, or maybe Ebon, who owns the hotel and cable television system at Point Barrow. I pulled the ticket out, and it was for a flight from Point Barrow to Prudhoe Bay. According to the ticket, Interior keeps a Howard and a pilot stationed at Point Barrow. I remembered that plane because it used to belong to the Ball brothers in Dillingham. Apparently Interior was a bigger outfit than I'd realized. I rummaged further and spotted several more tickets signed by Alvin.

Time was wasting. I checked the brunette's desk and found piles of invoices and letters. I was looking for the ledger I'd seen, but her desk was locked so I settled for the papers on top, scanned a few, got no ideas at all, and wandered into Reginald's office. I left the door open, but with Angie on guard I felt free to shine the flashlight around. His bookcase held an eclectic mix of federal publications, Jack London, Robert Service, Louis L'Amour, Baedeker's *Guide to Alaska*, and a bottle of Courvoisier with six brandy snifters. His desk drawers held stationery, a few folders that appeared innocuous, and a nickel-plated .38 revolver in the center drawer with the pens. I turned to the computer.

When Bushmaster gets rich, we'll buy a computer like that one. Reginald hadn't logged off; the computer was only sleeping. I tapped the space bar and the screen glowed with fifty icons taking up half the space. One of the few I recognized was Orbitz, the travel people, so I clicked on that one.

It invited me to sign in, so I typed in *Interior Air* and it asked for a password. Would Reginald use his wife's name, his mother's name? Did he even have a wife or mother? Then I realized this was a corporate account, not a personal one. The same account would be on Celeste's computer, Freddy's, probably the accounting office in Anchorage. I typed in Otter.

"You have entered an incorrect password."

"Skyvan."

"You have entered an incorrect password."

"Freight."

"Welcome, Interior Air."

I clicked on *My Stuff* and a listing of flights and hotels came up. I relied on Jody's estimate of two weeks. She probably tells time by counting thirty-dollar bottles, so she should know. I ran back fifteen days and found two first-class, round-trip tickets, Detroit, Fairbanks, with open returns.

I tried the most recent entry and it was two first-class, round-trip tickets from Seattle, also open returns. Each reservation had a name, but I didn't bother with them. I figured that hired guns probably travel with half-a-dozen phony picture IDs. I was in the right church, but which pew? Anyone with access to that system could have booked those flights. In fact, I could have booked Angie and me first-class to London with a couple of dozen keystrokes, and, with the account name and the password, I could even do it from Bethel.

I opened *My Documents* and was confronted with hundreds of files. I was in overload, no idea where to start, when Angie hollered. Sotto voce, but big-time urgency. "Hey, Alex, a big black Cadillac just stopped out front and I think someone is coming in." I heard her bump against the counter, then the door to the warehouse closed, but I had to shut down that damned computer. If I just pulled the plug it would be obvious someone had been prowling. I closed the file, pulled up *Start*, hit *Shutdown*. It said, *Closing files...Saving settings...* agonizingly slowly. I snapped off my flashlight, but the glow from the computer looked like a floodlight. The outside door opened, the drawbridge banged, and I dived under the desk.

Brisk footsteps came straight to the office, the door closed and the light snapped on. I tried to bury myself in blue shag. The desk was big enough, unless someone looked under it, but I didn't dare move a muscle or bat an eyelash. If I'd breathed, the desk would have gone up and down. Polished black oxfords came around the desk, walking fast, and someone tapped the spacebar on the keyboard. The computer must have made it to Off. That was a goof, because the computer had been left on, but I couldn't have waited for it to go to sleep.

He typed fast, so he knew the passwords. I heard a disk inserted. Twenty seconds later, more typing. Was he copying a file, or had he just ordered a new wave of gunslingers? The shiny black oxfords backed up, walked around the desk, the light snapped off. I breathed, the drawbridge dropped down, and the front door closed. I scrambled out from under the desk. The computer showed the desktop with icons, no clue to what the intruder had done. I hunkered down and ran to the front window without using the flashlight. Angie had been correct; it was a big black Cadillac, but it was pulling away without lights so I couldn't see his license plate. It must have been, very probably was, Dave Marino the campaign man, but like everything else in this screwy business, I couldn't be positive.

I opened the door to the freight warehouse and warbled, "Ollee ollee outs in free."

A flashlight snapped on behind the freight desk, a small circle of light in the massive dark cavern, and Cat Woman followed the beam.

"Kinda close, huh?"

"It's a good thing you made me shave. If I'd had whiskers, I'd have been caught."

"Well, the other good thing is that now we know who the bad guy is."

"Nope, Angie, what I know is he wears black oxfords and knows his way around Reginald's computer. All I could see was carpet pile and dust balls. Believe me, if I had so much as batted my eyes, I'd have been spotted, and no way could I get my pistol out from under that desk."

"Well, we know he drives a black Cadillac."

"Yep, and the campaign manager does that, but so do a couple of thousand other people in Fairbanks."

"Want to search some more?"

"I want a drink. What time does the bar at the River's Edge close?"

"Doesn't matter, we have our own in the room. Me heap big Indian bartender."

Chapter Thirteen

Sunshine warmed the edge of our table in the restaurant. The Chena raced by almost below us beyond the plate glass windows. I find rivers endlessly fascinating. The movement is constant but changes minute by minute. Rivers have unlimited power, they're unpredictable. Certainly rivers have made the populating of Alaska possible, both for the ancients and moderns. Fairbanks itself was first a fish camp for the indigenous people, then a river port for stern-wheelers.

That's changed with the arrival of the railroad, the highway, the airport. We were enjoying a breakfast that underscored the impact of jets on Alaska. Lox and bagels fresh from New York, cream cheese from Philadelphia, butter from Wisconsin, orange juice that still bore the tang of Florida, and Maui onions and Kona coffee from Hawaii. Life in Alaska was very different before the first Boeing 707 landed at Ladd Field fifty years ago. Angie and I were thoroughly enjoying the fresh lox, and an onion you could eat like an apple was beyond description.

Still, I was fascinated by the river. Apparently a swarm of gnats had dipped too low and foot-long silver grayling were leaping out of the water for their breakfasts. Mini-whirlpools came swirling by, then part of a wooden dock that had escaped from somewhere. Perhaps there's some Huckleberry Finn in me, but I couldn't help thinking that the drops of water going past our window would be in the Tanana tomorrow, the Yukon next week, the Bering Sea by next month, and then, who knows?

I was six years old when I first answered that call. A small creek flowed through our pasture outside Seattle. I built a raft of cedar fence posts, set a chair on it, stocked it with sandwiches, apples, and a mason jar of water, and set out for Zanzibar. That voyage ended two miles later when I came to a culvert under a highway and the raft wouldn't fit.

I still haven't been to Zanzibar, but the river was reawakening the urge. Angie pulled me back to Fairbanks by clearing her throat and pouring more orange juice.

"Is Sunday your day of rest? We could while away the hours by reading the tracts from Maranatha."

"Angie, remember the famous Sherlock Holmes quote, 'Come Watson, the game's afoot'? Well, you can think of this as a game we're in up to our eyebrows, it's just that the stakes are higher than usual. And no, I wasn't thinking of resting. Actually, I'm considering making the ultimate sacrifice."

"You mean letting me have the last of the salmon?"

"That, too, but you have no idea what lengths I'll consider to get information out of Interior."

Angie pounced on the last slice of salmon, slathered it with cream cheese, rounded up a few errant capers, and the last sliver of onion. She waved the saltshaker past it and closed her eyes while she savored. I had to content myself with finishing the orange juice, and we both sat back with coffee.

Cat Woman had turned into a contented kitten. Angie was almost purring. "You want to go back tonight and hit that computer again?"

"No point. Angie, there were a thousand files, and they all looked alike. Black Oxfords knew exactly what he was doing and copied only one file, so I'm more convinced than ever that the answer is in that computer, but there ain't no way we're going to find it."

"So, you have a more brilliant plan?"

"Angie, who knows everything that goes on in an office?"

"Oh no, don't tell me you're considering dating cheap perfume?"

"I said I was willing to sacrifice myself, and don't be selling her short. She's gorgeous, and *she's* not the least bit sarcastic. I don't have any better ideas, unless you'd like to date the new campaign manager?"

"No, you go right ahead. I'll stay home and read the tracts we got from Maranatha so I can save your soul, when or if you survive."

"Hi, Celeste? Alex. Listen, I can't get you out of my mind. I keep thinking about the way your fascinating blue eyes sparkle and the darling little dimples when you smile, and it's driving me nuts. Would you consider having dinner with me tonight?"

Angie rolled her eyes and made gagging noises, then turned over on her bed and pulled a pillow over her head. Our beds had big white comforters and three pillows each and she burrowed down almost out of sight.

"That's wonderful. How about seven o'clock? Any restaurant you fancy is fine with me.

"Great. Sure, you make the reservations. I appreciate that. I'll pick you up at six-thirty? Perfect, what's your address?" I wrote down the house number. It was on Wendell Street, a block from the bridge.

"See you then. You just made my day." I hung up the phone, reached over and gave Angie a whack on her cute little backside, the only part visible under the covers.

"Is it safe to come out?" she asked.

"What are you worried about? I'm the one sacrificing myself."

"Yeah, but it was getting pretty deep in here. Is that the way you always ask for dates?"

"Trust me, it works, and may the punishment fit the crime."

Celeste was out the door and striding down the walk the moment I parked. She wore a short red cocktail dress, and when she got close, her perfume smelled good to me. The earrings that peeked from under her blonde bob were blue stones that matched her eyes, and both were sparkling, but she stopped and stared at my new bandage.

"Alex, what happened to your cheek?"

"I got so excited when you agreed to go out with me that I cut myself shaving. Remember how it was in high school? We always got zits just before a big date? This is the adult version."

She didn't look convinced, but I opened the car door and she slipped in. She'd made reservations at Club Eleven, so named because it's eleven miles out of town on the Richardson Highway. It's not the most expensive restaurant in the area, but close enough, and the dining room is lighted for seduction, not eating.

She settled down just a little too close and crossed her knees under that short skirt. It was close, but I didn't drive off the road. From her smile, I think she noticed the swerve. "How did the Valdez charter go?"

"Educational. I had had the impression the pipeline carried oil, but now I think it may be Scotch whisky. Are those guys regular customers?"

"Yeah, pretty often. Weird bunch of ducks, engineers or something."

"Well, they kept me up past my bedtime. I dropped the key off yesterday and was confronted by that brunette who sits beside you. Does she hate all men, or just me?"

"Oh, Marlene? You didn't make a pass at her, did you?"

"Certainly not. Since I met you, other women are invisible."

"It's just as well. Don't quote me on this, but she belongs to Freddy. It's pretty interesting because they avoid each other like the plague at work, except when she goes into his office and closes the door. She finds about twenty excuses a day to do that."

"She gets lipstick on his collars?"

"No, but she sure looks happy when she comes out. That's the club on the left."

A maître d' bowed us to a table beside the dance floor. Several tables were occupied, some patrons in evening dress, some in Sunday duds. Celeste in her red cocktail dress fit right in. I was a little underdressed, but with Celeste at the table, no one was going to notice. A waiter in a tuxedo brought menus and asked if we'd like a cocktail. I let Celeste set the pace, and she ordered a margarita. That was a pace I couldn't match, so I ordered Captain Morgan and Coke. It's not that I don't like tequila. I love it. It may be the greatest flavor of all liquors and my mouth waters just thinking about it. The problem is that after a couple of margaritas I tend to go outside and bay at the moon, and I did have ulterior motives for this date.

Gazing into Celeste's baby blues by candlelight almost sidetracked me, but I forged ahead. "How long have you lived in Fairbanks?"

"Starting my third winter, and sort of looking forward to it. You know, this time of year is like the pause before you jump into a cold shower. You have to take a deep breath and force yourself, but once you're in, it isn't so bad. After that, it gets really lovely, you know? Beautiful white frost on everything, then Christmas lights reflecting in ice fog. In a weird kind of way, it's like living in a cocoon."

"Yep, know just what you mean. You bundle up, keep doing your thing, and every day is different."

"Is Bethel very beautiful, Alex?"

"On rare occasions, some storms are spectacular, but no, Bethel is flat bare tundra. Fascinating maybe. Beautiful, not likely."

"Then why do you stay there?"

The waiter brought our drinks and we hadn't yet consulted the menus. Celeste solved that problem. "Alex, they do a filet mignon that's out of this world."

"Terrific, let's do it."

She ordered salad with Roquefort, a baked potato with everything, and the filet rare, so when it came my turn I just nodded.

"Alex, why don't you pick the wine?"

"Sure. I've been thinking that a good Côtes du Rhône would hit the spot." Everyone nodded and the waiter bustled away.

"So, then why do you live in Bethel?"

"If you're not smart enough to get a real job and have to fly charter for a living, Bethel is the best place to do that. We have no roads, no connection with the outside world. There's only the Kuskokwim River between villages, and then only a few of the villages. Our area includes Nelson and Nunivak Islands, and half our customers live on the Yukon. Their choice is between a four-day snow machine trip or a one-hour charter, and in summer, they have no choice at all."

"So, it really is busier than Fairbanks?" She was sipping tequila with obvious relish and I almost envied her.

"Before the pipeline it certainly was. Bethel was the second busiest airport in America, no joke. Only Chicago's O'Hare had more takeoffs and landings in a year."

"Wow, I had the impression that Bethel was a small town."

"Oh, you are so right, and that's the rest of the story. The planes leaving O'Hare probably average a hundred passengers each, the planes leaving Bethel have one or two passengers. Still, if you're the driver, the pay is the same. So, you've been working for Interior for three years? I'm really impressed with your operation."

Our salads arrived. Celeste had finished her drink and pointed to her empty glass. The waiter caught the gesture. If I'd been bent on seduction, that would have been a very good sign. Come to think of it, seduction was not a bad idea, but remained secondary. We plowed into salads, and the Roquefort was sublime. It had hunks of cheese in it, but enough sauce to keep the tang manageable.

"So, how do you like working for Interior? It must be exciting working for a guy who's running for governor." A waiter brought Celeste a second margarita, followed immediately by another waiter with our wine. I sampled the wine, nodded approval, and he poured, so Celeste had a drink in each hand. I sent a silent vote of thanks to Angie for the red wine expertise. Celeste drank down the tequila as if it were water and shoved the glass aside. I finished my salad, and the waiter cleared plates and cocktail glasses.

Musicians came trooping in and started setting up on the stage. Celeste seemed to be contemplating my question.

"Well, Reginald is a stuffed shirt, you know? Pardon my French, but he can be a pompous ass. Thing is, the pay is good…and, I do meet some very exciting people." She toasted me with her wineglass. Our knees accidentally met under the table, lingered for a delicious second. I was pretty sure I hadn't moved mine.

Our steaks arrived, and Celeste had been right. Miniature filets two inches thick, tender enough to cut with a fork, and wrapped in bacon.

"What do you think of Reginald's campaign manager, what's his name?"

"Oh, you mean Dave Marino? Interesting character." She frowned, "He reminds me of a runaway bulldozer, but can't say I really know him."

"Isn't he a local character?"

"Nope, he showed up a few weeks ago, convinced Reginald that he needed a campaign manager, and took over advertising and stuff."

We had to stop talking, that beef was the clichéd melt in your mouth. It was ten minutes of ecstasy. Mostly the ecstasy was beef and the potato, but it included a couple of knee rubs before I got Celeste back to the subject of Dave Marino. In the meantime, the band eased into elevator music from the Sixties. The Côtes du Rhône was the perfect complement to the food and the music.

We finally sat back and sipped. "Do you think Dave is taking advantage of Reginald?" I asked.

"It's hard to imagine anyone doing that, but he certainly is pushy."

"And you have no idea where he came from?"

Celeste finished her wine. I picked up the bottle to pour more, but it was empty. "Shall we order another?"

"Let's not. It was perfect for dinner, but I'm ready for dessert. How about a Grasshopper? And mostly, I want to dance."

Our waiter descended, swiped away empty bottle and glasses. He'd caught the Grasshopper request, but I couldn't go along with that, either. I ordered another Captain Morgan. Crème de menthe probably has its uses, but imbibing isn't one of them.

The band struck up a cha-cha. Celeste was dancing in her chair, top half swaying to the beat, and I noticed some interesting movement inside her bodice. I did the gentlemanly thing and asked, "Care to dance?" She grabbed my hand and pulled me onto the floor.

Cha, cha, cha-cha-cha. We did the face-to-face with deep knee bends, then got creative, and Celeste danced like a dream, no bones in her body. When she twirled, I did notice that she was wearing garters and her panties matched her dress.

We segued straight to "Hey mambo, mambo Italiano, hey mambo…" Who cared if Dave was stealing the company?

We came back to a fresh tablecloth, a new candle, and our drinks sparkling in the light. Her green Grasshopper was beautiful, just not potable, but she seemed to like it.

"Oh, Alex, that was heavenly. Do you tango?"

"Not since my last one in Paris. I'll follow you. Did you say you think Dave is up to no good?"

She sipped and thought, and the colors were striking, sparkling sapphire eyes and earrings, spun gold bob, emerald drink and ruby lipstick, all reflecting the flickering candlelight. The dimples were there, and I'd been right to extol their allure.

"I hadn't really thought about it, but you might be right. Do you suppose Dave is blackmailing Reginald, or something like that?"

"Could be. Wouldn't it be fun to find out?"

"You mean play detective? Alex, did I tell you you're an exciting date?"

I didn't have to answer that. The band blasted into the tango and Celeste pulled me onto the floor. I kept reciting my mantra, "let-your-knees-go loose, loose, loose …" I didn't disgrace myself, and no one would have noticed anyway. All eyes were on Celeste, including mine. Interesting, she wore her panties over the garter belt. That was probably very practical. We were panting and beaming when we got back to the table.

It took me several seconds before I had enough control of my breathing to talk. "Maybe Dave has a history of fraud or extortion or something. We almost owe it to Reginald to find out."

"How do we do that?" She finished her Grasshopper. Apparently the waiter knew her because he brought her another when he took her empty glass. I nursed the rum, mostly because I was going to have to drive back to town.

"Well, one way would be his fingerprints. If you could snag something with his prints on it, I could get them checked out."

"Yeah, I could probably do that. Dave and Reginald sometimes have a glass of brandy together and leave the glasses for the janitors to wash. Would a glass be good for fingerprints?"

"Couldn't be better." The band struck up "The Skater's Waltz" and we were the first couple on the floor. We did the box, got the feel of each other, and Celeste floated away like a cloud. Dancing in space with a weightless partner must be like waltzing with Celeste. She even made me look good.

We finished the evening with a foxtrot, bodies fused together as if Super-Glued. I drove us back to town in a reasonably straight line, keeping the speedometer on sixty. My reflexes weren't up for any faster, but when you suspect you couldn't pass a sobriety test, you don't want to drive too slowly. That attracts cops like grayling to butterflies. Celeste was snuggled against my shoulder with thigh contact so solid I had to push back to keep my foot on the gas pedal.

We parked in front of her house and she melted against me like butter on hotcakes. A probing tongue, even one flavored by crème de menthe, does elicit an instant physiological response.

"Oh, Alex, that was divine. I wish I could invite you in for a nightcap, but my mother is here for a visit." She caught my hand and cupped it over her breast. It was infinite softness with an India rubber nipple against my palm and all the mystique of femininity. The physiological response ratcheted up, if possible, and something was about to rip.

I managed to croak, "You won't forget about the glass with fingerprints?"

"I won't forget a single second of this night, and I can hardly wait until next time. Oh, Alex, when mother leaves, it's going to be so wonderful." She detached from my chest, but reached down and squeezed the startled protuberance. "Call me." She was out of the car and running up the steps before I caught my breath.

Angie was tucked up in bed, leaning against pillows, wearing her pajamas and watching one of the late night shows. She switched it off instantly when I came in. No one wants to be caught watching that drivel.

"You survived. Did you remember to learn anything? Sorry you didn't get lucky."

"Why do you say that?"

"It's written on your forehead in capital letters."

"Angie, I never strayed from business for a moment and I'm immune to blondes. I kept thinking about your shining ebony tresses, your exotic amber eyes that suck men in like whirlpools, your…."

"Okay, knock it off, Cyrano. Maybe I'll have breakfast with you, maybe not. Did your blonde bimbo reveal any secrets that I'd be interested in?"

"Maybe. She's going to steal a glass with Dave Marino's prints on it. He's getting mysteriousher and mysteriousher."

"Now you're making up a new language? You'd better get to bed before you fall down and injure something besides your libido and your dignity. By the way, tomorrow night is my turn to howl."

"You are going to date Dave Marino?"

"Nope, a cousin and her husband are coming into town and I'm meeting them at the Silver Dollar Bar around seven."

"The Silver Dollar? Jeez, Angie, those native bars are dangerous."

"So, who isn't native, you racist son-of-a-bitch. You can just drop me off, if you're scared."

"Not on your life. If you're going to Second Avenue, I'm going with you and I'll be packing iron. But why there? We can buy your cousin a very nice dinner at Club Eleven."

"Not good enough. Maybe the native bars are just a little loud and frantic, but that is the whole idea. They'll be in town just one night, heading to Seattle the next day, Virginia Mason Clinic and sober propriety, or proper sobriety. In the village, they haven't had a drink or heard music to speak of for two years, and they have one night to make up for that."

"Okay, okay, they're from Crooked Creek?"

"No, Clyde and Angie Williams from Holy Cross, part of the Yukon contingent."

"I know Clyde, but another Angie? And she would be your cousin?"

"Right on. Must be a dozen cousins named Angela, spread for two hundred miles up and down the rivers. We're all named for our great-great, I don't know how many greats, grandmother."

"From Crooked Creek?"

"No, from Piamute. She had twenty-one babies with four different husbands, all of the babies boys, and eighteen of them lived to grow up."

"Twenty-one babies? You sure about that?"

"Yep, one every year from the age of fifteen until thirty-nine, but she missed a couple of years between husbands."

"Okay, she was a saint. Do Indians believe in fertility goddesses? No wonder you worship her. I can hardly wait to meet this other Angie."

"Alex, you have no idea. I predict a night you'll remember for the rest of your life."

Angie rearranged her pillows, slipped down between the sheets, and snapped off the light. I felt my way to my bed and passed out with my clothes on.

She did have breakfast with me. We had mushroom omelets to die for and enough coffee and orange juice to stifle my impending hangover. Service had been embarrassingly good because the last tourists had checked out. Angie and I were now the only residents of the River's Edge, with vacant cottages on both sides of us.

I dropped Angie at the Lathrop Building, promised to meet her in time for the party with her cousins, and didn't know what to do next. If ever a situation called for decisive action, this was it, but the only action I could think of was banging my head against a wall. I decided that wouldn't help.

What kept niggling at my mind were the two first-class tickets from Seattle that were on Reginald's computer. Two tickets from Detroit and two assassins from Detroit could not be coincidence, so someone with access to Interior Air's account had to have done the hiring. Then there were two more tickets from Seattle. There could be a dozen innocent reasons for those, but they could just as well be two more hit men. Worse, this time I wouldn't recognize them, but whoever hired them would certainly pinpoint me, and this time, Angie, too. For all I knew, they might have pictures of us.

Chapter Fourteen

Mostly, I spent the day worrying and trying to think. After I dropped Angie, I took a drive out the Chena hot springs road. This time there were no map-reading tourists at the club, and again, no cars beside the road. Turk was happy to see me. He was standing at the end of the drive with his tail wagging when I turned in, so the house was safe. I filled his water pan and found more dog food under the sink. He dived into the pans, and I didn't have to tell him to stay.

I turned right on the road and drove on into the hills, alternately trying to enjoy the fall colors and wondering what to do next. If determined killers were looking for us, how long could we avoid them in tiny little Fairbanks? I decided the one thing we were doing right was moving around and being unpredictable, until I suddenly realized that Angie came out the front door of the Lathrop Building every evening at six forty-five.

She had a low-profile job, but in a high-profile industry. How long before someone figured out her schedule, and if I met her, so much the better for them. We were even ripe for a drive-by shooting. It did seem like meeting Angie's cousin at the Silver Dollar should be safe. It certainly qualified as something we wouldn't be expected to do.

At six-ten I found a parking spot between the Lathrop Building and the bars, got the pistol lodged firmly in my belt under the windbreaker, and ambled back toward the corner to loiter under the theater marquee. People were already trickling in for the seven o'clock show, and another guy seemed to be killing time. If he was an assassin, he was good, cold calm, reading the posters for upcoming shows, and checking his watch every few minutes. He was between nondescript and good-looking, razor haircut and a snappy sports jacket. There was no bulge of a shoulder holster, but he could have a good-sized weapon in the back of his belt, like I did. He struck me as a shoe salesman, but that's the perfect disguise for an assassin.

I was between him and the Lathrop Building, and was satisfied that he didn't recognize me, so if he was waiting for Angie, I had him covered. When he crossed the entrance to check posters on my side, I strolled a few steps closer to Angie's expected arrival and leaned against the wall of Monty's Department Store, all casual, hands behind me but gripping the revolver.

Six thirty-five, ten minutes to go. A blonde dressed ladies-ready-to-wear, but with long sheer nylons came striding down the street, turned into the entrance, and caught my nemesis by the arm. He pulled two tickets out of his shirt pocket and the couple disappeared into the inner sanctum. I turned my attention back to the street, just in time. A boxy gray Volvo pulled into the spot right behind the Buick and the driver just sat. He was between me and Angie's door, and if he'd parked there because the Buick was known, he'd probably recognize me.

The driver seemed to be staring straight ahead, and he hadn't rolled down the window on the passenger side. He'd surely do that before he shot? I had a clear view of the back of his head, so if the window went down and a weapon came up when Angie appeared, I could take him out. The shot would be through the back window, but that's an advantage of the .357 magnum. The bullet will go through the window, through a head, out the front window and probably lodge somewhere in the Buick.

I edged a few feet closer to the door and could see the driver's hands resting on the steering wheel. As long as his hands stayed there, I could leave the revolver in my belt. The front door of the Lathrop Building swung open right on schedule and Angie emerged, earnestly discussing something with a fortyish woman wearing a tight cap of blonde curls and a sharp business suit. The driver's hand stayed on the wheel. The executive type gave Angie a little wave and crossed the sidewalk to climb into the Volvo. Angie spotted the Buick, looked around in surprise when she found the door locked and me not inside. I grabbed her elbow and dodged the traffic to steer her across Second Avenue into the Coffee Cup Café.

Angie went where I steered her, but her expression wasn't totally compliant. "What the heck was that all about? We could have been killed crossing the street."

"Angie, we could be killed anywhere, so watch out for banana peels in the bathtub. In the meantime, tomorrow night, if there is one, come out the back door of the building."

"Not just a little paranoid, by any chance?"

"Sure, paranoid and still alive. Remember the moose that always drinks at the same place? He will not survive the fall hunting season. It's just not smart to be predictable."

"Well, this qualifies. I never would have predicted dinner at the Coffee Cup." Angie was glancing around, and I saw her point. At a quarter-to-seven, several customers were already drunk and sagging over coffee. The general impression was between homeless derelicts and guttersnipes, but two stools were vacant at the near end of the counter. I steered Angie onto the end one.

I sat down next to the ancient mariner who was mumbling into his cup, mustard from his hamburger staining his beard. I turned my back on him, so my view was Angie, the front window, and the pinball machines that lined the far wall. They accounted for most of the din in the place. Traffic on the street appeared innocuous. The parking spot behind the Buick was grabbed by a young woman who ran toward the theater. Angie's view could have been me, and the curtained door at the back that led into the dark room with the peep shows, but she stared straight ahead. "Shall I order the lobster with Dom Pérignon?"

"May I suggest that madame try the hamburgers? Chef's specialty, and with that Doctor Price prescribes at least two glasses of milk."

"Milk? I quit drinking milk when I saw those horrible commercials with milk mustaches."

"That only happens to celebrities. The rest of us manage to get it all inside, and tonight it's important. Milk coats the stomach, makes it possible to keep the Coffee Cup hamburgers down, but it also cushions the blow of the first several gallons of beer. Take it from an old boozehound, milk before a binge creates the illusion that you can hold your alcohol."

"Boy, does that sound appetizing, but I'm lucky to be in the hands of an expert. Since when do you drink beer?"

The matronly waitress finished mopping the mess off the other end of the counter. Her worldly-wise expression indicated infinite but suffering tolerance. She wiped her hands on her apron, and came to take our order. She nodded at the hamburgers and understood exactly what the milk was about. She clipped our order slip to the wire that hung in front of the cook. He had his back to us, busily flipping hamburgers and buns on an eight-foot black iron grill. He paused to lift a basket of French fries from a cauldron of boiling grease and shake off the unabsorbed drops.

"Now, what was the question? Since when do I drink beer? Since we're going to the Second Avenue bars, that's when. Don't drink anything there that doesn't come in its own bottle and be sure to watch the bartender take the cap off."

The waitress set down two glasses of milk. We toasted each other silently and drank. No white mustaches, and it was good for milk in Alaska. About half of it is reconstituted, but mixed with fresh milk from Creamer's Dairy.

We scarfed down greasy hamburgers with wilted lettuce, and two glasses of milk each, but were running late. We jogged the block to the Silver Dollar Bar, but stopped at the Buick while I slid the revolver under the seat. One does not carry a weapon into a Second Avenue bar. If the Silver Dollar sounds familiar, it probably is. Bar owners are not big on originality.

This particular Silver Dollar was nestled between the Union Club and the Malamute Saloon, and those, too, can be found in every city in the northwest. The Malamute Saloon that Robert Service made famous by shooting Dan McGrew was probably in Dawson City, Yukon Territory, but today even tiny villages like Ester that have only one bar, have the Malamute Saloon. Music met us half a block from the bars, loud enough to rattle the parking meters when we got close. Every bar was blaring, each one different. You had to get inside to sort one out of the din.

When you step into a Second Avenue bar, you have to pause a moment while your lungs adjust to the alcohol fumes and perspiration in the atmosphere, and your ears go numb. It's dark, just enough light to read the label on your beer bottle, and fifty couples stomping out the beat on the dance floor keep the beer sloshing. The wooden building appeared to be over fifty years old, and the foundation was threatening to collapse.

Clyde was sitting halfway down the bar, next to two vacant stools. He was wearing a white shirt and sports coat, which I did not recognize, but Clyde is five feet one inch tall, and that's hard to miss. That's the only way he's small. He's been the BIA school maintenance man forever, and that's the best job in any village. Means he's a jack-of-all-trades, can handle plumbing, heating, electricity, carpenter work, whatever comes up.

He was watching for us, waved his bottle and indicated the empty stools. I waved at the bartender. He produced two Budweisers, popped the tops and traded them for a ten-dollar bill. One does not run a tab on Second Avenue. No one was speaking because the music was overpowering, seeming to vibrate the walls.

I recognized the woman with Clyde, but didn't know her name and had never made the connection. I'd seen her around Holy Cross, and once you've seen her, you don't forget. We bachelors aren't really knowledgeable about C cups and D cups. I don't even know if there is such a thing as an E cup, but it doesn't matter because she doesn't wear bras, just counts on the stretching sweater and a remarkably provident nature to hold her up.

Angie...I couldn't quite think of her as *my* Angie, so I dubbed her number one, went around and hugged Angie number two. She made introducing gestures, but a speaker right behind her had a ruptured cone and the buzz was so loud there was no point in her trying to talk. Angie Two reached behind Clyde to shake my hand, and we all settled down at the bar to suck beer bottles.

We finished that round and the bartender brought four more beers, trading for a twenty. Clyde reached for his pocket, I slapped his hand, and he capitulated gracefully. There's a lot of symbolism there, but it's a guy thing, and maybe Alaskan. His allowing me to pay without an argument meant that he was perfectly secure in his manhood, didn't have to prove anything, and he was correct about that.

The front half of the room was bar and dance floor, tables and more dancing toward the back. Most of those Second Avenue bars reach halfway through the block and connect with another bar on First Avenue. The Silver Dollar did that, but the First Avenue bars are quiet, at least comparatively, usually peopled by hard drinking working stiffs. There are seldom any women and definitely no dancing. Angie One, seated beside Clyde, did some pointing and beckoning, and the two of them got up to dance. I noticed that his nose came right to Angie's cleavage, so being height-challenged isn't all bad. That left two vacant stools between me and Angie Two, so I made the gestures and we met on the dance floor.

The way she snuggled against me would have been salacious in Seattle, unthinkable in Boston, but she was just being honest. In her view, men and women dance together to cop a feel, and there's no point in being coy about it. She led off, so I followed, and we did the Texas Two-Step. That's two gliding steps to the man's right, then one to the left, back to the right again. The woman is backing up and you slowly progress around the floor. It's not a very exciting dance, but it certainly makes for togetherness.

After two more beers and two more dances, four people got up and left a table. Clyde and Angie One grabbed the table, Angie Two and I shagged our beers, and we were finally established. At that point a waitress came around with more beers and collected more dollars. We took turns dancing, because one couple had to stay and guard the table, but it was so hot in our corner behind the bar that a little respite felt good.

Most tables were occupied by natives, both Indians and Eskimos, and all of them intent on having fun. The atmosphere was cordial. When you caught someone's eye they nodded and smiled. The few Caucasians scattered around, including me, were accepted and welcome. It was altogether a pleasant, if deafening, scene.

I found myself relaxing in a way that I hadn't since Stan's death, and was starting to think I was having fun when four big Caucasians came swaggering in. These guys were not assassins; they were from one of the military bases, I guessed military police, and they were radiating attitude. They were head and shoulders taller than most of the crowd, and if they had come to have fun, it was a different sort from the rest of us. They strode down the length of the bar, forcing dancers to dodge out of their way, and actually bumped a couple of guys.

It was like they didn't notice anyone else was there, or didn't concede anyone else the right to be there. They arrived at the end of the bar and grabbed an unguarded table. The table had been occupied by one couple, but they were dancing. The waitress came, moved the couple's drinks to the end of the bar, and served the newcomers. One of them patted the back of her skirt, she slapped his hand, and they all laughed, including the waitress. I didn't think she liked it; I thought she wasn't making waves, and that probably was smart.

The newcomers attacked their beers and the party continued, but the mood had changed. The new guys were lounging back in their chairs, taking up way too much room, so people around them had to adjust chairs and scoot tables. They were looking around the room, making remarks and gestures to each other, and it wasn't long before they focused on our table.

Clyde and Angie One got up to dance, and I didn't need to hear to catch the threat. The biggest guy stood up, crossed the floor in four strides, and picked Clyde up by the shoulders. He tossed Clyde aside like a rag doll, but when he turned back to reach for Angie, he found me instead.

I buried my left fist up to the wrist in his solar plexus, and it felt wonderful. He lunged forward with a satisfying *oof*, eyes and mouth wide open and leading with his chin. That requires finesse. As tempting as it is, you must never hit a chin with a closed fist, unless you're making a movie. In real life, you'll break your fingers and probably sprain your wrist. Use the heel of your hand, wrist stiff, roll your shoulder to get every muscle in your body behind the blow and raise up on your toes for the follow-through.

The point of the chin is the proper target; the skull snaps back, traumatizes the vagus nerve, and guarantees a half hour's nap. You do have to be careful because if you miss the chin and hit the nose at that upward angle, you'll drive bone fragments into his brain and kill him. Then again, sometimes it isn't necessary to be too careful. I hit the chin with predictable results. He staggered backward several steps before he hit the floor, but he was already unconscious.

A hand the size of a dinner plate clamped down on my shoulder and was pulling me around. I grabbed the thumb in my right, the little finger in my left, turned around, ducked under the arm. That turned him around and I jerked the hand up between his shoulderblades.

When your shoulder is being dislocated, your urge is to relieve the pressure and he did that by bending and lunging forward. I helped him right along. He stumbled past two chairs and we were traveling at a good clip when his head rammed into the wall beside the jukebox. Not that I was pushing so hard, but this guy must have weighed two hundred fifty pounds and he was trying to propel that out of the hammerlock. With all that weight on the move, the sudden stop cracked the plaster. He slid down the wall; I turned around. His two buddies were standing up, but they were facing a ring of Indians that would have looked familiar to General George Armstrong Custer.

They had their hands half raised, palms out and were backing toward the door. The path cleared, half a dozen guys followed them to the door, several others grabbed the sleepers and sledded them out through the swinging doors onto the sidewalk. The swinging doors flapped a few times, and the party reassembled. Clyde and Angie One resumed their dance. Angie Two took the chance of leaving the table unguarded and met me on the dance floor. If possible, the mood in the room was friendlier and more festive than before.

We weren't watching time or counting beers, but I did notice that an alcoholic fog was setting in. The first indication was when Angie One came back to the table and had to use both hands to hold the chair still while she sat. Angie Two and I got tangled up, would have fallen, but we slammed into a table. The occupants had seen us coming, were holding onto their beers, and cheerfully helped us back onto the dance floor. It was getting close to pumpkin time.

When we got back to the table, I made a head jerk toward the door. Clyde and Angie One nodded and stood, not swaying too much, and the four of us held each other up while we negotiated the party and made it through the swinging doors to the sidewalk.

Angie Two grabbed a parking meter and leaned on it. "Wow, that was fun." Those were the first words any of us had spoken since we met.

Angie One helped hold up the meter. "I'm so glad you guys came in. Too bad you can't stay a few days. Your plane is early in the morning?"

"Not too early." Clyde pulled tickets out of his jacket pocket and double-checked. "We need to be at the airport at ten."

Angie One beamed at him and caressed his cheek. "Wonderful, let's meet for breakfast."

Angie Two piped up. "Stay with us tonight. We have lots of room, right down the block at the Nordale."

That made a problem. I could imagine what she meant by *lots of room*, and they probably did have, by village standards. They were doing the Eskimo-Indian thing, sharing whatever they had. Any hint that what they offered wasn't good enough for us would have been the social gaff of the century. Then, too, I was in no condition to drive. If assassins were waiting, let them figure that one out. The two Angies linked arms and wove toward the Nordale, Clyde and I following.

We were dong fine until we got to the stairway. The Angies stalled, each clinging to a banister. Clyde and I got shoulders under derrieres, grabbed banisters ourselves, and we arrived at the top in a mass. The room was at the front, old-fashioned sash windows overlooking Second Avenue. Furniture consisted of one double bed, one chair, one dresser. The Angies disappeared into the bathroom. Clyde and I stood at the window.

"Headed for Virginia Mason?" I asked.

He was silhouetted in the light from the street; we hadn't bothered to turn on the room light. He nodded. "Angie and I decided it's time for babies. She had some female problems in her teens, we want to be sure everything is in place."

I put a hand on his shoulder, it didn't seem quite right to give him a hug, but I was conveying respect and understanding. The Angies came out of the bathroom and sprawled, crosswise, in the middle of the bed. Clyde took his turn, I watched the street below the window.

When Clyde came out, I ducked in. Both Angies were apparently already asleep. I did my thing, left the bathroom door open, light out. Clyde had stretched out beside Angie Two, and the three-foot space left for me at the foot of the bed was beside Angie One. I kicked off my oxfords and lay down. Any other time I might have noticed that my feet were off the bed from the ankles down, but just then it didn't matter. Angie One stirred, and her hand found my shoulder, but there wasn't any sexual tension. We were there to sleep, and that's what we did.

Chapter Fifteen

Breakfast at the Model Café was a solemn affair, close, friendly, but preoccupied. Clyde and Angie Two were probably thinking about Seattle, and Angie One and I had our own worries. We flooded impending hangovers with orange juice and coffee. When the check came, Clyde and I both reached for money. He slapped my hand. It was my turn to accept his hospitality graciously and be secure in my own manhood. I'm probably not as good at that as Clyde is, but he has better reasons to feel secure.

We drove them to the airport and waited while they retrieved their suitcase from the storage locker and dragged it to the Alaska Airlines counter. There was a spontaneous four-way hug. They turned toward the check-in line; we headed for the Buick.

We checked on Turk because Angie wanted to go to work before noon.

Turk was glad to see Angie, planting his paws on her window and licking the glass so she couldn't open the car door. I went around to help and together we overpowered Turk and got her extricated. She and Turk went inside, but Angie's trying to walk with Turk threading her legs reminded me of a fly fisherman walking in a swift current on a rocky bottom.

Trees were now yellow to the tops while the lower branches were starting to brown. The sun was out, but not much warmth to it. I strolled around back to check on the river. Turk had dug a hole in the backyard next to Angie's pottery firing pit, big enough for a foxhole if mortars were flying. Tiny tunnels away from his hole were the escape routes the voles had used.

The river was changing seasons. Thin skims of ice clung on the downstream side wherever the current was blocked. A few patches of clear ice floated by, so thin they bent when the water ruffled. Eskimos call that stage *new young ice*. I picked up the canoe, balanced it like an oversized hat and shoved it under the house. I judged the boating season was over.

Profound silence lay over the woods and the driveway. The world was getting drowsy, preparing for its winter hibernation. I caught a flash of movement in the woods and had the pistol on it, but it was a rabbit already turned white for the winter. He took a couple of tentative hops and another appeared behind him, so they must have had a burrow.

When the snow comes, they'll be as invisible as they were wearing their summer brown, but until then, they showed up through the woods like spotlights. I was glad to see them because they meant no assassins were lurking in the woods. Wolves will take advantage of the blown camouflage to fatten themselves up for winter, but probably not in Turk's territory.

Angie came out of the house dressed for work in skirt and blouse, heels and hose. Hard to believe she was the same person who had gone in wearing wrinkles from sleeping in her clothes. She told Turk to stay. He sat down, brushing gravel with his wagging tail, tongue lolling happily. I glanced toward the woods, but the rabbits had disappeared. We climbed into the car and I backed down the lane.

"What is that strange aroma? Did you fall into a spice cabinet or get dumped on by a truckload of flowers?"

"I'm wearing Shalimar, bush man. It's a selective repellent. Sophisticated city men appreciate it, but it keeps the bums away like Deep Woods Off repels mosquitoes. How are you going to amuse yourself while I toil in the salt mine? I assume your blonde bimbo has a daytime job?"

"Correct, and today she's going to risk her life stealing fingerprints for us. You could mask the jealousy a little by calling her Celeste."

A dark blur came out of the woods on the left. I clamped on the binders, started to skid, released the brakes, and snapped us out of it. A mama moose strolled casually across the road, apparently unaware of my throwing gravel and lying on the horn. I had time for one more brake, one more slide, then took the ditch on the left-hand side behind the moose and jerked us back up onto the road. The moose continued unperturbed, jumped the ditch, and pulled down an eight-foot-high branch to munch leaves.

Angie was no more perturbed than the moose. You get used to sudden evasive actions when you live in the Alaskan woods. We survived the slalom course and turned toward town on the Steese. In broad daylight, with no music blaring out, the Rendezvous looked sadly shabby and dusty. I used the Wendell Street Bridge, passed Celeste's house with barely a glance, and dropped Angie at the Lathrop Building on Second Avenue.

"What time shall I pick you up?"

"Forget it. I'm off after the six-o'clock news, but I'll grab a taxi. If you decide to fly off to Point Barrow, leave me a note, but I don't want to stand on Second Avenue waiting for you to get back."

There it was again, same lack of confidence in my scheduling that was keeping Connie turned off. There must be something fundamentally wrong with my genes.

"Okay, suit yourself, but do be careful. Don't come out the door until the cab is waiting, and pay attention to traffic. If a car follows you onto Boat Street tell the cabby you've changed your mind and have him take you straight to the cop shop."

"You think more assassins are lined up waiting to take a shot at us?"

"Angie, I'm almost sure of it. Someone at Interior bought two more tickets, this time from Seattle. I don't think they're for cousins coming to visit. You do have security at work?"

"Yeah, it's pretty good. We get stalkers and kooks harassing talent, and reporters get death threats now and then. Our receptionist has a button on her desk that sets off a buzzer in the shop. That brings the entire technical crew storming out waving wrenches and screwdrivers. I do get the message, and I will be careful. You just concentrate on staying alive to meet me for dinner." She swept the area with her eyes, hunkered down just a little, and scooted into the building.

When she'd asked about my plans, I hadn't answered because I didn't have any. Still, habit pulled me toward the airport. Maybe I should stake out the passenger terminal and see if Marino was meeting an army packing cannons. I stopped at the strip mall, found a copy of *An Infantry Lieutenant's Vietnam* by Ivan Pierce at Borders, a couple of Cokes at Safeway, and steeled myself for a long hard vigil.

The wisdom of the ages is to keep your friends close, but your enemies closer. I figured that meant keeping an eye on Interior and maybe following Marino if he came out. I parked between hangars to see what was going to happen next. The Otter was in its spot, and next to it a Skyvan had its rear ramp down.

An F-27 with Interior's blue-and-gold logo pulled off the runway and lumbered between rows of planes to stop in front of the freight shed. The building's overhead door opened and two forklifts emerged. They took turns, transferring the first six pallets into the Skyvan, then moving freight into the shed. A dozen pallets went in, different pallets came out and were hoisted into the F-27.

The forklifts retreated and the warehouse door closed. The left prop started to spin, wound up to a blur and billowed smoke when the turbine caught. The pilot used only one engine to turn the bird and started down the line before he cranked the right. Nice guy, he didn't want to sandblast the office, but his boss was inside so it made sense. The F-27 streaked down the runway, lifted off, and continued south toward Anchorage.

Reginald's Mercedes was in the lot. Dave's Cadillac was not. Several other cars were scattered around and one of them was a cute little teal blue Miata that I'd noticed parked on the street when I picked up Celeste, so I guessed it was hers.

Freddy came out of the office wearing coveralls, and trudged toward the Skyvan. I was too far away to see features, but his walk was familiar. Someone should do a study of that. I think walks may be as individual as fingerprints. He climbed into the Skyvan and a moment later the rear ramp swung up and closed. Turbines spun and smoked, the Skyvan lurched out of the line and waddled toward the taxiway. The Skyvan is a one-purpose airplane, fairly common in bush work but unusual elsewhere. It's a boxy-looking bird, short square wings, a turbine on each, and the body ends at the rear of the ramp with tail feathers mounted above it. The gear is short, but wide, so it looks as if it were dragging its belly. The only reason it flies is that the entire body is the shape of an oversized wing. It was carrying six large pallets. The Otter would have been strained with four, and boxy or not, the Skyvan is faster. He broke ground halfway down the strip, so he was heavy, climbed to five hundred feet, and turned north toward Alaska's newest bonanza.

I settled down with my book and was instantly transported to Vietnam. Pierce has a different perspective, not gung-ho or bloodthirsty, not concerned with the politics. He describes his life there with the same candor and word pictures he might have used to write about his former life on the Idaho farm. I cringed when the bullets flew, laughed when the sappers came, shook my head at the idiocy of military intelligence, and forgot about time until Dave's Cadillac turned off the airport road and parked at Interior. He didn't have any gunmen with him. My watch said four-thirty. I popped the second Coke, but it was warm and seemed to be all fizz.

At six-ten Reginald and Marino came out together, got into their respective cars and headed for town. Celeste's Miata was still in the lot, so I let them go. She came out ten minutes later, slipped into the Miata, and I followed her toward town. The exodus from the airport area was on, Fairbanks' version of rush hour, so there were a dozen cars on the road. She pulled into the strip mall, and when she came out with an armload of groceries, I was leaning against her car.

"Hi, Celeste, remember me?"

"Alex, gee, I'm sorry about the other night. You had my hormones in such an uproar I couldn't think straight."

"No problem, I can relate to that. Just call me Peg Leg. Any luck with the fingerprint detail?"

"Yeah, worked like a charm. Reginald and Marino left together early and when I took some papers into Reginald's office, there were two brandy snifters on his desk. I don't know which was which, so I brought both of them. Only problem is I have to replace them before morning because he'll miss them, and I'd be the prime suspect."

I opened the car door for her. She leaned into the car to set her groceries on the seat and came out with a brown paper bag.

I took the sack. "Good girl, well done. This might be interesting."

"Do you play cloak-and-dagger games all the time?"

"More cloak than dagger, but some of my charter customers are cops so I can sometimes wrangle a favor. How do I get the glasses back to you?"

"Could you just put them in my car sometime tonight? I wish I could invite you up to the house, but Mother wouldn't like that."

"She's a smart lady, but how did she learn so much about me?"

"It's not you, personally. She hates men with such a passion that I'd think she was a lesbian if I weren't evidence to the contrary. I think the main purpose of this trip was to warn me about men for the umpteen-jillionth time. She's still trying to raise me, you know?"

"Yep, I understand. My mother didn't make it this far, but she was still calling me her precious sonny and hinting that I should go into the ministry after I was a thirty-year-old disaster. Thanks for the glasses. I'll stick them under your car seat and call you in the next couple of days with a full report."

She stepped against me, so I wrapped arms around her and we kissed. It wasn't much like our date, but it definitely was not sisterly. She slipped into her car and drove away. I went to the pay phone and called Lieutenant Stella.

"Hi, Jim? Alex. Any chance you could run some fingerprints for me?"

"You have an idea who's hiring your executioners?"

"Maybe, bare possibility. Anyhow, there's a guy I'm wondering about and he doesn't seem to have a background. I have a couple of brandy snifters and one has his prints on it. Might answer some questions."

"Okay, drop them by the station. I can probably get you an answer by tomorrow afternoon."

"Ouch, that's a problem. I've got to return these glasses before morning and I do believe they're crystal. Might be hard to find substitutes tonight."

"Not a problem. We can lift the prints and give the glasses back in an hour or so. Alex, I won't be at the station when you get here, but I'll leave instructions. Just give them to the desk sergeant and wait."

"Can do. Thanks a lot, Jim."

"Happy to oblige, anything that will get you off our streets before you start shooting again." He hung up. I drove out to the state office building and presented the paper sack to the desk sergeant, who was surreptitiously watching Seinfeld on a small portable TV. I was sorry to interrupt him, but he didn't offer to let me watch, so it served him right. I plunked down in a hard wooden chair designed to torture prisoners, and finished the book. Pierce volunteered for three extra months of duty in Dak To in exchange for R&R in Hong Kong. Maybe he wasn't as smart as I first thought.

The sergeant answered his phone, disappeared into the inner sanctum and came back with the sack and glasses. I thanked him as if it had been his idea and drove over to Wendell Street. Celeste's Miata was parked in front of her house, doors unlocked. I stuffed the sack under the front seat and sneaked away without being spotted by her mother.

Angie had been right not to wait for me on Second Avenue, but I did think I was in time for dinner. I was just ready to turn off of Boat Street into the complex when I noticed a car parked across the street a couple of hundred feet past the drive. I could see lights on in our cottage so Angie was home, but that car didn't seem right. I drove on by.

Two people were sitting in the car, not Dick and Jane, more like Dick and Richard and they weren't doing anything obvious, just sitting and watching. I got a very uneasy feeling that they were waiting for me to come home. I drove two more blocks, turned left for one block, back four blocks, and raced to the service station and the pay phone on Cowles Street.

"Angie, stay put. Stay away from windows and don't open the door until you're sure it's me."

"Alex?"

"No time, explain later. Put on your Cat Woman suit and be ready to run."

I called Pizza Hut and ordered one large with everything to be delivered to bungalow number three at the River's Edge.

When the minivan with the lighted Pizza Hut sign came down Boat Street, I stepped out and hailed him. If we'd been in a city, he would have suspected a hijacking and driven on by. In Fairbanks, he expected I had a problem and pulled over, so he was surprised when I hijacked him. I didn't use the pistol though. I used a hundred-dollar bill.

"Look, buddy, my girlfriend is in that bungalow. Her husband is one mean son-of-a-bitch, will shoot me on sight, and both of us if he sees us together. Our job is to get her out so we can catch the evening jet to Vegas." The driver was nodding. Truth is, that's almost as classic an Alaskan story as the moose on the highway.

"What do I have to do? I ain't getting shot for no hundred."

"No danger. He's watching for my car. Just stop in front of the bungalow, park as close as you can, and loan me your hat. I'll make the delivery."

"Okay, but if anything moves, I'm gone."

"Right. Here's a retainer to show good faith." I tore the hundred in half and handed half to him. He took off his hat and passed it over while he turned into the River's Edge driveway. He stopped the van almost on the step, solidly blocking the view from the car that was still lurking beside the road. I put on the cap, took the "Stay Hot" pizza box and marched up to ring the doorbell.

"Hey, Angie, it's me. Open the door, then duck down and run to the van."

The door opened and a black streak went under my left elbow. I waited long enough to be plausible, closed the door and got back in the van.

"Okay, we're gone." The driver liked that. He spun us around so fast I was afraid he'd arouse suspicion, but we made it to the road and turned toward town. The mysterious sedan was still parked. There were only two seats in the front of the van, so Angie was crouched down between us, and the driver seemed to approve of my choice. He let us out next to the rented Buick. I gave him the other half of the hundred and the thirty for the pizza, and handed back his hat. I steered Angie into the Buick and handed her the pizza, but popped the trunk and grabbed the shotgun before I got in.

Chapter Sixteen

I leaned the shotgun between the seats. Angie handed me a steaming hot slice of pizza on a napkin. She was halfway through one of her own. "Hey, this is pretty good and I was starving, but isn't this the hard way to invite a girl out for dinner?"

She had a point. My stomach growled and I treated it to the tip of the pizza slice. I got anchovies, mushrooms and olives in one bite, and almost forgot the suspiciously parked car.

"Angie, remember your idea of shooting a few assassins every day before lunch? We missed this morning, so how about a couple during dinner?"

"You're not kidding, are you?"

"I wish to heck I was."

"You know, Alex, the most desirable and marriageable of all male attributes is being on time for dinner, but if you can't manage that, a hot combination pizza is a good substitute. After that, a girl does like to be surprised, and you've got that one down pat."

We drove back toward the River's Edge but turned inland a block before we got there, drove a block past, and parked on the side street. I had finished my slice, and Angie was halfway through a second. She ripped hers in two, handed half to me. We got out of the car and closed the doors silently. I carried the shotgun at my side between us as inconspicuously as a twelve gauge with a thirty-inch barrel can be carried, and we strolled up Boat Street toward the back of the parked car. It was dark, no streetlights, so the car was a silhouette against the resort. No buzzing insects, just the occasional hum from a passing car two blocks away on Airport Road.

We walked quietly on the pavement, and I hoped that if we were noticed we'd be taken for a pair of young lovers out for a stroll. I leaned close to Angie and whispered.

"Angie, here's the drill. The two guys in that sedan have been parked watching our bungalow for at least an hour. I'll take the driver's side, you take the other and you get the shotgun. We jerk their doors open at the same time and cover them, then see what happens next. If the door on your side is locked, blow the handle off with the shotgun, but I drove by earlier and they seemed to have their windows open. That's good enough."

Angie nodded, took the shotgun, and we split to walk up beside the car. The windows were open, engine running, heater blasting, and fifties music on the radio. I nodded over the car roof and we each jerked a door open. I had the pistol solidly in the driver's face. "Hands on the wheel and do not move." Angie had whacked the passenger in the temple with the shotgun barrel and he was shaking his head, trying not to black out, not sure at whom to look. "You, passenger, hands on the dash and stop breathing." He obeyed instantly. Who wouldn't? Angie was still pressing the gun barrel against his temple.

I spoke to the driver. "I'm the nervous type and my trigger finger itches. You move one eyebrow and this .357 will go through both of you." I reached into his jacket, pulled a .45 automatic out of his shoulder holster and tossed it into the back seat.

"Okay, Angie, your turn. Yours is a lefty so the pistol is on his right side."

"Say ahh," Angie said.

The passenger did. She shoved the gun barrel into his mouth until it hit the back of his throat, kept her right hand on the trigger and used her left to open his jacket and extract his pistol. She followed my example and tossed the automatic into the back seat.

"Okay, Angie, I've got them covered. You get in back." She pulled the barrel out of the poor guy's mouth and left him gasping like a guppy. She climbed in but rested the barrel against the back of his neck. I slammed the front door but kept my pistol on the driver while I climbed in beside Angie and nudged the back of his skull with the barrel.

"Okay, very slowly, right hand only, put the car in gear. Now both hands on the wheel, drive straight ahead, and any bumps will probably cause an accidental shooting."

I had the impression that these guys were pros, not terribly frightened or very surprised, and that was a good thing. They knew this was our turn and since we hadn't shot them yet, they had a chance to survive if they did what they were told. Amateurs might have panicked and done something stupid, but our driver followed instructions, straight to the cop shop. Angie got out first, still pointing that ugly shotgun at the front seat. I made the suggestion and both men got out with hands on their heads.

Each with a gun barrel against his spine, they marched up the steps and into the vestibule. The desk sergeant recognized me, sighed at yet another interruption to his TV.

"We came to see Lieutenant Stella."

"Right, he just came in." The sergeant punched buttons on his phone and whispered to it. Jim Stella came out of the back room.

"Now what?" he asked.

"You wanted me to stop shooting assassins, so we brought these two in for you."

"Preferring charges?"

"Well, we didn't wait for them to shoot us, but they were carrying concealed weapons. Both are wearing shoulder holsters and their automatics are in the car outside. Is that enough to hold them?"

"Yeah, that'll do it." The driver still had his hands on top of his head. Stella clapped a cuff on his right wrist, jerked it down behind his back, then cuffed the left over the guy's shoulder. "Pensguard?" Stella said. The desk sergeant jumped up, scooted around the desk, and cuffed Angie's prisoner.

"Their automatics and luggage are in the back seat, so you probably want to impound their car, but we could use a ride back to our hotel. Maybe if you pound their toes with a hammer, we'll find out who hired them?"

"Vee haff our vays," Stella said, imitating a terrible German accent. "Pensguard, get them a ride."

Pensguard ran back around his desk and punched buttons on the phone.

"We really are in a hurry," Angie said. "Our pizza is getting cold."

The toaster oven in our bungalow warmed the pizza two slices at a time. It wasn't entirely successful because it also dried it out a bit, but it was okay in an emergency. Our mini-bar didn't have Captain Morgan, but it had dark Myers. I wish I could describe the flavor of Myers. It puts me in mind of almonds, but that's not right. Perfect for pizza in any case, and Angie seemed to agree.

Angie sampled her pizza, wrinkled her nose, but then dived in. "Lovely dinner, sir. Shall I find some candles?"

"Nah, candles are an asset for blonde bimbos, but with the stark reality of your flawless beauty, the more light the better. Do you suppose it's time to move again? Mary Angela seems to have blown her cover."

"Is there any point in moving? There are only so many hotels in Fairbanks, you know. Of course we could go back to the Maranatha."

"We don't have to stay in Fairbanks. The 310 can set us at the Circle Hot Springs Lodge in forty minutes and we could commute."

"Could, but if we're going to commute, we could move back to the house. With Turk on guard we won't be murdered in our beds. I know, there's only one way in and out, but I could ride shotgun, literally."

"Well, there is one advantage to the house. The trick is to do something they won't expect, and they certainly won't expect that."

Angie finished her slice and drained her glass. "Okay, it's settled. Tomorrow morning, it's back to the homestead. Let's hit the sack, Alex. Something about ambushing gun-toting desperados takes the starch right out of me."

"Bathroom after you, madam."

"Thanks." She took her little bundle of pajamas with her and closed the bathroom door. I turned on my reading light and snapped off the overhead. I'd kicked off my shoes and removed my shirt and tee shirt, but I didn't feel good about getting into bed. The Chena was rushing past our window. It was a black snake with hints of foam and movement, but it was unconcerned. Were we safe for one more night? I felt the need to do something unexpected long before morning.

I bunched up the pillows in both our beds so there appeared to be bodies in them and snapped off the reading light. When Angie came out of the bathroom I put my finger to her lips in a shushing sign and caught her hand. We slipped out, barefoot and wearing nothing much, and padded across the grass to the next cabin. It wasn't locked. We didn't turn on lights, but I did lock the door from the inside, and we slipped into the beds.

Chapter Seventeen

It happened overnight. Jack Frost had etched the lower half of our window. He'd done a beautiful job with swirls and impressions of tropical jungles. If it had been colored, it would have looked like a New York subway car. Angie was bouncing on tiptoes, staring through the clear spot at the top.

"Better come have a look, author of my present predicament."

I joined her at the window. She hadn't bought pajamas for me so I'd been sleeping in my shorts, but fortunately this time I had included pants. The lawn was a white carpet of frost, the white Buick looked fuzzy, with no windows showing.

"Perfect," I said. "All part of my plan. Notice we can see that there are no footprints leading to our bungalow?"

"Yeah, I guess that's good, but we're going to have to make some and we are barefoot."

"Never fear, my lady. I, your self-sacrificing protector, shall brave the arctic and retrieve your shoes."

"Damn, I hate that macho bullshit. Let's go." She opened the door and we tore across the lawn, leapt up the steps, and slammed the door of our bungalow. I stamped my bare feet and scuffed them on the carpet. Angie sat down on the bed and massaged hers. I brought a towel from the bathroom, knelt by the bed, and dried her feet.

"Thank you, kind sir. You do get me into some miserable situations, but you're good at repairing the damage."

The proprietor was as sorry to see us go as we were to leave. I did use my card to check out, since hidden identities seemed passé. They had cut back to one waitress, but pigs-in-a-blanket and ham-and-scrambled were as good as ever. The river looked black and sullen, not inviting, and the ice floes were white and constant.

An ice scraper that Avis had provided was in the glove compartment. I rehabilitated the windows. Roads were bare, but fall was no longer beautiful. Trees along the hot springs road looked shabby and dying. Leaves were brown, black branches showing through. Turk was glad to see us, but Angie managed to open her own door. I went around back to the generator shed and started the three-thousand-watt Onan diesel.

The furnace was spotless. Stan must have cleaned it in the spring, and it would have had only occasional use during the summer. The electric-controlled furnace required the generator, and they would have run that only in the evenings. I turned up the thermostat on the wall and the furnace came to life with a satisfying roar. Angie ran water into the kitchen sink until the pressure pump kicked on. Blessed heat poured out of the floor vents. The only frozen thing was Turk's water pan. I fixed that with a stomp and a fresh pitcher.

"Planning to go to work today?" I asked.

"Well, one of us should do something constructive."

I'd noticed that Turk's plaster was no longer sitting on his scalp. It seemed to have raised up half an inch on new hair. "While you're lollygagging around the water-cooler at Channel Two, I could take Turk back to the vet. Looks like time for a post-operative check-up."

"Good. Leave the furnace on until you get back. Once the house is warm, it'll stay that way until evening."

I dropped Angie at the station, promised on my honor as an unreliable misanthrope that I'd pick her up at six forty-five outside the back door, and drove Turk to Creamer's Dairy.

The vet removed the plaster by dissolving it with something. Turk had a puckered strip of skin across his scalp but the new fur was coming in fast. Huskys do that. His winter coat would stay ahead of the dropping temperature and when the time came, he'd be comfortable sleeping outside at fifty below.

The house was comfy. I shut down the furnace, then the generator, and told Turk to stay. He sat down and wagged his tail, brushing the gravel into scallops. I drove into town and found Lieutenant Stella at the cop shop. He invited me into his office. It was spare, clean, masculine, with a wooden desk, one extra chair, and one window showing black leaves outside. Mandatory pictures of the governor, commissioner, and chief hung behind the desk. Otherwise the walls were faded wallpaper from the nineteen fifties. He indicated a chair for me and sat behind his desk.

"Did we apprehend two on the FBI's most wanted list?"

"Nope, far as I can tell, you accosted two innocent tourists who didn't know Alaska's gun laws. These guys are clean, have no priors. They arrived from Seattle yesterday, and have no idea about any plots or hits. They're not quite sure what the term *hit* means."

"You believe that?"

"Of course not, but that's not the point. If we slap them with a fifty-dollar misdemeanor for concealed weapons, you and Angie will have to testify. Not worth the bother, maybe even dangerous. Want to explain to the judge why you were out walking with a shotgun in the night? By the way, why didn't you tell me you're a private investigator?"

"When's the last time you cooperated with a PI?"

"You've got a point there."

"Okay, so the two thugs are actually Christian missionaries in disguise. What can we do?"

"No, actually they were both discharged from the same Marine unit with your former victims, which is a bit much for coincidence. I'll railroad them out of town for no visible means of support, but they can come back on the next jet if they want to. I'll convince them that's not a good idea, but the law is on their side."

"That's just dandy. Better luck with the fingerprints?"

"You batted your usual fifty percent. One glass was used by Reginald Parker, a regular Boy Scout. The only reason his prints are on file is his exemplary service as a Green Beret, honorable discharge, and decoration for valor. You do know he's running for governor?"

"Yeah, I heard. And the other glass?"

"Wiped clean, nary a print nor a smudge. Alex, that glass could have just come out of a dishwasher. Care for coffee?"

I nodded, he punched buttons and spoke to his phone. The door opened and a pert young woman in patrolman uniform came in with two steaming cups. Apparently it's good to be a lieutenant. She handed a cup to him, one to me, smiled at us, and departed.

"Could something have gone wrong in the lab?"

"Not a chance. Our print gal is the best. If she says the glass was clean, it was clean." He sipped, so I matched him. For institutional coffee, it was good.

"Good coffee, thanks. So, where does that leave us?"

"Interesting question. Consider this, what kind of a guy wipes his glass clean after he's just had a drink with a friend?"

"An obsessive compulsive?"

"Or one who is so paranoid he never leaves prints? Could be darn good reasons for that. Are you going to tell me who you suspected, or are you playing games?"

"No games, it's just that I can't explain a reason to suspect this guy. His name is Dave Marino, and he showed up three weeks ago to manage Reginald's campaign for governor. I don't suppose you can arrest him because I don't like the expression in his eyes?"

"Probably not, and keep in mind, that's not a good reason to shoot him, either. I'll see what I can find. Want to bet a hundred bucks that the name isn't phony?"

"No thanks." We'd both finished our coffee and I stood.

"By the way, we moved back to the cabin in the woods this morning. We've tried sneaking around town and it didn't seem to work. If we disappear, you can look for the bodies at the cabin." I set the empty cup on his desk. He gave me a rueful nod that I did not take to be encouraging.

I stopped by Fairbanks Electronics, bought two motion sensors, a power supply, two five-hundred-foot rolls of zip-cord, and a bell like the one that had summoned me to grade school classes. Back at the house, I set the power supply and the bell in the spare bedroom, tied the ends of the rolls of wire to the bed frame and set them on the windowsill.

Outside, I just pulled the reels and let the wire lie on the ground beside the driveway. Two hundred feet reached to the road. I left one reel, turned toward town, and followed the road until the reel ran out. A sturdy birch limb made a good mount. I scrambled up, taped a motion sensor to the limb, focusing it on the road, and connected the wire. The other reel and the other motion sensor went an equal distance toward the hot springs.

I was setting us up for false alarms if a moose crossed the road, but anything that moved within five hundred feet of the drive in either direction was going to ring the bell. That made the house seem more like a fortress than a trap. A smart intruder might be able to neutralize Turk with a poisoned beefsteak or a silenced shot, and maybe I was being overly macho again, but with the pistol in my belt, and Angie backing me up with the shotgun, I figured we could handle an invasion, so long as we had some warning.

For no reason I could think of, I drove out to the airport and parked between hangars. The morning frost was gone, the sun trying to make up for it but with minimal success. The Skyvan was missing, Otter tied down. Reginald's Mercedes and Celeste's Miata were in the lot, Dave's Cadillac was not.

The morning jet from Anchorage arrived, rocking the car and damaging eardrums when the pilots honked on the reverse thrusters to stop. It used three quarters of the runway before it turned around and screamed its way back to the passenger terminal. There's a good reason why bush pilots refer to the Boeing 737 jet as Fat Albert. It doesn't use the taxiways, taxis right down the middle of the runway to the far end, then shakes buildings and airplanes when it takes off.

It did occur to me that if I'd followed yesterday's hunch and staked out the passenger terminal, I might have seen Dave meet the innocent tourists. That would have given substance to some unsubstantiated suspicions. I was debating with myself about making the same mistake two days in a row when the F-27 from Anchorage arrived on schedule and pallets were jockeyed back and forth, but none went into the Otter. The F-27 closed its door, the door of the freight shed slammed down, and the F-27 again used only one engine to sandblast the front of Interior Air.

I did keep an eye on the road, but Dave's Cadillac didn't come from the passenger terminal with a fresh wave of commandos. I was wasting time and getting half frantic. I needed a good idea, or at least a plan, and as usual, when I tried to think, nothing happened. I like to pretend that I get my share of good ideas, but they come when I'm driving or flying, or sometimes just sitting on the commode, not when I'm trying to focus and think.

The temperature had sneaked up well above freezing so it was a good time to do some housekeeping I'd neglected. The 310 needed the gas tanks topped off, oil checked, and winter covers over the engines, just in case the bottom dropped out of the thermometer. I strolled down the flight line to the 310. Bright green, hundred-octane gasoline poured out of the fuel tank drains and the fuel strainers on the engines, so there was no water in the system, but that is a danger when the temperature is flipping up and down. If the tanks aren't topped off, air fills the space, and air has moisture in it. I checked the oil; both engines were down half a quart, very good for air-cooled engines.

I taxied the bird over to Sea Airmotive's gas pumps, topped off tanks, and bought one quart of oil from the gas boy, who imagined himself in training to become a 747 pilot. He was as anxious to get on with his career as I was with mine. I added half the quart of oil to each engine, parked the plane, and dug the orange quilted cowling covers out of the baggage compartment. It wasn't much, but I was doing something. No good ideas popped in when I stopped trying to think.

The Skyvan came home. Freddy climbed out and strolled into the office.

Reginald came out of the building at twelve fifteen, climbed into his Mercedes, but turned left toward the passenger terminal and coffee shop. He wasn't meeting anyone because no planes had arrived in the last hour, so I let him have lunch in peace. Apparently the rest of the crew brown-bagged it because they didn't come out.

Reginald returned at one-ten. The cars sat in the lot, and I guarded them. Persistence is the watchword for successful surveillance, so my afternoon must have been successful. Anyway, no one stole the cars. Reginald came out and drove toward town at six-oh-five. Celeste and Freddy came out and stood between their cars to banter for a minute, then Celeste headed for town in her Miata.

Freddy lounged beside his pickup and the brunette of the locked desk came out. What was her name? Muriel? Marlene? The crew from the freight shed dispersed, the brunette typist took thirty seconds to lock and shake the doors, and I was guarding an empty building. She strode to the lot, where she and Freddy glanced around and apparently decided the coast was clear. They locked into an embrace with kisses that made me blush before both slipped into Freddy's pickup and headed for town. That put a new slant on Freddy, and I should be ashamed to say, added a whole new interest in the brunette.

I was Johnny-on-the-spot, parked behind the Lathrop Building at six-forty-five when Angie came out.

She glanced at her watch while she climbed in. "Amazing."

"Yep, that's me, thoroughly domesticated. How was your day?"

"Stinking. Your friend Dave Marino was in all afternoon trying to weasel the cheapest spots for Reginald. He had our top salesman crying, and the rest of us shagging availabilities."

"Where would you like to have dinner?"

"Supposing, just for a change, I cook something?"

"Darn, I have this image of you as a high-powered executive. Don't make me change to a household drudge."

"Well, you could think of me as an executive chef. I can whip up a world-class beef stroganoff in twenty minutes. You can flirt with me instead of trying to make out with every waitress we've had."

We hit the grocery store. Angie knew what she wanted. I just hovered, but there is something intimate about buying groceries together. It's kind of a grown-up version of playing house. I asserted my macho ego and paid the tab, but it was interesting because everyone must have assumed we were married. Connie and I have done a lot of things together, but I couldn't remember ever shopping for groceries. Maybe we should try that. I tried to picture grocery shopping with Celeste and got nowhere.

It was starting to get dark by the time we approached the house. We had half a mile to go when a furious barking, and then a howl like an air raid siren startled us. I slammed on the brakes, and Turk bounded across the ditch, pawing at the car. Angie reached over the seat to open the back door and he jumped in.

"What the devil are you doing here, big boy? I told you to stay." I dropped the car into gear and started to roll. Turk whined like his heart was breaking. I stopped.

"Darn, I wish you could talk, fella."

"He's certainly trying, isn't he?" Angie asked.

"Big time, and I think I'm getting the message. Has he ever met you on the road before?"

"Never."

I popped the trunk and jumped out. The shotgun was wrapped in towels. I shook it free of its travel wrapping and handed it to Angie. "You're driving. If anyone tries to stop you, blow them away." I dug Lieutenant Stella's card out of my wallet and handed it to her. Angie scooted over under the wheel and took the card.

"Go back to the nearest phone, probably the Rendezvous is open, and call Stella. Don't come back without the troopers."

"What are you going to do?"

"Don't worry, nothing stupid or macho. I'll just skulk around and try to decipher what Turk is telling us."

Angie backed around in a half circle and spurted gravel. I got my pistol in my hand and stepped off the road into the trees.

Chapter Eighteen

I paralleled the road. If any cars came from Angie's driveway, I wanted to get a look at them. Leaves had fallen but they were damp rather than crisp so I could walk without crackling, and sight distance was much more than it had been during my last foray. That was a two-edged sword. I felt naked between trees. Bushes that had made a blind a week ago were bare sticks, and I could see, and be seen, right through the low tree branches. I used the squirrels' technique, moving fast between shelters then freezing and scanning from each new perspective.

That works for squirrels. You see a blur of movement but they're invisible when they freeze and you begin to doubt what you saw before they move again. Mostly I was counting on whoever was there to be expecting a car and concentrating on the drive rather than the woods. Problem was that they would be set, not moving. I got close enough to see there were no cars in the drive, but that only meant they had been dropped off. I started seeing shapes that could be men with rifles crouched under bushes, but each time I studied one it turned into a log or a branch that still wore leaves, and definitely, nothing moved. The woods were totally, eerily silent except for my breathing.

I dropped down and crawled for the last fifty yards until I came to a big cottonwood that looked bulletproof. I had a clear view of the edges of the drive, and could see a man lying beside the track with a rifle sticking up. He would have been an easy shot, but I couldn't spot his accomplices. Once I shot, I'd be the center of attention and I didn't see a suitable bunker close by. The cottonwood was good, but not that good. I did a slow scan, both sides of the drive, then the trees, and I couldn't spot them. There had to be at least two men, maybe three. Why not ten or twenty? I came back to my original target and he had turned into a log with a branch sticking up.

I decided they must be inside and crawled toward the house. It was too dark to see into the house, but nothing showed in the picture window. I lay flat behind a mound of leaves and just watched over the gun sight.

Ten minutes crept by in slow motion. It seemed like forever since Angie had left, so surely the troopers were on the way. The house looked peaceful and inviting, but those solid walls also looked impenetrable. Anyone inside would be warm and comfortable, could spend the night if necessary. When I stopped moving I noticed it was cold, and I wasn't dressed for it.

More time crept by. My feet were checking out. I took the pistol in my left hand and warmed the right one in my pocket, then switched and rubbed my undamaged ear but was worried about staying invisible. When squirrels freeze, it usually isn't literally. I was wondering about backing off and waiting for the troopers on the road when something moved at the end of the house.

It was a strange rocking motion, a gray blur the size of a washtub. It passed the house and turned to cross the drive, then another appeared behind it. A pair of porcupines waddled past the house and disappeared into the woods. I got up and stamped my feet, then stumped around back and fired up the generator. The hot exhaust from the muffler felt good so I basked in that for a few minutes before I went inside and started the furnace.

Turk's food dish and water pan were empty and there were porcupine quills in both of them. I was sitting on the front steps with a cup of coffee when the school bell in the spare bedroom announced time for classes. A minute later two state troopers came slinking down the edges of the lane with rifles at the ready.

"Hey, Jim. Nice night for a drive. Can I offer you a cup of coffee?"

◇◇◇

The troopers were nice about it. They declined coffee but Jim seemed relieved that I hadn't shot anything, not even porcupines. They shouldered rifles and walked back up the lane. The school bell rang to announce their departure, then rang again and Angie drove in with Turk still in back. She carried the groceries inside. I opened the car door for Turk, but he refused to get out. We had a tug of war, me pulling on his collar, him trying to dig his nails into the seat. Eventually I won, kept a grip on his collar and dragged him around back. He whined and bolted into his doghouse.

I took the pans inside, washed and refilled them, then set them just outside his house. He crouched and sniffed, walked all the way around the pans, but finally took a few slurps of the water. I went inside where the kitchen already smelled like a French restaurant.

Angie's beef stroganoff was superb, lots of sour cream, and it complemented the generous dollop of bleu cheese on the salads. So did the pinot noir. The dining table was against the rear wall, the windows overlooking the backyard and what would have been a view of the river, if it hadn't been too dark. Turk was once again master of his domain, settled down in his house, but chin resting on his paws outside. Across the room toward the front, the drive was just discernable. I did trust Turk to raise an alarm if anyone came within half a mile of us, but the silence of the bell was reassuring.

"Angie, this is wonderful. I'm so sorry we wasted all those meals in restaurants."

"Not bad for a silver-tongued, lying Irishman. Want to rhapsodize about my eyes sparkling in the flattering glow of the overhead lights?"

"Yeah, that was the next subject."

"Can it. You can help wash the dishes if you promise not to break anything."

"Yeah, I've always heard about diners who couldn't pay their bills and had to wash dishes. Mere money couldn't begin to cover this experience. Can I set a drink on the drainboard, just to look at it and salivate while I perform this menial task?"

"Watch your mouth, buster, there is nothing menial about maintaining home and hearth." Angie went to the refrigerator for ice and mixed two frosty rum and Cokes, but she set them on the drainboard while she washed and I dried. We carried our drinks into the living room. The wood Stan had laid in the fireplace was still waiting for a light. I looked the question, Angie nodded, and I touched my lighter to the paper under the kindling.

It was a companionable time; the fire was a perfect focus for our thoughts. Angie mixed more drinks, but we didn't have a lot to talk about, and I kept getting distracted by the aggravating need to think and my total lack of fresh ideas.

"Alex, I'm beat. Long day in the halls of commerce, and the excruciating exertion of preparing gourmet meals has done me in. Can you find the guest room?"

"I think I'll spend the night on the couch. I blew the day watching cars in the parking lot, so may as well spend the night watching the Buick in the driveway." Angie parked her empty glass by the sink and disappeared into her bedroom. I mixed one more drink and settled down on the couch to waste the night.

When we pulled onto Second Avenue at five minutes after eight, Reginald's Mercedes was parked in front of Monte's Department Store. I drove on by and found a vacant meter six spaces ahead of him.

Angie gave me her perplexed nose wrinkle. "What's the matter? Lost in this bewildering metropolis?"

"Not yet. Angie, that's Reginald's car in front of the store, and we need to know why."

"You think it's suspicious that a car is parked on Second Avenue?"

"Sweetheart, I've spent the last two days watching that car sit in the parking lot at the airport. Compared to that, this is earth-shaking. Maybe he's having breakfast at the Coffee Cup...." That got a vigorous headshake from Angie. "Maybe he went up to the station, but that's Dave's provenance. The movie doesn't start for eleven hours, so he probably isn't waiting in line. Besides, he should be at the airport in a few minutes, so something different is happening. If he needed a new handkerchief or a pair of socks, he should have bought those last night. Be a good girl, nip into the store, and just check on what he's doing in there."

"Gee, I don't know. I don't have your training and expertise as a gumshoe."

"No problem. Turn your collar up, and there's a false beard and mustache in the glove compartment. Slip those on so no one will notice you, and pretend to be shopping. You have a master's degree in that."

She slanted a skeptical glance from the corner of her eye, but climbed out and marched bravely into the store. Ten minutes dragged by, Reginald came out stuffing a paper sack into his overcoat pocket, climbed into his car and drove away. I impersonated an empty car and seemed to get away with it. Two minutes later, Angie was back.

"Was he buying machine guns?"

"Nope, he was at the jewelry counter looking at gold chains."

"Aha! A present for his wife, so he has a guilty conscience."

"Alex, don't you ever watch the political ads? His wife died of cancer ten years ago. He's running as an eligible bachelor, so he must have a girlfriend."

"Is she in the ads?"

"No, why should she be?"

"Angie, one of the best things about Governor Bill is that Bridey has been buying his neckties for almost forty years. Every morning she sends him out to run the state with a peck on the cheek, so he's always in the right mood. Also, we know that if he ever does anything dumb, Bridey will give him hell. He comes with a built-in system of checks and balances, and voters can relate to that."

"Would having a girlfriend be a bad thing for the election?"

"No, a little romance might be a good thing, but it depends on the girl. If he were going to present us with a Jackie Onassis or a Princess Diana, she should be in every commercial, so why isn't she?"

"So, maybe she isn't Miss America. Alex, what does that have to do with people trying to kill us?"

"Depends on whose wife she is. Might be enough to get us killed and him, too. You go to work, I'll take over the assignment from here."

Angie treated me to a scowl and I peeled out. I'd seen Reginald turn left at Cushman Street, and that was toward the airport, but I didn't want to lose him if he had another destination in mind. I made the stoplight, and spotted the Mercedes waiting for a light three blocks ahead. We convoyed sedately to the airport and Reginald parked in his usual spot. It was looking like a replay of yesterday until the F-27 finished unloading and Reginald came out of the office and climbed up the steps into the airplane.

I left the Buick and sprinted for the 310. By the time the F-27 trundled down the taxiway, I had the engine covers off, engines running and was pulling out to follow him. The pilot was on the radio copying his instrument clearance to Anchorage via Blue 27. I was right behind him filing a VFR flight plan for Nenana. He was cleared to go, I was cleared onto the runway and hold. The moment he broke ground it was my turn, and I jammed the throttles to the firewall.

He climbed up to his assigned seventeen thousand feet. I leveled off at ten thousand and set a high-end cruise. He had wanted the higher altitude for speed and engine efficiency, but all airspace above twelve thousand feet is controlled, so he had to follow Blue 27 and that took him on a dogleg directly over Summit Lake, where he had to report his arrival. I set a ruler line for Anchorage and rocked in my seat, trying to go faster.

I was actually ahead of him before he reached altitude, but then he inched away and angled off to the left to follow his clearance. When I passed Nenana, I called Nenana Radio and cancelled my flight plan. Reginald just might be in the cockpit of the F-27 and if he was, he'd hear me on the radio. He probably wouldn't recognize my tail number, but why take chances?

"Eight Four Zulu, are you on the ground?"

"Yeah, are you asleep? I'm just parking on the village end."

"Roger, Eight Four Zulu, flight plan closed."

When I passed Mt. Denali Lodge, the F was a speck on my left, going over Windy Pass. I bored straight through Mt. Denali. That's not as unlikely as it sounds. The picturesque profile we view from a distance, the one Sydney Lawrence painted, is actually a whole group of mountains ranging from fourteen thousand to seventeen thousand feet. Denali itself is a misshapen spire like the Matterhorn with glaciers winding between mountains like snakes.

I took snow off Mt. Silverthrone with my left wing, off Browne Tower with my right, and ignored the up and down drafts that tried to rip off the wings. I was over Willow when I saw the F-27 coming up on me from behind. I dropped the nose to lose two hundred feet a minute and kept the power on. That almost held our positions.

I reported Cape Mackenzie at four thousand feet and was cleared for a straight-in approach. Twenty seconds later, the other pilot reported the Cape at ten thousand and was vectored over Fire Island. I made a high-speed turnoff at the first intersection. A vacant transient parking spot by the tower was meant for loading. I locked up the parking brake and ran for the terminal.

Luck was in. Trish was at the Budget Rent-A-Car desk. I'd met her that spring, and I was in a hurry then, too, because the entire Russian Mafia was right behind me with Kalashnikovs. I laid such a line of blarney on her that time that she now assumes I'm the head of the CIA.

She saw me sprinting down the hall, assumed that civilization as we know it was threatened unless I got somewhere fast, and held out a car key for me. I handed her a credit card when I whipped by.

"Chevy Malibu, first stall."

"Thanks, this afternoon." I grabbed the key and kept right on running.

Chapter Nineteen

The F-27 was already parked at the Interior terminal, forklifts doing their dance, and Reginald was nowhere in sight. I had parked the Chevy and was still calming down when a Mercedes, the twin of the one in Fairbanks, pulled out of the employee parking lot and hit International Airport Road. Reginald was at the wheel and I locked on two cars behind him.

He turned right on Minnesota, left on Dimond Boulevard. (Yeah, spelled correctly. It's named for Judge Dimond, not the gem.) We drove halfway to the mountains and turned right again on the old Seward Highway. The town tapers off and stops after the Peanut Farm Lounge, so we were headed for the Rabbit Creek Inn. Good choice for an assignation. Good restaurant, a view of the mountains across Turnagain Arm, and discreet unless you bumped into an acquaintance on a similar project. I should bring Connie there next trip.

We drove right on by the Rabbit Creek Inn, passed the flats, and continued on the crooked shelf of Seward Highway. That's an exciting drive. The Chugach Mountains on the left try to squeeze the highway into Turnagain Arm and occasionally spill rocks onto the pavement. The Arm itself is either a picturesque fiord or a disgusting mud flat, depending on the tide, and the mountains around Hope on the other side are worth the drive. The road is so crooked that I didn't have to worry about being spotted until we got to the million-dollar mile. That's a straight stretch, entirely built on fill after the '64 earthquake submerged the old road.

At Girdwood, Reginald turned left into the valley. Two cars coming from the Portage direction made right turns to follow him, and I survived the left turn behind them. Maybe he was headed for the Double Muskee Inn, wonderful romantic spot, view to rival Switzerland and food to dream about. I should definitely bring Connie there next trip.

Forty-foot spruce hung over the road, but through the gaps, a view of Alyeska Mountain reared up on the right. It was scarred by almost annual avalanches, and by the ski lift that rose above it all. Reginald turned right and headed toward the ski lodge. One of the cars ahead of me went straight, the other turned, and I was number three pulling into the gravel lot in front of the massive log lodge.

That was the perfect place for an assignation. Ski season was still a month away, but the lift was running so tourists could ride up to the top of the mountain and down again. The view from the top of that mountain is more than worth the twenty-minute ride and the freezing year-around wind. You're surrounded by mountains with a glimpse of the Arm and far enough away that it always looks good. The restaurant is wonderful, its big picture windows looking up at the mountain and the bunny slope, and the bar is suitably rustic with a massive stone fireplace and a predictable Alpine motif. Perfect place for an après ski toddy. Definitely have to bring Connie here.

Reginald drove right through the lot and turned right on the service road toward the ski lift, then right again behind the row of detached chalets. It would have been a little pointed to follow him there, but the road only ran fifty yards behind four matching units. I parked in the lot facing the lodge and rolled down the passenger window. I saw the Mercedes pass behind the first two units, but it didn't come out from behind the third.

A young athletic type bounded down the steps from the chalet and strode around the corner toward the back. This kid was a Norse Adonis, if that's not too great a cultural stretch. Just over six feet, long blond hair, and a wisp of blond mustache. He had the slender athletic build of a professional ski instructor. In one minute he was back, and Reginald was right behind him. The kid opened the door and ushered Reginald in, but just before he disappeared, Reginald reached back and squeezed the kid's bum.

I didn't upchuck. I spun the Chevy around and burned the pavement back to the airport. I was strolling down the hall toward the rental booths this time, and Trish gave me her glorious smile.

"Hi, Alex, did you make it in time?"

"Yep, thanks to you. I can't talk about it, but you and I averted an international incident."

"What's the matter with your face?"

"Just a little gunshot wound, nothing to worry about. How much for the car?"

"Company reimbursing?"

"Yep, deepest pockets in the world."

"I thought so. I charged you for a full day, is that all right?"

"Trish, the only thing that mattered was speed, and we did it. We'll let the General Accounting Office pick up the pieces." I signed the contract, solemnly folded the copy into my pocket, retrieved my card, and thanked her with the ten-thousand-watt official smile. She blushed with pride. I stomped back through the building and out to the airplane.

I made it back to Fairbanks, refueled the plane, and was again on duty as the lot watchman by a quarter to three. I'd barely had time to get bored when a sleek Piper Apache with the gold star logo of Cordova Air landed. That was a good excuse to move my vigil to the coffee shop at the terminal. I made it to a seat by the window just as the passengers deplaned from the Apache. The plane taxied across the ramp and parked on the tarmac. The pilot climbed out and strode toward the terminal. I had been hoping it would be Tommy Olsen, and it was.

Tommy and I got to be good buddies down in Juneau. We'd both delivered legislators for an emergency session, got in just ahead of a storm, and were weathered in solid. We spent two days hunkered down in the Baranoff Hotel, most of it in the bar. A Taku wind tried to rip the islands out of the channel and deposited ice about two inches per hour on everything. That old hotel creaked and groaned, ice and water were screaming sideways up Franklin Street, but the bar was warm and very well stocked. I don't remember a lot about those days, except that the waitress was named Donica and was the prettiest little mixture of Russian and Haida Indian ever born. Other than that, Tommy and I shared our life stories, sometimes drunk, sometimes sober, but the bond was established.

"Hey, Tommy, over here."

"Alex? Kinda far from home, and what's with the bandage? You prang an airplane?"

"Nah, Second Avenue bar and no backup. You here for a while?"

"Long enough to scarf down a hamburger and a cuppa joe. You?"

"Little longer, personal business."

Tommy waved down a waitress and ordered a hamburger. I asked for coffee.

"I gather you've spent some time here recently. I noticed you made a flight for Interior."

"No, not that I remember. I've been through a few times, seasonal fishermen heading home and such, but I haven't stayed over."

"You sure? You never flew that new turbine Twin Otter of theirs?"

The waitress brought our coffee and Tommy sipped. "Alex, I'm pretty sure. I have forgotten a few things. Sometimes I can't remember which bars I've hit, and once in a while I can't remember who I hit them with. That's particularly awkward when she's still in bed with me in the morning, but no, I don't think I've forgotten any flights."

The waitress slapped his burger on the table when she ran past with an armload of plates destined elsewhere. He glanced at his watch and stuffed his mouth full.

"My mistake. I thought I saw your name on a flight ticket, must have been someone else. Business good?"

He chewed and took a sip, but still had his mouth full. "Too good this week, probably nothing next. I've been to Kodiak, Anchorage, and now here since six o'clock this morning, and if I don't get a two-hundred-mile-per tailwind, I'll be late for a flight to Homer." He shoved the rest of his burger into his mouth, tried to wash it down.

"I'll get the check. See you around."

"Thanks, Alex, I'll look for you at the Baranoff." He skipped out, still chewing. I signaled the waitress for a refill and watched Tommy almost run across the apron and scramble up into the Apache. He fired engines and was rolling. I could see him talking on the radio while he taxied toward the runway. He made an intersection takeoff rather than taxi back to the end, and he was gone.

I was perplexed. I was positive I'd seen Tommy's name on a flight ticket at Interior. I remembered being surprised, but it didn't seem like I could have been mistaken. I finished the coffee and paid the tab. The waitress was a pretty little thing with one too many buttons open on her blouse, so I tipped her two dollars.

A jet slammed down and shook the terminal when the pilots honked on the reverse thrusters. I made the excursion down to the passenger area and watched the arrivals, but didn't see Dave or any obvious assassins.

I gave up my vigil and met Angie at the back door of the Lathrop Building. When she got in, I made a U-turn and headed back to our old haunt at the River's Edge for an evening of nostalgia.

"You're tired of my cooking already?"

"Angie, at the peak of gustatory delight, you need to stop and cleanse the palate. Besides, I'm developing dishwater hands."

"By proxy? All you've done is dry. Did you find Reginald's paramour?"

"That I did. Very attractive, slender six-footer with long blond hair, real athletic type. You'd have been impressed."

"So, why isn't Reginald showing her?"

"Bit more complicated. Maybe because his mustache is a little wispy?"

"Reginald's?"

"No, his lover's."

"Oh no, don't tell me."

"I thought you insisted on all the frightening details."

"Okay, so tell me. Could that have been what Stan overheard?"

"Possible, but the lover isn't the wolverine type. I still think it was Dave that Stan overheard."

"You don't suppose Reginald and Dave are lovers?"

"Possible, but how about this? Suppose Dave knows Reginald's preferences and is blackmailing him?"

We arrived at the River's Edge. The receptionist looked as if she was going to kiss us and took us straight to our usual table. We ordered the lamb but Angie wanted a bottle of pinot noir. I think she was expanding my horizons. The wine was served along with bread and butter. We sipped and did the smiley face thing. Our Caesar salads were almost instant.

Angie tore a chunk of bread and buttered it. "Do you suppose Dave has his eye on a political office if Reginald is elected?"

"I doubt it. I think Dave knows that Reginald's chances of election are written on a snowball in hell. I think it's more immediate, something to do with the business, and consider this. If Dave thinks that we know, and we might blow the whistle, there goes his blackmail scheme, and that just might be valuable enough to kill for."

"Not trying to worry me with bombshells?"

Our dinners arrived and we dug in. When I had my mouth empty again, the subject was still hanging in the air.

"Angie, that was just a little bombshell. After that, I was going to worry you with a very strange conversation I had today."

"New blonde, or more of the same?"

"No, kind of a grizzled dishwater with gray around the edges. A pilot I know from Cordova stopped by for a snack. What's bothering me is he said he'd never flown the Interior Otter, but I could swear I saw his name on a flight ticket.

"Another strange thing keeps bothering me. Interior keeps a Howard and a pilot standing by at Point Barrow, but why would they do that? If freight was sent to Point Barrow on the mail plane he could shuttle it to Prudhoe, but the mail planes are Interior's competition. Interior flies the Skyvan direct, Fairbanks to Prudhoe almost every day, so why keep a plane at Point Barrow?"

"Maybe he's shuttling the other way? Picking up stuff they drop at Prudhoe and taking it to Point Barrow?"

"Possible, but there couldn't be enough to justify a full-time pilot unless there's something very illegal and profitable in the shipments."

"You mean like drugs?"

"Could be. Barrow's a good-sized village. Drugs on mail planes get sniffed out by dogs and such, but freight to Prudhoe isn't suspect, so a shuttle would get it into the village."

Angie was considering and nodding. She poured the last drops of pinot noir into our glasses.

"Alex, it could be the other way. Walrus ivory used to be a big export from Point Barrow, but now it's illegal to sell raw ivory. Natives can possess it, but it has to be a work of art if they sell it, so it has to be scrimshawed. That only raises the price of raw ivory and it's really valuable now."

"Okay, one way or another there could be big bucks coming out of Barrow. Maybe not enough money to kill for, but illegal enough. Maybe I should run up to Barrow in the morning and have a chat with Mr. Alvin Hopson."

"Really? Can I come with? I've never been north of Fairbanks."

"Sure. Can you get the day off?"

"Very likely. Let me work on it."

"Fine, I'll appreciate the company, but bring a good book with you. We're talking about hours of boredom here."

Chapter Twenty

We blasted into a clear blue sky at eight thirty in the morning. The Skyvan was already missing and I wondered where he'd gone. I opted not to file a flight plan because those are public and anyone in the air can hear the radio. Flight plans aren't for the benefit of the aircraft; they're for the benefit of the searchers if something goes wrong. If you put a plane down and need to be found, you have a locator beacon on board for that purpose. I didn't want Interior to hear me file a flight plan to Point Barrow.

Angie was glued to the window so I stayed low for the view. That cost us some speed and a little extra fuel, but made the flight a lot more scenic. Angie was wearing her leather jacket with the faux fur nestled around her cheeks and was so darned attractive it was hard to keep from staring. Someday when we're both sober, I should really try to tell her what a lovely lady she is. Meantime, I fudged right of our course and flew through the White Mountains.

They have some spectacularly rugged areas, and flying up the creeks rather than over the top is fun. We spotted Dahl sheep on several hillsides, then waterfalls where new snow was melting and gushing down cliffs. Angie was beaming and pointing every which way.

"Alex, why did you say it was boring? Oh, look, there's sheep on that hillside."

"Just wait. We've got two hours to go."

"Wonderful, I could do this forever."

The mountains tapered off and the Yukon Flats spread out. That's interesting too, because the river divides into a dozen channels at that point, and altogether is close to twenty miles wide. Moose and beaver would be old stuff to Angie, but fall colors still carpeted the flats so I dropped down to a thousand feet and got the full effect of the twisting river and sloughs.

The village of Beaver was hugging the northern bank of the main channel on our right. I realized we were farther east than I'd intended, and was about to turn back toward Barrow when I noticed a moving speck in the sky above us. We were catching it fast, so I stayed behind it and climbed up a bit. It was Interior's Skyvan on a direct course for Prudhoe Bay.

Angie was studying the plane above us. "Is that who I think it is?"

"Yep, that's Interior making their morning milk run. Might be fun to beat him to Prudhoe. If the pilot is Freddy it will be awkward, but if we catch him offloading cocaine, it will be awkward anyhow, and if the Howard is there to meet him, mission accomplished. Besides, it probably isn't Freddy. The plane left Fairbanks too early for that."

Angie shrugged and turned to watch the village go by. A dozen log cabins were scattered along the riverbank. A yellow wooden frame building was the BIA school, and the larger log building on the west end was the store and general community center. What looked like a dirt road paralleled the river, but it was only a quarter-mile long and had an orange windsock flapping against a pole beside the east end.

I dropped us right down to the deck and used the descent to pick up speed. We were indicating two hundred knots when we passed the Skyvan, a solid fifty knots faster than he was and six thousand feet below him. I figured there was very little chance of us being spotted and no chance at all of being identified.

The river dropped behind, the ground started to rise and support a few spruce trees. "Angie, see that bright red stripe on the ground?"

"Where?"

"Right there at the edge of the trees."

"I don't see anything. What the heck are you talking about?"

"Darn, you missed it. We just crossed the Arctic Circle."

"Alex, I may be a dumb little girl from the bush, but no one is stupid enough to fall for that."

"Angie, you'd be surprised. I've even had passengers who claimed to see it. Anyhow, you're officially in the Arctic. I'll have Vickie mail you a certificate when I get home."

"Is that part for real?"

"Yep, suitable for framing. Good grief, look at that beaver dam." The dam must have been a quarter of a mile long and backed up a lake big enough to support half a dozen resorts. The ground climbed fast, the Endicott Mountain Range was coming up, and tendrils of fog instead of waterfalls were leaking out of the valleys. We followed the ground up, and the higher we got, the more clouds I could see against the far mountains. At ten thousand feet there was a gray carpet below us with occasional eight-thousand-foot peaks sticking through like islands. That cloud layer appeared to reach clear to the North Pole.

"What do we do now?" Angie asked.

"Hey, me heap big Gussak honey bee. We fly straight to Prudhoe Bay, what else?"

"You have X-ray vision?"

"Sort of. That's what all these little clocks on the dashboard are for. They're not very exciting now, but as soon as we pass the mountains, they'll all start to flash and beep and whistle and lead us right down to Prudhoe."

"It's a good thing I know you never exaggerate."

Mountains tapered off and stopped sticking through, but the cloud reached on forever. First the automatic direction finder (ADF) swung around to point at the non-directional beacon (NDB) at Prudhoe. I corrected three degrees east and centered the needle. Then the VHF omni-directional range (VOR) flag began to flicker with a signal from Point Barrow. I turned the compass indicator to west and the *To* flag settled down, but the needle was off scale to the right.

"Angie, these are the hours of boredom. You did bring a book with you?"

"Yes, I brought a good book, but it's hard to concentrate when you're terrified."

"Yeah, that's why I never read while I'm flying." I keyed the microphone. "Point Barrow Radio, Cessna Eight-Zero-Eight-Four Zulu out of Bethel requesting current Barrow weather."

"Eight-Four Zulu, current weather five hundred feet and one mile. Altimeter two-nine point nine-five, wind north at seven. Please state your destination."

"Barrow Radio, no particular destination, just a sightseeing trip. Thanks." I switched the radio to the Prudhoe Unicom. The Barrow VOR was straight magnetic west of us. Geographically, Barrow is north of Prudhoe, and if you live in Kansas City, you may think there isn't much difference between magnetic and geographic directions, but that close to the pole, the difference is eighteen degrees. When the VOR said Barrow was magnetic west, I reduced power and dropped down into the cloud. It bumped a little, not bad. I kept the ADF needle centered on Prudhoe.

"Alex, can we go back to boredom?"

"Any moment now. We're down to four thousand feet. See, this needle here is pointing toward Prudhoe Bay. We just keep it centered."

"Oh, goody. I feel much better."

The needle wavered, then swung around to point behind us.

"Now what?"

"Now, we're over Prudhoe at two thousand feet. We fly straight ahead for two minutes while we drop down to five hundred feet, turn around and go back."

"How do you know we won't hit a mountain?"

"Because there's nothing taller than an oil derrick within fifty miles. Be quiet and read your book."

I started a two-minute turn to the left. Angie grabbed her seat and took on that morning-after-the-Wagon-Wheel pallor.

"Prudhoe Radio, Cessna Eight-Four Zulu, initial approach fix."

"Eight-Four Zulu, authorization, please."

"Interior Air Freight, second section."

"Eight-Four Zulu, we have a Skyvan authorized, we do not have a Cessna."

"Can you check it out? I'm on final approach. The Skyvan is the first section and he's right behind us, we're just a little faster."

"Better break off. If you land, the aircraft will be confiscated, and you with it."

"I'm declaring an emergency. Not enough fuel to return."

"Fine. Same difference. Land and your ass is grass. Suit yourself."

We were down to three hundred feet, white frosty tundra flashing by below us. "Angie, look sharp. We're going to fly right down their runway. We're looking for a Howard, a red boxy airplane with one big radial engine on the front. You look on your side, I'll watch the left."

"Are we really out of gas, Alex?"

"Heck no, and he knows it. Here comes the runway."

I slowed us up to eighty but didn't drop gear or flaps. We flew the length of the strip at fifty feet. Half a dozen aircraft were tied down, none that remotely resembled a Howard. Tan buildings with round corners went by, self-contained metal affairs that looked as if they were designed for a lunar colony, which might be close to true. I poured on the coal and climbed back into the cloud.

"I didn't see it." Angie was shaking her head, half negation, half shock. "Now what?"

"Now, we grab some lunch. How about a hamburger patty at the Barrow Road House?"

"Do we stop this time, or do I grab it while we fly by?"

We climbed to a thousand feet and turned magnetic west, sky the consistency of a vanilla milkshake. Angie was biting her lip and staring at the white windshield. "You do have some idea where we're going?"

"Sure, smell the hamburgers? We just follow the aroma to its source."

I didn't bother to climb, so it took five minutes before the Barrow VOR locked on. "Barrow radio, Eight-Four Zulu. We decided to stop for lunch, estimating Barrow in ten minutes."

"No reported traffic. Everyone else is too smart to be flying. Are you enjoying your sightseeing?"

"Immensely. We've taken a thousand pictures. We're over the middle marker."

"Eight-Four Zulu, cleared to land."

Landing gear came down with a satisfying clunk and three green lights glowed. Flaps whirred down to twenty degrees, engines protested the adjustment to high RPM, but slowed us down. White cloud below us changed from milk to cottage cheese, then morphed to tundra, and the outlying approach lights whiffed beneath us. The tarmac runway was still black, not yet frosted over. Single-family houses went by on our left looking like storm survivors, which they were, but that wasn't the cause of the irregular shapes. Each house had been built by its owner out of whatever materials came to hand. The results were solid and snug, but strange by suburban standards.

We flew more than halfway down the strip before we touched down and still had to taxi a hundred yards to the apron. Barrow is not the usual Eskimo village. Because of its location, it's a regional hub with a runway that can handle anything flying and has instrument landing capabilities. There's a lot of airline traffic over the pole, and Barrow is the first possible landing for a plane in trouble. Also, Barrow is home to the Holmes and Narver Arctic Research Center maintained by the navy.

The research center is located five miles from the village on the last possible spit of land, with more of the moon-colony type buildings and a road to get there. That accounted for the occasional rusting hulks of dead pickups in some front yards. We taxied into the tie-down area, surrounded by half a dozen

Piper Cubs and Cessna one-eighties, a Cessna one-seventy-two, and a Beech Barron, but no Howard.

"Kinda big, huh?" Angie was looking at the cluster of houses around the runway, and they were a confusing mass, maybe ten times as many as a typical Eskimo village. True to the Eskimo custom, they were arranged without regard to surveys and seemed to huddle together for warmth. The first impression is of dark clutter, but that's not fair. Houses aren't painted, but there might not be two days a year when paint would dry in Barrow.

One house had two beaver hides and a seal skin nailed to the wall, the beavers a circle, the seal an oval. They added to the impression of clutter, but to their owner, they were money in the bank. A couple of buildings were two stories, looming over the usual low-roofed jumble. Those were the store and the Road House, both owned by Hopsons. Angie was staring at a whale vertebrae beside a house. It was the size of a chair and probably used for a seat. I caught her hand and pulled her toward an opening between houses.

"Come on, I promised you a hamburger, remember?"

"Oh yeah, still following the aroma?"

"Yep, it's leading toward that big building on the right." We wound between houses and tromped up the wooden stairs. The first door opened into an Arctic entry, bare wooden floor and plywood walls. The next let us into a low-ceilinged dining room with six long wooden tables under fluorescent lights.

The room was capable of seating sixty people family style, but only one chair was occupied. A bear of a man, sporting a shock of white hair and wearing overalls over a red wool shirt, sat at the table nearest the kitchen. Old Eben wore a two-day accumulation of white stubble and his usual satisfied smile. He well deserved the smile, lord of all he surveyed and revered by every soul on the North Slope.

"Hey, Alex, welcome to God's country. You got yourself a wife?" He turned to shout toward the kitchen. "Ellie, need two hamburgers and two coffees." He hadn't bothered to ask because anyone who arrives in Barrow hasn't had food for several hours. His specifying hamburgers was because I'm a Gussak (Caucasian). The Road House has plenty of variety but mostly local Eskimo foods. Gussaks either wouldn't like them or their systems couldn't stand them, so he didn't take chances. If you think I'm kidding, try a plate of muktuk or blubber, or maybe a beaver with the head on and the eyes staring at you. Black fish the size of sardines are served in the round. That makes good sense because the Eskimo diet is short on vegetables. The fish has been eating plankton, so if you don't clean the fish, they will prevent scurvy. The bones are soft enough to crunch and if you're squeamish you bite the head off and swallow it whole.

Angie was hanging back so I pulled her by the hand again. "Eben, this is my sister-in-law, Angie." I needed to squelch the wife assumption because it wouldn't play well in some villages.

Eben stared, his smile flickered off, and his features turned to stone. He had registered that Angie was Indian. He had to work fast, replace thousands of years of animosity with the new veneer of tolerance, before his smile inched back up. Angie was having the same reaction, almost cowering behind me and gripping my jacket, but when Eben got control, she relaxed and came around beside me.

"Hi," was all she could manage.

"Hello, well, come sit, come sit. Will you be staying the night?" He was still wrestling with why a formerly respectable pilot should be traveling with an Indian. He wasn't necessarily buying the sister-in-law scenario, but he could see one possible excuse for my being there with Angie.

"No, no, just stopped for a bite of lunch. Heading right back to Fairbanks."

"You just happened to be in the neighborhood?" That was such a good joke we both had to laugh. Even Angie smiled. Eben reigned at the head of a table, and we took chairs on either side of him.

"Actually, I was hoping to talk to Alvin for a minute."

"Alvin?" He was clearly perplexed.

Ellie bustled out of the kitchen with two plates, doled them out, and picked up Eben's half empty cup. She carried it to the thirty-cup pot on the sideboard and filled it and two more large brown mugs for us. She delivered the coffee and slipped back into the kitchen. Ellie wasn't being anti-social, but she doesn't speak English, except for *hamburger* and *coffee*. She's sensitive about that and avoids strangers. When you get to know her, she's delightful and joins right into the repartee with a wicked sense of humor, but with Eben translating.

Our hamburgers were thick juicy patties between slices of homemade bread, very good and very welcome. The usual Eskimo condiments were on the table, salt, pepper, ketchup, Tabasco, and a little bottle of seal oil. I skipped those, but Angie grabbed the seal oil and sprinkled her hamburger. Eben's smile ratcheted up to full welcome.

Angie dug in with obvious enthusiasm and I hoped she knew what she was doing. If your system isn't used to seal oil it's disastrous, especially if you're going to be in an airplane with no bathroom for a while. Every Eskimo table along the coast has seal oil, but it would be a rare treat in Angie's Indian home village, three hundred miles up the Kuskokwim from the ocean. Apparently she knew what she was into, because if you don't, about two bites will do you in, but she kept right on munching and smiling around her mouthful.

Eben went back to his quizzical mode. "You want to talk to Alvin?"

"Yeah, Alvin Hopson, the pilot?"

"You came the wrong direction. He lives in Seattle, flies Boeing seven-twenty-sevens for Alaska Airlines."

I had to swallow hamburger. "I must have made a mistake. Who flies the Howard?"

"Nobody, at least not lately. It's rolled up into a ball out beside the navy highway."

"An accident?"

"Sort of. Alvin had been flying it one night, came home late in a snowstorm and his tie-down anchors were buried. The snowplow was handy, so he tied the Howard to it and went home to bed. Early next morning Charlie goes out, fires up the grader, and takes off to plow the road. By the time he noticed that he was dragging the Howard, it didn't even look like an airplane anymore. He just scooped it out into the tundra and it's still there. Want to go see it?"

"That was a while ago?"

"Few years I reckon. How's the hamburger?"

"Best hamburgers in the world. Give Ellie a hug for me."

Angie was nodding enthusiastically. "Really wonderful. Don't know how many years since I've had seal oil, what a treat."

Eben positively beamed. I think Angie had just repaired several thousand years of animosity between races. If you're wondering about seal oil, it's a relative of Worcestershire sauce, both with a fish-like base, but when seal oil is fully ripe it's about ten times stronger.

We finished our burgers and licked our fingers. Then Angie put one more drop of seal oil on a fingertip and licked that off. She closed her eyes in ecstasy, then jumped up and gave Eben a hug. I think he blushed, but his complexion is pretty dark, so it's hard to tell. Fair is fair. I went into the kitchen and hugged Ellie. That earned me a glorious sunny smile and a pat on the shoulder.

"I wasn't kidding, we really do need to get back to Fairbanks." I laid the appropriate twenty-dollar bill on the table.

"Well, don't be a stranger, and bring...your sister-in-law up when you can stay longer."

We waved and smiled and backed out. Ellie peeked out of the kitchen for the last wave. We closed the doors and tromped down the stairs.

"Alex, what in the devil is going on? I thought you said Alvin was here and flying the Howard."

"Yeah, that's what I said, that's what I thought, but now I think something in Denmark is rottener than ripe seal oil. I just don't know what."

"Hey, don't knock seal oil. When I was a little girl, we got one bottle a year at Christmas time. We had a cousin in Chevak who sent it, and us kids fought over every drop."

"You had a cousin in Chevak?"

"Hey, you think Eskimos can't marry Indians? You some kind of racist, or just a century behind the times?"

"Probably both." We were back at the airplane. I let Angie climb up onto the wing first, then had to squeeze past her. She followed me in and buckled her harness. I reached across her to close and lock the door.

Chapter Twenty-One

At ten thousand feet we were flashing in and out of the cloud. At twelve thousand, it spread out below us, soft white cotton bunting from horizon to horizon.

"Okay, this is the hours of boredom I warned you about."

"Yeah, maybe, but it *is* beautiful, you know? Sort of amazing that twenty minutes ago we were in super-bad ugly weather and now we're in bright sunshine. I guess I can say I've been to the North Slope, but all I really saw were a couple of dozen houses."

"Not too bad, that's about all that's there. I don't know why it's called the North Slope. It's flatter than Kansas from the mountains to the ocean and that's about a hundred miles. Of course there are a million lakes there, but most of the year they're frozen so you can't tell them from tundra, anyway."

"So, it looks pretty much like Bethel?"

"If there's a difference, I've never noticed it."

"Maybe we were lucky that it was all fog." Angie sat back, but she was watching the cloud below us, and it was about as interesting as tundra. It's a mashed potato, or tapioca pudding effect.

I had trimmed us out, full cruise, and expected the cloud to last for thirty minutes, at least until we had crossed the Brooks Range. Mountains were below us, but no longer poking through the cloud. I would have said I was relaxed and not paying attention, but apparently that's not entirely true. The instruments are clustered, engine gauges on the left, navigation in the center. So long as the gauges are where they're supposed to be, a pilot really isn't aware of them, but if one gets out of place, it jumps out at you. It was the oil temperature on the left engine, and it was climbing. It would normally sit at one hundred ninety degrees. It got my attention when it passed two hundred.

I checked for pilot error, but no such luck. Cowl vents were at forty percent, appropriate for the ten-above-zero outside temperature. Exhaust gas temperature on every cylinder was in the green so the mixture was correct, no spark plugs were fouled. Oil pressure was steady at eighty pounds, no plugged filter or failing pump. Oil temp had climbed to two hundred five. I cranked the cowl flaps open full and it dropped back a degree, then climbed again, faster now.

The most likely scenario was that a main bearing was going out, getting hot and heating the oil, but the engine was smooth, no hint of a vibration, no loss of power. It didn't make sense. The cloud cover stretched ahead of us, at least thirty miles that I could see, and it didn't seem so scenic and friendly anymore. Two hundred ten degrees, two fifteen. The temperature seemed to be going up like the second hand on a clock. Two twenty, twenty degrees from redline, and the oil pressure started dropping off. That was the bad sign I'd been afraid of.

When a problem comes up, your priorities are first to save the passengers, then the airplane, then the engine. If it had been a single engine plane, I would have run the engine until it seized up, trying to get out of the mountains. In a twin, the situation isn't so critical. With only two passengers and now less than half a load of fuel, the 310 would easily maintain altitude on one engine. Meantime, if the problem with the left engine was a bearing and the bearing seized up, the sudden stop would bend the crankshaft. No reason to take that chance.

I put on my calm, competent pilot's expression, backed off the power on the left engine, feathered the prop and shut it down. It's not quite that simple, I was standing on the right rudder to compensate for the asymmetric thrust, but cranked the horizontal trim, trimmed us up four degrees and increased power on the right engine from sixty to seventy percent. We were still cruising level, only ten knots slower than before.

"Hey, what did you do that for?" My cool expression hadn't quite fooled Angie.

"Standard procedure. Saving gasoline. No point running two engines when we only need one."

"Alex, that sounds like bullshit. Dammit, if we're in trouble, tell me so I can help you worry."

"If you really want to help, you can climb out on the left wing and see why that engine was heating up, but no, we are not in trouble. We can fly all day on one engine, so go back to being bored."

I was telling her the truth, but only part of it. True that the 310 would happily cruise to Fairbanks on one engine, if nothing else went wrong. With an unexplained problem, one that didn't quite make sense, did I dare trust the right engine to keep running? The engines had the same time on them and both had thirty hours since the last hundred-hour inspection. Both had been filled at the same time with the same oil. There's nothing interconnected about the oil supplies, but still...

We were twenty minutes from the Yukon Valley and several villages. If I bypassed them it would be another hour over another mountain range to Fairbanks. When we'd left the Yukon three hours before, the cloud was spilling over the mountains, but the valley had been, might still be, clear.

When I'd told Angie her Kahlua eyes sucked men in like whirlpools, I'd been kidding, but there they were, looking at me with quiet trust. Many passengers would have been screaming and clawing at the door. Angie believed that I would take care of her, and suddenly I wanted to get that lovely girl on the ground as soon as possible.

We'd been homing on the KFAR radio transmitter in Fairbanks. I tuned the automatic direction finder radio to the nondirectional beacon at Fort Yukon and made the turn. The village of Beaver was closer, but has no radios and precious few amenities. Stevens Village, where Jeannine, the new schoolteacher, was presumably settling in, was a few miles to our right, and she might appreciate a visit from Angie. However, Stevens has only a dozen houses, no lodge, no radios, and since Jeannine's arrival, probably no vacant rooms. Fort Yukon has a lodge, a general store, and a radio beacon. The beacon locates the village for you, and you can use it for an approach, but it's not much related to the precision instrument landing facilities at Point Barrow or Fairbanks.

If Fort Yukon was fogged in, then we were on the way to Circle City, and if we couldn't land there, the Circle Hot Springs Lodge was a possibility, and at least we'd be over the Steese Highway. Landing on a highway is not a good thing, but it beats the heck out of landing on the tundra, and it's infinitely superior to running into the side of a mountain. I figured thirty minutes to Fort Yukon, and the cloud ahead did seem to be tapering off.

"You know, Alex, I'm really not bored anymore. Why did we turn?"

"Scenic route. Thought you might enjoy a look at Fort Yukon."

"Wow, you bet I would. I've got cousins there I haven't seen since I was a little girl. Now you can tell me the real reason we turned."

"Angie, there are old pilots and there are bold pilots, but there are no old bold pilots. I don't know why the left engine heated up, so the cowardly thing to do is land and check it out." What I wasn't telling her is that there is no such thing as a single-engine takeoff. If we landed, it was fix the engine or hitchhike home. That might be inconvenient, even expensive, but with Angie's well being in the balance, it didn't matter.

The overcast ahead was tapering off and breaking up. Tendrils ran down into the valley, but I was getting glimpses of the river. I figured we were almost out of the mountains, twenty minutes from Fort Yukon, when the right engine started to heat. I was paying attention that time, and caught it the moment it started up. I opened the cowl flap wide and reduced the power.

"Are we going down?"

"Well, sure, we're at twelve thousand feet above sea level. Fort Yukon is only six hundred. Naturally we have to go down."

"Alex, we're going to hit that cloud."

"No problem, it's soft and fluffy, and I promise, the mountains are behind us." Not entirely true, but nothing below us could reach six thousand feet and we were still at ten thousand when we plowed into the final cloudbank. I slowed us down to a hundred and twenty knots, the best angle of glide, but retained enough power to keep our descent gradual. The oil temperature settled at just over two hundred degrees and seemed to stay there.

"Have you had a good life, Alex?"

"Yeah, no complaints. What brought that up?"

"Well, mine is flashing before my eyes. Not too bad, really. My childhood in Crooked Creek was probably the best available on the planet, you know? So much love, so much happiness. Every adult in the village was raising us, but they all liked us and none were critical. Us kids climbed the mountains and played in the river like a bunch of wild Indians, which I guess we were. You know, I was twelve years old when I shot my first moose, and I was helping haul in king salmon when they were bigger than I was. Daddy was killed, broke through the ice on his snow machine when I was eleven, but then Momma married his brother, Uncle Jack, and he seemed to love us just as much.

"Damn it, why did Stan have to die? We would have made such beautiful children together…but the three years I had with him were better than most people experience in their lifetimes." Angie subsided. I kept my eyes glued to the instruments. I'm not wise enough to comment at times like that.

I wished that cloud would end. We were down to four thousand feet, oil temp at two oh five. I was guessing fifteen minutes to Fort Yukon, but that was only a guess. The radio would tell us if we passed Fort Yukon. I knew we were out of the mountains now, over the Yukon Flats, but it wouldn't hurt to have the radio confirm that. I decided I'd drop down to a thousand feet, but if we passed Fort Yukon still in the cloud, it would be dead reckoning to Circle City, no more radios this side of Fairbanks and no way were we going to climb out of the valley with one engine and it getting hot.

The ADF needle was getting persnickety, and that's a good sign. The closer you get to the station, the more critical it is, and I was guessing less than ten miles. We were down to fifteen hundred feet, still in the cloud, when the temperature gauge started that second-hand sweep, going up like an escalator. I trimmed us down, let the speed build to a hundred fifty knots. That was wasting altitude, but it didn't matter anymore. It was make Fort Yukon or land on whatever happened to be below us when the engine seized. The temperature passed two hundred ten degrees and went right on up.

One thousand feet, windshield the color of fresh laundered sheets, and the ADF needle reversed, we were over Fort Yukon. I circled to the south, and slowed us up. At seven hundred feet above sea level we were one hundred feet above the river, still nothing showing below us.

The Fort Yukon runway starts at the river and runs north with the beacon beside it, so if you head toward the beacon with your compass showing north, you will cross the end of the runway. There's no indication of the distance, so you keep your turns tight, but not too tight. If you pass the beacon again before your heading is established, you've blown it. I locked us onto a thirty-degree bank for a two-minute turn.

The ADF needle slowly swung to the right. When the NDB was straight north, I jerked us around and headed for it. If the altimeter happened to be exactly right we were fifty feet above the river. Then a gleam of water, a flash of trees on an island, more water, and the oil pressure was heading down. I held us steady, let the speed drop to seventy to preserve altitude. The engine was slowing down by itself, too hot to operate.

Seventy is minimum speed for a light twin. Try to stretch a glide by flying slower and you're in for a pancake stall and probably dead. Decision time. If you land short of a runway you want the landing gear up, let the plane slide on its belly, and it will stay right side up. Put the gear down, and especially if you land in water, which was below us, you'll end up on your back.

Too low, too slow, water still going by. I advanced the throttle. Destroying the engine didn't matter anymore. Drop twenty degrees of flaps, extend the glide. Engine speeded us up, seventy-five knots, and faded. Feather the prop and shut it down, a wind-milling prop will act like a brake. Twenty feet above the water. I glanced over at Angie. She'd tightened her harness and was bracing herself against the panel.

A hazy black stripe turned into the riverbank. I hit the landing gear switch. Short brush had been cut to clear the approach. We were left of center. I jerked us right and raised the nose, let the speed go. We were skimming over the ground so a stall wouldn't be lethal. The gear slammed down, three green lights glowed. The main gear was clipping brush. I hauled the yoke all the way back, held us off, and suddenly there was gravel below us.

"Welcome to Fort Yukon. I hope you enjoyed your flight. There is no need to remain seated while we taxi because when we stop rolling, that's as far as we're going to go."

We whiffed past the normal tie-down area, but the loading spot next to the lodge was coming up. I stood on the right brake, turned us into the clearing, and clamped down both binders. We slid to a stop ten feet from the edge of the clearing.

"Want to give me that lecture again about hours of boredom?" Angie leaned back and closed her eyes.

"I thought you knew all about that now. Did you finish your book?" My pulse was dropping toward normal, but why spoil a macho image? "Want to get out and smell the roses?"

"I wouldn't mind putting my feet on the ground. Are you sure this is Fort Yukon? All I saw was a couple of spruce trees."

"Hey, me heap big Gussak honeybee, remember? Right now I can sniff fresh coffee and it's coming from a big log lodge about a hundred feet down that trail between the trees." I reached past Angie to pop the door. She loosened her harness and climbed out onto the wing.

"If that smell is Fort Yukon coffee, I don't think I want any."

I followed her out and closed the door. She was right about the smell, or rather stink of hot oil. It was almost overpowering. I slipped past Angie and climbed down. The underside of both nacelles and the wings behind them were coated in oil, the right side still hot and dripping.

Angie climbed down and shook her head. "Kinda messy, huh?"

"Yeah, the airplane needs a good washing." Oil behind the left engine was no longer dripping. I walked under, reached up through the cowling vent and found the nut was loose above the quick-drain valve. That's a half-inch steel line right from the bottom of the oil pan, and that one-inch nut had not loosened by itself.

I wiped the oil off my fingers on a tuft of dry grass. "Come on, I still smell the coffee and it's great. You just haven't developed your senses properly so you've got your odors mixed."

The trail led between stately spruce, their tops invisible in the cloud. Needles had fallen to carpet the dirt path, and in fifty feet the spruce smelled more powerfully than the oil. The Fort Yukon Lodge made its picturesque two-story silhouette against the murk.

"What happened to the airplane, Alex?"

"Sabotage. Someone reached up through the vents and loosened nuts on a main oil line."

"In Point Barrow?"

"Possible, but I think Fairbanks. If they'd been opened enough to leak, I'd have spotted that before we took off. They just nudged them loose and let the engine vibration finish the job."

"It couldn't have happened during maintenance, or something like that?"

We'd reached the wooden steps and started up toward the porch. "No, it could not. Manny did the hundred-hour inspection thirty hours ago and he does not leave nuts loose. In fact, we have him to thank for us being here instead of down in the mountains hours ago. When Manny services an engine it doesn't vibrate, so it took six hours for the nuts to work loose when one hour would have been normal."

I banged on the big rough wooden front door and shoved it open. "Hey, anybody home? What does a customer have to do to get a cup of coffee here?"

Debby came bustling out of the kitchen, apron over house-dress, arms spread to give me a hug, but she saw Angie and stopped short, cupid's bow mouth wide open. No animosity this time. We were in Indian country, and Debby's smile was about to crack her sweet, motherly face.

"Mary Angela?"

"Debby Parent?" The two women ran together and were hugging each other as if each was the last life preserver on the Titanic. The heck with that. I took a cup off the hook and drizzled a cup of rich dark Yuban out of the thirty-cup urn. The first table had a white cloth and was set for two. The other six tables were bare, so I pulled up a wooden chair at the second table. Debby dragged Angie into the kitchen. They'd forgotten that I was there.

The bare wooden table matched the rest of the room, hewn log walls, open beam ceiling, wooden staircase to the second floor. Everything but the yellow curtains and the throw rugs had been made by Joe. Debby had made it bright and cheerful.

Chapter Twenty-Two

Joe and I sat back with glasses of homemade cranberry cordial.

The table was meant to seat twelve, so the four of us were clustered at the kitchen end. We'd finished off a five-pound moose roast and a big tray of home-grown vegetables, and Joe and I each had two pieces of blueberry pie. Joe is big for an Indian and gives the impression of a collection of circles, round face, round chest, arms like connecting rods on a locomotive. He has Debby's cooking to thank for the roundness, and a lifetime of hard work for the rest of him. A little gray was threatening his thatch, but that, too, might have come from trying to work himself to death. Like many a villager, he's as at home repairing an engine, a furnace, or a generator as he is netting salmon or building log houses.

The two women were still working on their pie, but that was because they hadn't stopped chattering from the moment they met. Joe jerked his head, indicating the front door. We wandered out under the spruce trees and strolled toward the airport. The women didn't notice us leaving. Joe packed his pipe with mixture seventy-nine, struck a wooden match on his pants and lit up. The sweet smell of tobacco blended with the spruce.

"Airplane sabotaged, huh? How bad?"

"No problem at all, just have to borrow a one-inch spanner, tighten two nuts, and refill the crank cases. Might take a gallon of gasoline to clean the oil off the wings."

"Pretty serious business, sabotaging an airplane. Isn't that a federal crime?"

"Yeah, whereas murdering us is only a state crime. Thing is, except for the luck of the Irish, we'd have gone down in the mountains, and if the plane was ever found, it might have passed for an accident."

"So, someone tried to kill you? Sounds a little extreme, even for someone with your bad habits. I always expected it would be a jealous husband that did you in, so what is it this time?"

"Joe, that is the weird part. This is the fourth or fifth attempt and we don't know why or who. Even my Irish luck is starting to wear thin." We were walking in a profound sort of darkness, feeling the trail with our feet. Fog was caught in the trees, trailing down like Spanish moss, and it seemed to have turned from white to black. Joe's pipe glowed like a beacon. We came out of the trees and the plane was a black silhouette, still stinking of hot oil.

"Come on, Alex, brainstorm a little. Don't tell me you have no ideas."

"Okay, I'm getting a glimmer. There's something fishy about the bookkeeping at Interior Air Cargo, but I can't imagine it's worth killing, or trying to kill, three people. This oil thing confirms the airport connection. Whoever did this knew airplanes, knew exactly how to sabotage one. Someone is desperate to keep us from telling something or doing something, and we don't even know what that might be. The whole thing simply makes no sense."

Joe knocked the ashes out of his pipe into his hand to be sure they were cold before he dumped them on the ground.

"Doesn't have to make sense, you know." We started back toward the lodge. "People who kill are insane by definition, so their motives don't have to add up in a normal way. Follow the money, Alex, and remember that's a sliding scale. You and I wouldn't kill for a million bucks, or at least we think we wouldn't. Maybe it's good we don't get tested very often, but on skid row men get killed for fifty cents."

An owl let out a screech right above us and whirred away through the trees. Somewhere in the village a lone husky set up a howl and was joined by an entire chorus of dogs. They joined in one at a time until maybe fifty of them were wailing their mournful ghostly song. The women were sipping coffee but showing no sign of tapering off the chatter. Joe shook his head at the impossibility of transcending the gender gap. "You take the room at the head of the stairs. Angie can have the next one, if she goes to bed at all tonight." Joe turned toward the first floor suite he shared with Debby. He was on the villager's schedule, would be up and working on something when the sun rose, but saw no reason to stay up after the sun set.

I climbed the stairs, solid two-by-tens with a homemade banister. The bathroom was one door to the left with several fresh towels on a shelf. My room had a cot the size of the one at Maranatha, but infinitely more comfortable. The dogs were in the village a quarter mile away, and the howling was filtered through trees and the thick log walls. It's a soothing sound really, an indication that all is normal, and when you get used to it, serves as a lullaby.

It's strange to wake up to total silence. No motors running, no sirens in the distance, no noise from the neighbors because there aren't any. The door to the next room was closed, so Angie had gone to bed sometime. The coffee in the big urn on the sideboard was fresh, and beside the pot Joe had left a one-inch, open-end, Snap-on wrench with a twelve-inch handle. That was Joe, right tool for the job, and the best that money can buy. He had probably been out for several hours working on whatever his current project happened to be.

The coffee knocked the cobwebs out of my brain. Fog had fallen out of the trees and turned to a layer of frost on the porch and the trail, but the sky was still an ugly dark gray. Frost made little crunching sounds underfoot. The plane carried a dusting of white, and no longer stank. Oil had stopped dripping and the coating under the wing felt like black Gummy Bears. I started on the right engine.

The quick-drain valve and the loose nut were four inches above the cowling vents, and I had left those wide open. It was a matter of reaching up through the vent and tightening. The nut turned several turns by hand before I had to put the wrench on it. It came snug, and the final pull on the twelve-inch wrench handle produced the squeak that means metal has bitten into metal and the nut is locked.

The left engine was even easier because I'd shut it down sooner. Five minutes and the plane was repaired, except that the oil pans were empty and everything underneath looked as if it had been paved. The esthetics were no big deal, but that much oil that close to exhaust pipes was a fire danger. Best to start from the top and clean things thoroughly. I climbed up on the right wing, leaned over the nacelle, and popped the Zeus fasteners with my pocketknife to remove the top half of the cowling. The engine looked as if it had been undercoated, or maybe covered with that Rhino stuff they put on pickup beds.

My Casio said eight-thirty, so the village store was likely open. Not that villagers pay much attention to clocks. Probably several households don't even have clocks, but the morning was progressing, and that they would pay attention to. I crunched along the edge of the runway toward the village.

Frost was disappearing, not so much melting as evaporating. Tufts of brown dry grass struggled through the gravel. Majestic spruce lined the runway with the crimson remains of blueberry bushes under them. The first building, across the runway on my right, was the Episcopal church. It may have been designed in, and shipped from, New England; it was surely the only white clapboard building within hundreds of miles. It did look a little out of place with forty-foot spruce hanging over it, but it was an icon. Next time you're in Fort Yukon, check out the bleached white moose-hide altar cloth with the native beadwork. It's a beautiful thing.

Don't go looking for other churches in Fort Yukon. In the 1800s when missionaries from every Christian sect descended on Alaska, they opted for a peaceful approach. They must have met in conference where they divided up the villages, so Bethel is Moravian, St. Mary's Catholic, Kotlik Pentecostal, and so on. Fort Yukon was, and is, Episcopalian.

Another fifty yards of spruce, cabins beginning to appear under them, and the main village spread out along the Yukon. I stopped and marveled at the river, as all travelers have for the last several thousand years. The dark brown water rushing past the village was half a mile wide, but that's less than half the Yukon. It's split into a dozen major channels, many more minor ones, and all together, counting the islands, it's at least ten miles wide at that point.

A well-worn footpath led past the end of the runway. The city dock on the left consisted of creosoted piling driven into the mud and down to permafrost so barges can be tethered against the bank. The village store on my right was sixty feet long, maybe forty feet wide, most of it warehouse. Fort Yukon is the northern terminus for the Yutana Barge Line, the hub for thousands of square miles where trappers, homesteaders, and prospectors can get supplies. The last boat of the season was long gone. The diesel-powered, steel tunnel boat, the *MV Yukon*, would have shoved her barges down the Yukon and up the Tanana to Nenana where the railroad meets the river. Like the rest of the outpost's inhabitants, I was counting on the store's having what I needed.

Three wooden steps where several old-timers of both sexes were seated led up to the loading porch and ran the length of the building. The oldsters were watching the river and socializing. They gave me pleasant nods but didn't speak, probably because they had very little English.

Bare wooden floor, low ceiling with light bulbs hanging down from cords, all wonderfully rustic. Head-high racks of everything imaginable were squeezed into the space. The first case inside the door contained jewelry, and I had to stop and look. Fort Yukon is famous for beadwork, and I was seeing the reason. Brooches, pendants, medallions, earrings, miniature woven grass baskets, all exquisite, colorful, beautiful. One pair of earrings caught my eye, tiny fur mukluks, an inch tall, with a minuscule ruff and intricate beadwork.

I was thinking how good they'd look next to Angie's smooth cheeks and almost reached for them before I noticed they were for pierced ears. Were Angie's ears pierced? I couldn't remember. She wore earrings to work, but were they snap-on? Women always complain that men never notice things, and they are so right. I turned back toward the household section.

I gathered up six quarts of Dawn liquid dishwashing detergent and headed toward the hardware. Two full racks were packed with all sorts of liquids and additives, but of course, no aviation oil. Several cases of outboard oil were stacked next to equal piles of snow machine oil. One stack of outboard oil was forty-weight non-detergent. That's the equivalent of uncompounded aviation oil. Maybe there's a difference, maybe not. The oil was $2.50 per quart, or a case of twenty-four quarts for fifty bucks. I took the case, paid cash at the register, and lugged my treasures back to the airplane.

It took thirty minutes to coat both engines and the wings with as much detergent as I could get to stay. The soap that dripped off was black, but the engines didn't change much. I tromped back to the lodge, grabbed another cup of coffee when I passed the sideboard, and carried it to the kitchen.

Debby's kitchen is an experience. The entire south wall is windows for maximum sunlight above a countertop. Washer, dryer, and dishwasher are tucked under the counter, three stainless steel sinks and cutting boards and such on top. The southwest corner is taken up by a two-hundred-gallon hot-water tank heated by the cook stove. The stove is black iron, four feet wide, eight feet long, with two ovens, and roaring with a fan-fed oil fire.

Debby was kneading a massive mound of bread dough at the six-foot-square island of counter in the center of the room. She wore an apron over a housedress, and had her bonnet of black silk tucked under a knitted cap.

"Mornin', Alex. Sleep well?"

"I feel like I've been reborn. That was the best dinner and the most comfortable bed I've had in years. Did you and Angie stay up all night?"

"Most of it, lot to talk about." She paused to sprinkle flour on the counter and attacked the dough again.

"Yeah, I noticed that. You seemed to be enjoying yourselves."

"Alex, it was like a trip in a time machine. Angie's six years younger, so she was like a little sister to me, but we were together every day from the day she was born until she was fifteen. That was the year that Joe came down the Kuskokwim on a raft of logs, heading for Bethel. He stopped in Crooked Creek for a meal, and when he left he just picked me up and took me with him. You can imagine that I wasn't struggling much."

"Makes perfect sense. Lot of bread dough."

"Yep, six hunters from Germany will be on the mail plane tomorrow. Joe will take them upriver for moose, probably take three or four days to get a trophy for every one of them."

"Wow, an international connection?"

"Yep, Germany, Japan, sometimes Russians, lots of Americans from the east coast. It's good for the village because all the hunters want is the horns, so the meat gets distributed around, and I'm ashamed to tell you what we charge them." She stopped kneading dough, turned to face me, and looked right into my soul.

"Alex, are you going to marry Angie?"

I didn't stop to think. I blurted out my gut reaction. "Debby, I couldn't. I love her dearly, she's the most remarkable woman I've ever met, but she was the wife of my best friend. It would be like incest. She's my sister."

Debby searched my eyes for a long time before she nodded and turned back to her bread. "Yes, I suppose that makes sense to you. In the village that would be the reason you should marry her. When Angie's father was killed, her mother married his brother, Jack, and when Jack was killed, she married the next brother, Willie. That was correct and proper, but I guess it was another time and another culture. You need some breakfast?"

"No, at the moment, I need a couple of buckets of hot water."

"Help yourself, buckets under the sink, tap water's almost boiling. Scrub brush beside the buckets." She attacked that mound of dough, and I wondered if she was vicariously pummeling me.

It took six trips for more water, but it was working. No problem pouring water on an aircraft engine because the fuel is injected, so there's no carburetor, and the ignition is from magnetos. Those and the sparkplugs are sealed and shielded so tight they don't even leak radio interference.

Each engine holds eight quarts of oil. The right engine took seven quarts, the left six. I started them up and let them idle. Oil pressure leaped up to normal and the right engine sounded fine, so I probably hadn't hurt it. I shut the engines down and added one more quart each to compensate for the oil that was pumped into the coolers and the propeller controls.

When I lugged the empty buckets, brush, and the extra oil into the lodge, Angie was in the kitchen. She and Debby seemed to be discussing something very seriously, the festive mood gone. Angie handed me a plate with two fried duck eggs, a hunk of reindeer sausage, and two biscuits. I carried it out to the table. I didn't think they needed me at the moment. Angie's ears are pierced, by the way. Now if I can just remember that.

Chapter Twenty-Three

Our leave taking was solemn, not sad. That is the bush way. The women hadn't seen each other for ten years, and might not again for ten more, although I suspected I'd find excuses to drop Angie off at Fort Yukon now and then. No need to wait for or say goodbye to Joe. We wander in, we wander out. If we were back in a year or five it would be as though we'd never left.

Angie and Debby hugged long and hard, and Debby gave me a hug, but a little more tentative than usual. I don't think she'd quite forgiven me for being of the wrong culture. She didn't escort us out. She simply turned back to her baking.

We paused on the porch while Angie inhaled the fragrance of spruce. She was looking up at the trees and nodding. "Funny, Fort Yukon is just like Crooked Creek, but we're above the Arctic Circle, aren't we?"

"Yep, that we are. It's the rivers that do it. They thaw the permafrost and you get real trees, only that doesn't work for Bethel because the Bering Sea is too close and too cold."

We came out of the trees next to the plane and Angie sniffed. "Smells like my kitchen sink."

"Thought you might be getting homesick. Want to play tourist?"

"Sure. Now that I've crossed the Arctic Circle, all I have to do is sleep with a bear and wrestle an Eskimo to become a sourdough...or is it the other way round?"

"I think that part is optional. There is a certain biological connection you're supposed to make with the Yukon, but maybe we can skip that one. Come on, something to show you."

We turned toward the river and angled across the runway. The church gleamed white through the trees. Angie grabbed my hand and pulled me after her. The path from the airport was worn inches deep from a hundred years of the feet of the faithful, and was carpeted by spruce needles. The trees arching over us were already inducing the feeling of a cathedral.

"Alex, give me your handkerchief."

"Huh?"

"Give me your handkerchief. I want to cover my head."

"Angie, this church is Episcopal, not Catholic. Anglican, you know? Bishops, no Pope."

"Shut up, Alex. God is inside and I need to talk to him. You go peddle your papers." She took my handkerchief, draped it over her head and marched up the stairs. I felt I had been dismissed, so I sat down on the steps to wait.

A miniature altercation was in progress under one spruce tree. Two chipmunks seemed to be fighting over one cone, although there were a dozen under the same tree. I was just thinking how human that reaction was when the cone turned sideways. One 'munk was holding the cone and rolling it, the other busily digging inside and removing tiny white kernels. They made a pile, then gobbled them up, pouching out their tiny cheeks, and scampered back into the trees making a blurred series of McDonald's arches.

They were back in a minute, and had attacked another cone, when a whir through the trees announced the arrival of an owl. That's one good thing about owls, if you're a chipmunk, bad if you're an owl. They're so heavy and short-winged that they don't fly silently, at least not when they're navigating through trees. The 'munks disappeared. They didn't run away, they just vanished, like a conjurer's trick. Now you see them, now you don't. The owl perched on a large branch thirty feet up and sat there blinking yellow eyes. He looked too fat to be hungry.

When Angie came out twenty minutes later, her countenance did seem to be radiant. I think that's the biblical terminology. She handed back my handkerchief and we turned toward the runway. "Thanks, Alex. That was really special. Have you seen that altar cloth? It's unbelievable."

"Yep, I've seen it. That's what I wanted to show you. Did you...uh...find anything else inside?"

"You bet I did. I lit a candle for Stan and God told me Stan is fine but just a bit worried about me. God says that as long as I'm okay, Stan will be happy to wait for me. Stan knows you're taking care of me and he appreciates that. He also says not to blame yourself about the bomb because you couldn't have suspected it was there. "

We turned toward the village and walked in silence. Angie wasn't quite on this planet at the moment, and I certainly had no comments.

At the store, Angie stopped on the steps to speak to several of the old-timers and elicited a lot of grins, many of them toothless. I pulled her up the steps and over to the jewelry counter.

"Oh, Alex, look at those mukluk earrings, they're darling."

"Yep, and they were made for you. Kitty wanted them to nestle against your cheeks."

"Kitty?"

"Kitty Carter."

"Another old girlfriend?"

"Nope, but she did go to high school in Fairbanks and she stood out in the crowd. She was doing beadwork even then, and everyone knew she'd be famous someday. When you put on these earrings, her day will have come." I took the little fur booties out of the case and carried them over to the checkout counter.

Angie had slipped them from the card and put them on so I was buying the small square of paperboard. The clerk was smiling. I looked at Angie, and we were all smiling. I turned back to the clerk. "When you see Kitty, would you tell her thank you from Alex Price?"

The clerk nodded and reached for the box of frozen strawberries the next customer was proffering. Angie and I turned back and walked along the side of the airport to the plane.

"Alex, are you a romantic, by any chance? That was a nice gesture for a hard-bitten, scruffy old bush pilot."

I didn't have an answer for that, so I pointed her up the steps. "Jump in, it's off we go, into the wild blue yonder...."

"Are you colorblind? That sky is charcoal gray."

"Give me twenty minutes." I did take a little extra time running up the engines and exercising the props, but all systems were go. We blasted off and climbed like preachers during the rapture.

The cloud was only a thousand feet thick and as soon as we topped it, the Crazy Mountains were ahead of us, cloud packed against their northern edge, new snow gleaming in sunshine. I have no idea why those mountains are named Crazy, but someone was serious about it, even naming the East Crazy Mountains and the West Crazy Mountains. There is a plateau between them and the White Mountains, so maybe they deserve their own name. We were fifty miles east of our previous crossing, but the mountains were just as rugged. With two happy engines humming, the mountains were spectacular, not threatening.

Angie was fascinated again, and this time, by staying at six thousand feet, we had the whole panorama of mountains around the Tanana Basin. We left the cloud behind, the Crazies glistened in sunshine, snow fields almost too bright to look at, castellated by basalt or granite spires worthy of Sydney Lawrence. Snow-covered mountains ringed the entire horizon.

Angie's neck was in serious danger from swiveling. "It's so beautiful and so big. Can you imagine prospectors covering these mountains before they had airplanes and helicopters?"

"No, I can't imagine it, but they did. There isn't one creek down there that someone didn't walk to and prospect. Remains of cabins are scattered all through those valleys."

"Did they find gold, Alex?"

"About one in a hundred, maybe fewer. They hunted and trapped and lived off the land, but no. For every dollar that was invested in Alaskan prospecting, about eighty cents worth of gold came out. That doesn't count the years of labor, sometimes whole lifetimes spent with nothing to show for it."

"But you hear stories...."

"Yep, and most of the stories are true. A few people got fabulously wealthy, and those are the stories you hear. It's exactly like Las Vegas. When someone wins a million dollars, the casinos are delighted and very happy to pay. Newspapers and local TV stations pick up the account, twenty million people read the stories, troop to Vegas, and lose their shirts.

"The people who really made money off the gold rush were in the support business, transportation and such. Have you heard of Cap Lathrop?"

"You mean like the Lathrop Building and Lathrop Theaters?"

"Yep, almost every theater in Alaska at the time, the Midnight Sun Broadcasting Network, Fairbanks Air Service, Usibelli and Suntrana coal mines, whatever, if it made money, Cap owned it."

"And he got his start gold mining?"

"No, he got his start with fifteen one-room log cabins lined up along what is now Eighth Avenue, with a Jody in every one of them."

"Stan spent a few years prospecting. Was that foolish?"

"Not at all. You know Stan spent two summers digging up the creeks between Flat and Crooked? Last year someone dug ten miles upstream from the last spot Stan tried and found what may be the richest deposit ever discovered. It's a crapshoot, Angie. The gold is there, and so are the million-dollar jackpots in Las Vegas. You get lucky or you don't, and there's nothing you can do about it."

"Did I do a bad thing when I talked Stan out of prospecting?"

"No. He missed the big bonanza by ten miles. In another season he might have missed it by one mile. No, Angie, you were the best thing that ever happened to Stan. He wouldn't have traded you for truckloads of gold. See that rise on the left with the highway running across it?"

"Where? Oh, yeah."

"That's the Steese Highway crossing Eagle Summit. It's below the Arctic Circle, but because it's high, you can see the midnight sun from there."

"How far are we from Fairbanks?"

"Maybe eighty miles, but it's a beautiful drive. What everyone does is set a camera on a tripod and starting around eleven at night in late June, snap a picture every fifteen minutes. You know, like a double exposure but eight or ten of them. They show the sun dipping right down toward the horizon and going back up again."

"That's neat. So there was no chance of Stan getting rich?"

"Sure, there was always a chance. We both knew it was a long shot. We never kidded ourselves, but if you don't buy a lottery ticket, then you will not win the lottery. If you do buy one, you won't win it anyway, but you tried. Oh, my gosh, Angie, look at that plateau."

"It's moving, what's wrong? It looks like it's covered with ants."

"Not ants, hang on." I chopped the power, did a wing over, and dived down to skim the plateau. Fifty thousand caribou made a river of horns, a hundred yards wide and no ends in sight, all trotting southeast toward their winter home in Canada. Angie's mouth had dropped open and maybe, for a change, she was struck speechless. We swung back toward Fairbanks and climbed over the next ridge. Valleys ahead of us dropped away toward Fairbanks.

"Is that the Tanana Valley?"

"Yep. Fairbanks in twenty minutes."

"Wow, eighty miles?"

"Not any more, that was five minutes ago. We're descending under full power."

"Never mind getting technical. Aren't you supposed to radio in or something?"

"Not this time. Angie, someone in Fairbanks thinks we're dead. Let's keep it that way, and maybe they'll stop trying to kill us. We can't land at International without reporting the control zone on the radio, but Phillips Field is almost outside the control zone. We can get away with landing there with no radio, so let's do it."

"Phillips Field?"

"Yep, general aviation. Hawley Evans' Fairbanks Air service, Horace Black's flight school, Jess Goldstein's repair facility, and about a hundred private planes tied down for half the price at International."

"Then why do some people use International?"

"Lighted runways, instrument approach, radio control, all depends on what's important to you."

We passed the gold dredge at Fox, skimmed over the final hill low enough to be in the radar clutter. I backed off the power, slowed us down. We whiffed by the KFAR Radio tower on Farmer's Loop Road, swung over the college, and I lowered the flaps to twenty degrees.

"So, where's this airport?"

"Right there, beside College Road."

"Alex, that's not an airport, it's a cow pasture."

"Maybe you should read your book for a minute." Landing gear came down with a satisfying clunk. At high RPM, the engines were straining but slowing us down. Fifty-foot spruce trees passed under us. Slam the flaps down full, chop the power, sideslip down to the end of the runway and lock up the brakes. Nothing to it. We taxied up to Jess Goldstein's hangar.

The hangar's sixty feet long with one big door that hinges out in the middle when it's raised, so the effect is like the bill on a baseball cap, and serves about the same purpose. Four airplanes inside were works in progress: a Piper Cub with no fabric on the fuselage, a twin Beech missing one engine, a Cessna 180 in the process of receiving a new wing, and a Taylor Craft that probably needed everything.

Jess was at a portable workbench, rebuilding the engine from the Beech, but he wiped his hands on a rag and came out to meet us. He wears overalls and plaid shirts, so you'd take him for a farmer instead of the very fine mechanic that he is.

"Hi, Alex, what's up?"

"Jess, need to flush the engines and change the oil. It might be contaminated."

"Sure, but might be a couple of days. I've got to get that Beech out. Want to just buy the oil and do the job yourself?"

"Nah, a couple of days is fine, if you'll rent us a beater."

"Only thing I've got at the moment is an old Dodge Power Wagon. She ain't pretty, but she'll take you around town. Say thirty bucks a day?"

"Sold. Where shall I park the bird?"

"Leave it. Call me in a couple of days." He sauntered over to the wall, reached up to pluck a key ring from among several hanging from nails on a sheet of plywood. He tossed me the keys and turned back to his engine repair.

Angie had been standing on the wing, not sure which way we were going, but climbed down and followed me around the hangar. The Power Wagon was parked beside the gravel road behind the hangar, and Jess was right. It wasn't pretty. The khaki color was reminiscent of army surplus, and the body wasn't quite straight with the wheels, so it had probably been rolled over, but the doors worked. We climbed in gingerly and sat on the old army blanket that almost covered the broken springs in the seat, but the engine caught instantly and purred.

Angie was wriggling her tail between springs to get comfortable. "Shall we head for the airport and pick up the Buick?"

"No, this is transportation for a few days, and it's perfect. Remember, the Buick is parked in the tie-down slot where we got the 310. Someone knows we took the 310 out, and they may or may not know where we went, but they aren't expecting us to come back. We'll leave the Buick right where it is, sort of a decoy. Meantime, this rig looks as if it could belong to any dirt farmer around Fairbanks, and notice we didn't sign anything. What say we check on Turk?"

Chapter Twenty-Four

For breakfast Angie served grits, ham, and biscuits and gravy. I was surprised and delighted. "Hey, there's a southern belle lurking inside that stoic Indian exterior."

"Little antidote to coming winter. Smell the magnolia blossoms?"

"Love 'em. Notice the cotton has been blowing outside?" I do love a bowl of grits with a generous mound of butter melting on top and a liberal sprinkling of salt and pepper. Can't explain that because I don't have any southern roots, only the occasional visit to the sunny south. Some things are just universally good.

Angie was alternating between grits and gravy. "Remember the Robert Service poem, *The Cremation of Sam McGee*? He was from Tennessee where the cotton blooms and blows."

"Yeah, I think about him sometimes. *Why he left his home in the south to roam 'round the pole, God only knows.* Have you ever been south?"

"Only in dreams. Maybe someday. How about you?"

"A few times, Mardi Gras and such. When you said you and Stan were whiffing down Hurricanes at the Maranatha, I thought maybe it was a New Orleans thing."

"It was. Stan was planning to take me outside this winter."

"Angie, we could do that this winter. I could get away in February. Charter business stops and all we do is try to keep the planes from blowing away."

"Maybe, let's talk about that later. How long do we have to play dead? Can I go to work?"

"Yeah, that might be safe. I need to call Jim Stella, so he'll know we're alive. We only have to be dead at the airport...I think."

"Oh, I love those positive statements of yours. Want to be a sweetheart and rinse the dishes while I dress for work?"

I dropped Angie at the back door of the Lathrop Building. Being dead might take the heat off us, but I couldn't help scanning traffic for snipers.

I drove the Power Wagon to the airport, parked between hangars and just watched Interior. Both the Skyvan and the Otter were tied down, engines covered, as if in winter hibernation. The sky was dark, but not the black of a blizzard, just punctuated with occasional snowflakes. Celeste's Miata was in the lot with a dusting of snow on it. Reginald came, Marino came, Reginald and Marino left in Marino's car, they came back. It was every bit as exciting as watching paint dry or grass grow.

That detective course I took warned about time spent on stakeout being the longest hours you'll ever live. It also suggested that you keep an empty gallon jug in the car so your bladder doesn't burst. I'd forgotten that nicety, so when I was threatened I drove up to the passenger terminal, solved the problem, and had a cup of coffee in the shop to restart the cycle. Same waitress, different blouse, still unbuttoned. I tipped her a dollar and drove back to my blind between hangars.

Airplanes were still tied down, cars in the lot, little more snow on them, I hadn't missed a thing. The Buick still sat in the tie-down spot where the 310 was missing and I wondered how long it would be before Avis would have found it, if we really had been killed. Undisturbed snow on the Buick had a macabre connotation. Whoever had loosened the nuts on our oil lines must see the Buick every day. I wondered if they viewed it with satisfaction or a twinge of conscience.

Angie came out the back door of the Lathrop Building at six forty-five. I had the Power Wagon parked next to the dumpster, where it looked right at home.

I shoved the door open for her. "Hi, did you have a good day in the salt mine?"

"Tolerable. Did you solve any crimes or shoot any assassins?"

"Very few. I really didn't do anything to deserve the hunger pangs that are killing me. Want to hit a restaurant and fix that?"

"Chicken-fried steaks tonight, the beef is already thawed. Pop on the siren and the flashers and get me home. I'm wearing a new bra and it's killing me."

I checked traffic and pulled out. "Hang on tight, we're on our way. All this concern about killers, but me dying of hunger and you dying of a bra...unworthy anticlimax."

The city streets were tracked up, ugly brown slush, but the Steese had just a few tracks, and after the Rendezvous, we were making the first marks in virgin snow. I tried to stay cynical, but it was sort of magical so long as the heater kept pumping and we stayed on the road.

With no tracks in the new snow, we didn't have to worry about an ambush. Angie was out of the car and running toward her bedroom before the engine died. I tromped around back, fired the generator, and took Turk's pans in for refills. The furnace had kicked on automatically when the generator started. Angie was in the kitchen wearing jeans and a smock. It wasn't really obvious that she wasn't wearing a bra. She filled Turk's food bowl, I filled the water, and delivered the pans back to the doghouse.

When I got back inside, she tossed me a paring knife and pointed toward two potatoes. I peeled them, then dug ice out of the freezer and mixed two rum and Cokes.

"Angie, remember that one of the ways I wasted time a couple of days ago was setting up an alarm system. If a school bell suddenly rings in the spare bedroom, don't jump out of your skin. It just means a moose has crossed the road."

"I thought we were safe now that we're presumed dead."

"Probably, but you know the macho drill, layer upon layer of safeguards." I handed her one of the frosty glasses. "You know the shotgun is still in the Buick at the airport, but the .30-06 is in the closet. Naturally, you're a world-class expert?"

"With the .30-06 I can shoot the mustache off a gnat at fifty yards and leave him smiling. Go worry somewhere else. I'm busy here."

Angie took a sip and set her drink on the drainboard where she was busily pulverizing a couple of flank steaks. I carried my glass to the living room and watched a new snow flurry cover the Power Wagon.

I was doing some serious internal examining. The comfort of coming home with Angie and the quiet domesticity were very different from my usual evenings alone in the cabin in Bethel. At home I'd be drinking the same drink, maybe pounding a steak myself, but compared to knowing Angie was in the kitchen, my life seemed pretty bare. Connie invited me to dinner now and then. She's a terrific cook, sets a classy table, and dresses as if we'd gone out for the evening, but I always had the feeling of being a guest.

Connie was just too good for me. Her forty-foot trailer in Bethel was immaculate, everything polished and shining. Angie's house was clean, but I wasn't afraid to step on the carpet. Connie had ceramic knickknacks and curios, so I was a little afraid I might break something. Angie's house had two pictures on the mantle, her extended family, which was every soul in Crooked Creek, and her wedding to Stan, also in Crooked Creek with her mother and her uncle/father Willie. I remembered Connie's bed, and yeah, I do know about that. White satin sheets, down pillows, down comforter, clean, clean, clean, and classy. The bed's an experience, even if Connie weren't in it and an experience in herself. At times like that, Connie is the answer to all my dreams, and I think we'd be contented together forever. Maybe we would be, if we could spend our whole lives in bed. I'm only too happy to spend a night with her when the details work out, but I don't think I've ever relaxed there. Even in the bed, I had the feeling of being a guest, a welcome one, but I couldn't feel proprietary.

I finished my drink, wandered back to the kitchen. Angie's was down to half, so I replenished both, then on an impulse, I caught her from behind and gave her a hug. Her hands were covered with flour, she was anything but dressed for going out, and she struck me as the prettiest sight I'd ever seen.

She leaned into my embrace for a moment, then pointed toward the cupboard. "Why don't you set the table? You've obviously got too much time on your hands, and I have flour on mine."

I set the table with plates, knives, and forks, but resisted the impulse to set out a candle. Linen napkins were in the drawer below the silverware, wineglasses in the cupboard, a bottle of cabernet sauvignon on the sideboard. I pulled the cork and let it breathe. Steaks were simmering in a covered frying pan. Angie stuck a fork in the potatoes and replaced the lid on them. I carried the wine out to the table. Clearly, my life was being wasted by staying single, and the profound sense of what Angie had lost was really sinking in.

I wondered if I should grab Connie by the shoulders, shake her, and insist on getting married. Maybe the two of us could make dinner together and I could hug her when she had flour on her hands. Still, her memories of marriage were not quite the idyllic picture I was conjuring up, and could we compromise to the point that I could wear muddy boots into the house?

"Alex, grab the gravy boat and the potatoes." Angie was carrying the platter of steaks in both hands and I noticed she was wearing hot mitts. I scrambled for the two bowls on the kitchen counter. Angie removed the mitts and we sat down. I reached across the table to pour the wine.

I don't know which was better, the dinner or the quiet camaraderie. It wasn't a time for banter; we were both shoveling in food, but there was a lot of smiling going on.

A sudden clanging from the bedroom had me jumping up and reaching for the pistol. Angie took another sip of wine. "I thought you said I shouldn't jump out of my shorts if the bell rang."

Car lights whiffed past the end of the drive and the bell rang again. I shoved the pistol back in my belt and sat down.

"Why did the bell ring twice?" Angie wasn't ruffled, just curious.

"It rang once when he was coming, and again when he was leaving. If he stops and comes back, it'll ring again. You could humor me by showing some concern. Diving for the rifle would be good."

"Okay, got it. Two rings you panic, one ring we both panic."

"Panic may not be the right word. *Assume a protective stance* sounds better."

"Sure thing, we've got to protect that fragile male ego."

We stuffed ourselves and took the last sip of wine. Angie carried dishes to the kitchen and came back with coffees.

"Angie, that was fantastic."

"Naturally. I told you, I'm a world-class chef. Why don't you look relaxed and happy?"

"Oh, happy I am. Relaxed is a little tougher. I need to get into the freight office one more time, just to verify what we already know. You've been accusing me of not making positive statements, and I'd like to change that."

"So, you want to sneak back into the office and have another look? Do I get to sit on my cushion again?"

"Seems indicated. This time I won't turn on the computer, so if we get invaded, I'll beat you to the freight shed."

"Good enough. Tonight, instead of the generous tips you always leave, you can help wash the dishes."

More domesticity. She washed, but I dried and put things away. I was enjoying it until I noticed that Angie was crying. I put down the dish towel and pulled her into a hug. She rested her head on my shoulder and sobbed.

"Oh, Alex, I miss him so terribly. Will I ever get over it?"

"No, sweetheart, our lives will never be the same again, but we will learn to live with it. There aren't any more men like Stan, and we were both lucky to have had him for a while."

"Damn, we were talking about having babies and I wish we had. If I had his son or daughter, it would be better, you know?"

"Angie, nothing in this world lasts except memories, and you have those." I squeezed her until her ribs bent, and it seemed to help. She finally stepped away, picked up the dish towel and dried her eyes.

"Okay, I'm all better now, you may lead the innocent lamb to the slaughter."

We drove slowly past the office, no cars, no lights. I parked the Power Wagon in an empty tie-down spot and we hiked back. Angie had loaned me one of Stan's coats; the jacket season had definitely passed. I noticed that my oxfords were out of season, too. Angie was sleek and warm in her Cat Woman suit with the leather jacket, faux fur collar nestled around her incredibly smooth cheeks.

I looked both ways, no security truck. The office door creaked a little, we stepped inside and snapped on flashlights. Angie assumed her stance, I ducked under the counter and parked at Celeste's desk. The folder for today's flights was missing. Otherwise they were up-to-date. I checked the brunette's desk and the current folder was there, so she must have been doing something with it.

I did slip into Reginald's office and tapped the spacebar on his computer. The screen came to life. I called up Orbitz, clicked on *My Stuff.* No more first-class tickets, so if there were more assassins around, they were locals. Maybe our already-dead act was working. I closed the file and left the computer to go to sleep.

I went back to Celeste's desk, spread the first folder out and started through the flight tickets. The first ticket was the Howard, two hours, Barrow, Prudhoe and return. No mistakes. Yesterday's date, Alvin Hopson pilot, aircraft tail number Zero One Victor. Charge, four hundred fifty bucks. The second ticket was the Otter, three hours to Stevens Village with a five o'clock return. Funny I hadn't noticed it was gone. Then another Otter flight, four hours to Copper Center at ten in the morning, and I had been sitting out front watching the Otter at that time. I got the picture and started adding hours.

By the time I'd worked through folders for the last ten days, I'd passed seventy hours that I was sure hadn't been flown, and another ticket was signed by Tommy. Then I found one signed by me that I hadn't flown. Finally the low hours on the Hobbs meters made sense, and at eight hundred dollars per hour, the Otter had earned over twenty thousand dollars for the month, and as far as I had seen, most of it without ever being untied.

"Jiggers, security pickup." Angie hit the deck. I snapped off my flashlight.

"Hey, Angie, did I remember to lock the door?"

"Hell of a time to think of it." She crawled over and reached up. I heard the lock snap and ten seconds later a guard's light flashed through the office and the door rattled. I kept my head on the desk until we heard the pickup drive away.

"Damn it, Alex, are you trying to give me a heart attack?"

"Nah, a little adrenaline is good for you. That's what keeps you so young."

"Are you doing any good, or is all of this just for my beauty treatment?"

"Angie, we did it. I found the smoking gun and it's money, lots of it. Just one airplane must have earned two hundred thousand this year, and if that's a pattern, there must be millions."

"I thought airplanes were supposed to earn money."

"Yeah, but in little dribs and drabs. Someone is willing to kill for that much money. Has to be a conspiracy: Freddy doing paperwork, Celeste doing billing, surely Dave Marino as mastermind. Marino must have been around a lot longer than Celeste said, and now we know what Dave is blackmailing Reginald for, control of the company and silence while he steals a few million bucks. We just have to figure out how to prove it."

"Can we do that in the car? I've had enough adrenaline for one night."

"Is the pickup gone?"

"No, he's over at a hangar past the airplanes."

"Maybe we should wait. Cops need coffee and doughnuts every fifteen minutes." I replaced the files and closed the drawer. Celeste's desk did smell good to me but I didn't want to start an argument I'd be sure to lose. I joined Angie at the window. The pickup worked down the line of hangars and roared away toward the coffee shop. We ducked out and ran.

The Power Wagon's heater squeaked and belched dust, but it felt wonderful. We unzipped jackets and cracked windows. Turk didn't meet us until we pulled into the drive, and then he came around the house wagging his tail. I forgave him for my ordeal stalking porcupines in the woods.

Angie turned on a couple of small lamps, popped a tape of Vivaldi's *Four Seasons* into the deck, and disappeared into the kitchen. She was back in a minute, handed me a rum and Coke, ice cubes floating, and settled down on the couch with one of her own. I parked at the other end of the couch and sipped. It was Captain Morgan.

"Alex, this is pure masochism. I'm going to sit here and cry while you figure out what the money is about. I know you're going back to Bethel eventually, so I want to get times like this out of my system while I can still get a hug if I need one. Does that make sense?"

"Perfectly. I know I've been harping on your beauty, but did I ever tell you you're one smart cookie?"

"It never occurred to me you realized girls had brains. Don't talk, flow with the music."

Angie did cry at times, but she also smiled occasionally. When the tape ended she took our glasses into the kitchen, came back with refills and inserted Tchaikovsky's *Andante Cantabile* into the player. It featured Itzhak Perlman on the violin, and I almost felt like crying, too.

The tape ended. Angie stood and gathered the empty glasses. "Thanks, Alex, that was what I needed. You know where the guest room is?"

"Yep, but I think I'll spend the night on the couch. It's comfortable and I want to be able to see the driveway. I know,

Turk is on guard, the bell will chime, but still it's a sop to my macho ego."

"One more hug, Alex."

I hugged her, long and close. She brushed my cheek with her lips and slipped away into her bedroom. I set the pistol on the stand beside the couch and was still wondering where the money was going when Morpheus slipped in.

I dreamed Celeste was laughing and dancing, pulling hands full of money from her bodice and tossing it up like confetti. Her partner was twirling and twirling her, her skirt flying, and her partner was Dave Marino. He was laughing and leering and he started tossing money. That woke me up.

The house was silent, the Power Wagon the only thing in the drive, with just enough light from the sky to show its outline. I turned over and went back to sleep.

Chapter Twenty-Five

I'd promised to call Celeste with a report, but now I was playing dead, and her sparkling eyes and dimples had taken on a very different connotation. No way could she be innocent and sit there day after day, tallying up Otter hours while the Otter was parked outside her window. That shed new light on everything, and I wondered about her visiting-mother story.

I dropped Angie half an hour early and drove down Wendell Street. Celeste's Miata was parked in front of her house, and a black Cadillac was parked around the next corner. I cursed my incompetence for failing to get Marino's license number. I parked on the next side street with a view of the house. Celeste came fluttering out, lacy white blouse with ribbons, straight dark skirt well above her knees. She wasn't tossing money, but she did look happy to be going to work, and that's suspicious.

I figured that if the Cadillac was Marino's, they wouldn't leave together. He seemed to set his own schedules, so I watched the Cadillac for an hour before a little old man in a business suit came out of another house and drove the Cadillac away. It was not only cold, it was overcast and threatening. I'd been running the engine and the heater in ten-minute bursts, but windows were frosting over. I crossed the bridge and found a pay phone at Piggly Wiggly. Celeste's phone rang eight times before it was picked up. "Hello?" It was the voice of a broken violin, definitely feminine and at least a hundred years old.

"Sorry, wrong number." I hung up the phone, but I did want to know where Marino was staying. Apparently it wasn't too hard to find us when we were registered under an unknown name, so with the right name, that trick should work in reverse.

The store had a customer service counter in back. A sweet little lady who looked, but didn't sound, like Celeste's mother traded me a roll of quarters for a ten-dollar bill. I sat down with the phone book and tied up the instrument for an hour calling every hotel in the greater Fairbanks area, even the Maranatha. I wondered about the description of *greater area*, but it may apply someday.

"Hello, I need to speak to Dave Marino, please."

"I'm sorry, sir, we have no Marino registered."

After eighteen tries, I had that speech memorized and there were no more hotels in the yellow pages. I still had a pile of quarters, so I dialed state police headquarters and asked for Lieutenant Stella.

"Good morning, Alex. What's the problem? You have a raccoon treed?"

"Hey, sorry about that. What can I tell you?"

"No, you did the right thing. We can't *all* be smart. How may I waste the state's time and resources on you today?"

"Did you have any luck tracing David Marino?"

"Oh, yeah, lots. None in Alaska, but nationwide there are nineteen thousand of them. Would you like the David A's, David B's...I even have a David Z here, so take your pick."

"How about the Detroit area?"

"Yep, two hundred and nineteen and no David Z, so that narrows it right down."

"Thanks a lot. I don't know what I'd do without your cooperation." The phone beeped for another quarter, but I decided Stella wasn't worth it.

I stomped next door to the bowling alley and plunked down at the counter. I'd already wasted most of the morning, might as well finish the job. The fry cook was also manning the counter. Most of his gray hair was under his cap, and his apron was probably clean yesterday. He was smoking a cigarette while he cooked, but was careful with the ashes. I ordered a cheeseburger and coffee.

Angie had produced Wheat Chex and milk for breakfast, and toast topped with her homemade blueberry jam, so we ate like royalty, but it was wearing off. A few people were bowling and the crashing pins suited my state of mind.

The thing that was bothering me was Celeste's statement that Marino had shown up three weeks before, but the over-billing scam had been going on for months. The Otter would have passed its Hobbs meters six months ago if the hours that were billed had actually been flown. But, if Celeste was a thief, and she obviously was, then why trust anything she said?

Did Marino really wipe his glass clean, or did Celeste do that to cover for a partner? Was Celeste plotting to have me killed while we were dancing? Even more pertinent, would she succeed? That thought was hard to take. So was the coffee, but the cheeseburger was fine and the fries no more soggy than noodles. I mixed Tabasco with the catsup for the fries. That helped.

When I stepped outside, I was slapped in the face with blowing dust, and by the time I got to the car it was mixed with tiny snowflakes. I took a drive out to the airport. The Otter and Skyvan were both tethered at Interior. Reginald and Celeste were parked in the lot, Marino was not. For the heck of it, I drove through the lot at the passenger terminal, but no black Cadillacs jumped out at me. I got to thinking that Fairbanks was a small town so maybe I could drive around and spot Marino. That wasted the afternoon and I was fifteen minutes early to pick up Angie. By that time the snow was sticking and I was peering out of the double arches the wipers made. I got out and cleaned the back window and mirrors, but they were covered again by the time I got back in the car. Before my hands were warm, the evidence of my efforts had disappeared.

Angie came out wearing a long gray coat that almost covered her nylons. Her collar was turned up, but the coat was hanging open, flying in the wind. She had a cute little matching stocking cap perched on her head like a crown. She pulled the cap down tight, but opened her arms to embrace the snow before she bent to open the car door.

"Oh, Alex, isn't it beautiful?"

"Real white," I agreed.

"But it covers everything, all the ugliness in the world is clean and sparkling."

"Yep, including our rear window and the mirrors." I rolled down my side window, braved the blast to stick my head out and look back. Snowflakes melted on my face and watered my eyes. I let one taxi go by and pulled into traffic.

On Hot Springs Road, the snow was streaking by sideways. Leaves were gone from the trees, the branches black, but they did have snow plastered against them. Maybe they were *ridged inch deep with pearl*, but it looked to me like a creeping fungus that was attacking the world.

Turk was in the lane to meet us, but he was distracted, snapping at the flakes. He turned around and around, shaking his head when flakes piled up on his fur. Angie gave him a pat and brushed snow off his back. He was busy trying to figure out where the white things were coming from.

I went around back and started the generator. Ice was flowing steadily in the river, and snow had turned it white. It was a pinto effect, white shapes on black water. Turk gave up biting the snow and crawled into his house. I went inside and cranked up the furnace.

Angie was watching the snow through the window, humming to herself. She had two gigantic orange salmon steaks on the cutting board. "Feast tonight, Alex. These are king salmon, almost fresh from Emmonak."

"Little out of season?"

"They were flash frozen an hour after they came out of the Yukon, and they've been frozen until I set them out this morning. They're almost fresh, and this guy is so fat he doesn't need the pan lubricated." She fired the propane broiler on the cook stove, set the salmon steaks on a cookie sheet and shoved them under the flame. She went to work grating pickles and onions to make tartar sauce.

"Can I help? Peel potatoes or something?"

"Potatoes are boiling in that pot, but there's a bottle of chenin blanc on the back step. You can check if it's cool enough."

I judged that it was, brought it in and found a corkscrew in the silverware drawer. That salmon smelled so good my mouth was already watering. Angie pulled the sheet out with a hot mitt, flipped the steaks over with a spatula and slathered mayonnaise on them before she stuck them back under the flame.

"Here, mash these." She took the potatoes off the fire, dumped the boiling water and ran cold over them, then dumped that and handed the pot to me. An old-fashioned potato masher like my mother used was peeking out of a squat ceramic jar full of knives and spatulas. I had the spuds half mashed when Angie dropped in a stick of butter and went to set the table.

It was magic, salmon steaks, homemade tartar, asparagus, potatoes, and wine. Angie lit candles and turned off the overhead light.

"The candles aren't for me, Alex. They're in honor of the salmon and the snow."

I was thinking that was the best meal I'd ever tasted and snowflakes by candlelight aren't too bad, so long as they're outside and I'm in. It didn't seem right to talk, we were having a religious experience. I stuffed myself miserably full, but could not stop until my plate was polished. It didn't seem possible, but Angie stayed right with me.

When we finally leaned back to sip the last of the wine, I was in a golden haze.

"Angie, this is heaven, and you're an angel on earth."

Her eyes popped wide open, she burst into tears, and ran for her bedroom. I was flummoxed. That might have been the first really sincere compliment I'd ever paid anyone. She'd left her door open, and was lying on her bed, hugging a pillow and sobbing her eyes out. I went in and fidgeted beside the bed.

"Angie, I'm so sorry, I meant...I didn't mean...."

She reached out to take my hand and smiled through her tears. "It's okay, Alex. I know what you meant. It's just that your compliment was exactly what Stan used to say. Oh, damn, I'm not sure I can make it, Alex. I'm not entirely sane, you know? I kept thinking I was preparing dinner for Stan. It was his favorite and I'd been saving the salmon for some special event with him. Then you sat back, just like Stan would have, and said what he would have said, and I just lost it."

I sat on the edge of her bed, released her hand and kneaded her shoulders. "It's going to be okay, Angie. Why don't I take you back to Crooked Creek? You could visit your mother, get your feet on the ground."

"I don't know, Alex, I don't know what to do. Sometimes I think I should sell the house and start over, but then Stan is here and I couldn't leave him." She buried her face in her pillow and bawled.

I kept massaging shoulders, making soothing noises. Eventually her sobs lessened to the occasional hitching breath and she was asleep. I tiptoed out, rinsed the dishes, and left them in the sink. I sat on the couch. The snow continued to fall. Maybe it was covering the ugliness outside, but it couldn't touch the ugliness inside people. I knew what I had to do. I didn't have all the answers, but enough to know what was rotten. I paced for a while, then just sat down and stared out at the snow.

Chapter Twenty-Six

Angie woke me with a fragrant cup of coffee, so I must have slept. "Thanks for last night, Alex. You're the best brother a girl ever had. I am going to be fine. I took your suggestion and talked to my mother last night."

"You what?"

"Had a chat with Mother, never mind the details. I told you, me Indian medicine woman. Mother reminded me that she's lost two husbands, and she loved them both. When it happens to other people, we expect them to deal with it. When it happens to us, we flop around like a fish out of water. Mother would have been ashamed of my performance last night, so it won't happen again. Wonderful of you to help me over the rough spots, but now let's stop all this maudlin foolishness and get to work."

Snow had stopped falling, but the world was white and it was going to stay that way for the next seven months. I dropped Angie at the station and drove out to the airport. Reginald and Celeste were parked in their usual spots, and Dave Marino's car was in the lot. The Otter and Skyvan were tied and covered, so all of the principals were in that building. I used the pay phone at the entrance to call Stella.

"Jim, I've got a whole tree of raccoons cornered. I don't know all the answers, but I know how to find out. Can you very quietly get into the freight shed at Interior Air Cargo in the next half hour?"

"You won't even see me slip in."

"Good, stand beside the connecting door between the warehouse and the office, and I think you'll hear everything you want to know."

"I'm on the way." He hung up, so I did, too. I waited twenty minutes, hoping Dave Marino wouldn't leave, and wondering how I was going to lure him back if he did. Just for insurance, I parked the Power Wagon so it blocked the lot entrance.

Celeste gave me her smile, but didn't rush to the counter. I raised the leaf and invited myself in. She didn't seem happy to see me, but she wasn't surprised, so she apparently didn't know I was dead. The brunette turned around and did a double take when I stepped through the counter uninvited, but turned back to her desk and buried her nose in papers. It seemed I just wasn't her type.

"Hi, Celeste, can I tear you away from your ledgers for a minute?"

"Sure, what's up, Alex?"

"We need to have a chat with Reginald. Is he in his office?"

"Yeah, he's in, but he's meeting with Marino at the moment. Maybe we shouldn't interrupt them?"

"This will just take a couple of minutes. Maybe Freddy could join us?"

"Well, I don't know...."

"Aw, come on, invite him. He might feel left out."

She picked up her phone and pushed buttons. Freddy came out of his office and did a double take. He was surprised to see me, but he didn't register the shock I was expecting. If he had thought I was dead he was a consummate actor. He shook his head to clear it and recovered admirably. "Hi, Alex. I thought the storm would chase you back to Bethel."

"Very soon. We just need to touch base with Reginald." Celeste was still seated. I took her arm, half urged, half lifted her to stand and gestured for her to precede me. Freddy shrugged and stepped over to tap on Reginald's door. I shepherded Celeste ahead of me, and opened the door to the warehouse as I passed.

The warehouse was silent. I hoped Stella was as good as his word. I left the door to Reginald's office open when we entered.

Reginald and Marino were hunched over the computer. Reginald looked up with a flash of annoyance, but he instantly shifted to campaign mode. "Hello, people, what's up?" Marino backed away from the computer and stood in front of the Nixon photo.

My throat was constricted. I had to clear it. "I'm afraid I called this meeting. The five of us need to go over some details of flight scheduling and billing."

Reginald stood, Marino backed toward the end of the desk, and Celeste looked ready to cry. I glanced down and noted that Marino was wearing black oxfords.

Reginald was prepared to bluff it out, an expression of concern and perplexity on his movie star mug. "What's wrong, Alex? Didn't you get paid for your flight hours?"

"Yes, I got paid for the hours I flew, but not for the sixteen hours that have my name on them that I didn't fly. Maybe Freddy can explain how the Otter got over a thousand hours of billing but only three hundred on the Hobbs meters?"

Freddy was shaking his head. "Did the Hobbs meters fail? Probably a blown fuse. You can check the aircraft log if you like."

"No, I'm sure the log matches the billing, but the meters worked perfectly when I flew the bird, and I personally saw the Otter tied down half a dozen times when flight tickets said it was flying. Let me guess. Interior is bilking the consortium out of a million or more a year. Anyone doubt that?"

I was expecting a reaction from Marino, but he didn't flinch. Reginald seemed to be having a heart attack. "What the hell are you talking about? Have you lost your mind?"

"I'm talking about several hundred thousand, maybe a million dollars' worth of fraudulent billing."

"Get out of my office. I'm calling the cops." Reginald reached for his phone. Freddy stepped forward and waved his hands like an umpire declaring a runner safe.

"Calm down, Reginald. You've been so wrapped up in that governor scheme, you wouldn't know if the business was bankrupt. Alex what the devil *are* you talking about?"

I was standing with hands behind me, but had a grip on my pistol. "I'm talking about a scheme to rob the consortium. I'm talking about hired assassins who killed Stan and have been trying to kill me. Don't play dumb, Reginald. I know Marino and Celeste have been blackmailing you, but that's going to end right now."

Reginald bent over and opened the desk drawer. He fumbled through papers, but came out lifting a nickel-plated .38 revolver.

I jerked my pistol out and had it pointed at his face. "Drop it, Reginald. Leave the gun in the drawer. Don't make me shoot you."

"Alex, I don't know what you're up to, but there's too much at stake, the governorship, the business. I can't let you stop me. Freddy, if Alex wants money, give it to him. Don't endanger my reputation."

I took one step forward, letting Reginald look down the gun barrel. "Reginald, you're forgetting one detail. This isn't about money. This is about conspiracy to commit murder. I don't care how many millions you make, they are not worth Stan's life. You imported assassins and had him killed."

Freddy groaned. "Alex, that was an accident, not my fault. I answered an ad in a magazine, just looking for some muscle. All powerful men have their enforcers. Do you think Nixon didn't? I just wanted to protect Reginald. I thought his boyfriend might cause trouble, or there might be a union problem. I wanted some muscles who could threaten and intimidate. I didn't realize those guys were killers.

"When your friend overheard them talking, they said they'd take care of him—well, I didn't know they meant to kill him. I told them it was all a mistake and I didn't want to hire their services, but they told me to get stuffed. No way could I control them."

"So, it wasn't your idea to have me and Angie killed?"

"Alex, I didn't know anyone was going to be killed. I didn't even know the connection between you and the pickup explosion until the night you introduced Angie, and then the two mercenaries got killed. I thought that was the end of it."

"But two more showed up from Seattle to take their place."

"I know, they charged their tickets to the company, but I had nothing to do with that and I never even saw the second two."

"So, you're just an innocent victim of circumstance?"

"Alex, millions are being wasted on the pipeline. It just makes sense to grab our share while we can. If Reginald becomes governor and leaves the business for me to run, we'll all be set for life, you've got to see that."

"What I see is that Marino and Celeste were blackmailing Reginald, but you were all in it."

I was expecting Marino to make a try for me, or pull a weapon of his own, but it was the brunette who stepped through the door and stuck a gun in my back.

"Come on, Freddy. Grab the phone, jerk the wires out of the computer, and let's lock them in the office. All we need is enough time to get to Canada in the 310 and we'll be home free. I stashed a fortune in the Caymans while Marino dithered around trying to connect Reginald to the scam. Couldn't believe that a mere woman could do it, could you, Marino? Alex, drop the pistol or you're dead."

I glanced down at her feet and saw open-toed sandals. I dropped the pistol. That two-pound chunk of steel landed on her toe. She screamed and bent over. I grabbed the pistol out of her hand when it went by. Freddy lunged, grabbed the barrel with his right hand, my wrist with his left and used his momentum to swing me around. I didn't fight him; I helped him, and tripped him as he went by. When my gun wavered, Reginald jerked his up and shot. I don't know if he was shooting at Freddy or me, or just shooting from sheer frustration, but the bullet hit Freddy in the shoulder.

Freddy's head slammed into the wall. He lost his grip on my arm and slid down. Reginald had dropped his gun to his side, not understanding what had happened. When he raised it again, I shot it out of his hand. He shrieked and stuck bloody fingers in his mouth. Freddy was trying to get up, so I stood on the middle of his back. The brunette was bent over whimpering and rubbing her foot. Her big toe was turning purple and blood seeping out around the painted nail.

I snapped my attention back to the desk. "Marino, get your hands up. If you go for a gun, I might miss it and hit your heart. Celeste, get over there beside him. You're in this up to your pretty little false eyelashes, and your signature is on papers that will put you away for twenty years."

"Alex, no, I...."

"Can it, get over against that wall." I gestured with the pistol. "Now, nobody moves but Celeste. Pick up the phone and dial nine-one-one."

"No need." Jim Stella stepped through the door behind me. "Put the gun away, Alex, before you shoot someone else." He knelt and put the cuffs on Freddy, so I stepped off his back. Stella pulled another set of cuffs from his belt and advanced on the brunette, but she was wailing and massaging her toe. He cuffed only one wrist and handed the other end of the manacles to a cop who had come through the door behind him. "I'm arresting you two for grand theft. Your lawyer can work out the wording."

Reginald was moaning around his fingers. He suddenly looked old, deflated.

Stella looked at the crease in Freddy's shoulder, then around the room. "Does anyone here want to testify that Reginald shot Freddy?" No one spoke. Stella nodded. "I didn't think so." He pulled a note card out of his shirt pocket. "Fredrick and Marlene, you have the right to remain silent...." He read off the Miranda spiel and the cop pulled Marlene toward the door. I grabbed Freddy by the cuffs and jerked him to his feet. He could stand. He wasn't badly injured, but I was mystified.

"Jim, Celeste had to know. Marino was blackmailing Reginald, but...."

"Alex, maybe you haven't been properly introduced. This is David Marino, special agent from the Federal Prosecutor's Office. Like you said, Interior is stealing millions, and Celeste blew the whistle. I think you should stop waving your gun at her and apologize. In fact, I believe that's Marlene's gun, so I'll take it."

I handed him Marlene's .32. "Jim, there's a lot more going on here than grand theft. Freddy must have tried to kill me by sabotaging my airplane."

Jim was nodding his head. "So, that's what happened. The day after we railroaded your two gun-toting missionaries out of town they came back on the early morning jet, but didn't rent a car or take a taxi to town. They caught the next flight back to Seattle and left that evening for Honduras. I thought they had lost their nerve, but now we know how they spent the hour between jets."

"But why? If Freddy didn't hire them to kill us, what was going on?"

"Blood feud, Alex. The original two must have thought you knew something they needed to kill you for. Then you killed two of their group so they had to kill you. That's the real meaning of honor among thieves. Now, if you'll excuse us, we have a date downtown." Two more cops appeared in the doorway and ushered the prisoners out. I sank down into one of the leather chairs, then remembered to pick up my pistol and shove it in my belt.

"Alex, my eyelashes are not false."

"I know, I know. You're absolutely beautiful and the best dancer on the planet. I was just hurt when I thought you were trying to kill me. I guess I was lashing back. Marino, my apologies."

"Not necessary. I knew you were getting close when I noticed you'd been into the computer and were hiding under the desk, but no harm done. I've collected more than enough evidence for the fraud case, thanks to Celeste. I'm glad you went ahead, because I wondered about the murder but I wasn't prepared to charge them with it."

"But you met with the two assassins at the Rendezvous Club."

"I met with two men who flew in from Detroit to help with the campaign. I didn't see much use for them, but I had no idea they were murderers."

Reginald had sunk down into his chair. "That was my fault. They were friends of Freddy's and he wanted me to give them a job. Apparently I've been an old fool and blinded by ambition. I sound like a Shakespeare character, and I guess I feel like one, too. I just don't understand how it could have gone so far."

"Am I really a good dancer, Alex?"

"Celeste, you are divine, but it was you who wiped Dave's glass clean, wasn't it?"

"No, I wondered about it, but I thought you were bluffing, you know? Trying to impress me. Lieutenant Stella matched the prints, checked with Dave, and decided we shouldn't tell you. We all thought you might be planning blackmail, and I was afraid that's what you came for today."

"But you kept the ledger. How could you not be in on it?"

"Alex, the ledger I keep is just for office expenses and payroll. Invoices and flight tickets are numbered and I filed them in order, but Marlene did the billing. That's why it took me forever to catch on."

"So nobody trusted anybody? I'm going back to Bethel where life is simpler."

"Alex, you could call me next time you're in town. We really do dance well together, and Mother will be leaving soon."

"You can count on it. We'll find a mutual friend to introduce us and start all over."

Chapter Twenty-Seven

Jessie had parked the 310 in the hangar. The Beech and the Cessna 180 were gone, the Piper covered, and he had the cowling cover off the Taylor Craft.

"Hi, Jess, 310 ready to travel?"

He wiped his hands on a rag and came to lean against the 310's wing. "Yeah, she's pristine. Why did you think the oil was contaminated? It looked brand-new."

"Just a hunch, never take chances. When I'm flying, that's dangerous enough without aircraft problems."

"Yeah, that's what everybody says about you." He pulled a clipboard down from the key rack. "Three hundred twenty bucks. Fuel tanks were almost empty, so I filled them, and price includes the car rental. You got cash?"

"Sure you wouldn't rather have a credit card?"

"Why leave paper trails when there's no need?"

That was between him and the IRS. I pulled out the roll, and it would have been short without the extra income from Interior. As it was, there were very few bills left and I suspected several of them were singles. I traded him the cash and the car keys for the keys to the 310. He brought a little gadget like a gasoline-powered hand truck, hooked it to the nose wheel and pulled the airplane outside. He turned it so I could start it without blasting his shop.

I flew the plane back to International and traded it for the Buick, then drove to the Jeep Chrysler dealer. I had an idea about how to spend some more serious money, and that idea felt really good. They took a check and a promise, and agreed to deliver the Jeep.

When Angie came out the back door, I had the Buick parked beside it. I reached over and shoved the door open.

"Wow, on time three days in a row? Maybe men really can be reformed. I'll call Connie and tell her you're a new man. Hey, where are we going? And where's that classy limousine from Phillips Field?"

"Limousine's returned to Goldstein, and the airplane's ready to fly. We'll have to make do with the Buick tonight."

I'd turned right on Cowles Street instead of left toward home and hearth. "We're headed for The Broiler, of course. We have reservations in twenty minutes and they have another bottle of nineteen seventy-one."

"And we're celebrating?"

"It's over, Angie. Next time Turk meets you on the road, you may assume it's porcupines." I parked in the lot at The Broiler beside a brand-new Jeep Wrangler. We were escorted to the same table we'd used before, and the sommelier met us with the Pouilly-Fuissé in a silver ice bucket. He poured, we saluted each other and sipped.

"It's really over, Alex? You found out who's been trying to kill us?"

"It's over, Angie. All packaged and delivered to the cops. I suspect you're going to have a little problem canceling campaign ads, though."

"It was Reginald?"

"Nope, Reginald is as innocent as any politician can be, but the scandal is going to end his ambitions, if it doesn't actually kill him. It was Freddy's girlfriend Marlene, but Freddy went along, and I didn't really believe it until he confessed."

"Alex, you said, 'when Turk meets me.' You're going back to Bethel?"

"Unless you'd like to take me up on the offer of a ride to Crooked Creek. If you'd like to do that, I'll help you close up the house and such."

"No, you're right, I'm staying here. I'll have to pick up a car, but I do have a good job and I love the house. I'm through going crazy."

"Car's taken care of, Angie. That Wrangler out front is yours. Here's the keys." I handed them across the table. She hesitated, reached for them, pulled back. "Why, Alex?"

"Because I want my sister to ride in style, and I may want to borrow it next trip, if I date a blonde."

"Thanks, brother. So you will be visiting?"

"Angie, anytime I'm in Fairbanks, the first and last dinner will be right here with you. The occasional blonde in between is possible. Remember we talked about the Mardi Gras? I can always get a few weeks off in February."

"You're kidding. Wouldn't you rather take a blonde?"

"Nope. The thought of you and me strolling down Bourbon Street, sipping Hurricanes from paper cups and listening to the music will keep me warm all winter. Ever hear of Preservation Hall?"

"Bunch of guys about a hundred years old, playing jazz? Sure, everyone's heard of them. Do you have the whole trip planned?"

"Yep, rooms at the Royal Sonesta, fried oysters in their coffee shop...."

"Just one room, Alex. I rather like listening to you snore in the other bed. But why me?"

"Not to put too fine a point on it, but blondes come and go. You're the only sister I've ever had, and I'm really getting into this family thing."

We both reached at once, clasped hands in mid-table and squeezed.

The waiter brought our lobsters. I'd ordered them in advance, along with the wine.

"I'll hold you to that, Alex. If I catch you with a blonde before you check in with me, hell hath no fury."

We shed the lobster shells, a solid fork thrust under the tail, a quick twist, discarded the husks and dug in. The lobsters were perfectly done, flaking off by the forkful, and the garlic butter was lightly salted and smoking hot.

"You said you really like your job at the station?"

"Yes, actually I do. Fun people, interesting work, advancement on the horizon."

"And it pays pretty well?"

"Oh, oh, I see where this is going. Alex, you don't have to worry about me. Yes, the job pays very well, the house is paid for, and Stan was a fanatic. You know, even when we had plenty of money, he had that macho hang-up, always worried about taking care of me. I tried to talk him out of it, but a stubborn macho male he was. He bought a life insurance policy for half a million dollars, then fussed and fumed about whether it was enough. So, no, dear brother, you don't have to worry about me. I'm accepting the car as a gesture of love and a symbol of the bond between us, not because I need it. Is that what you had in mind?"

"That's perfect, and speaking of perfect, how's your lobster?"

"Couldn't be better, but you're not drinking your share of the wine."

"No, it's a nefarious plot to get you drunk. And then, too, I'll be flying in an hour, one glass is my limit." We'd eaten every bite of lobster. That seemed to be a habit with us. "So, I'm to drink the bottle and then drive home?"

"The Jeep is four-wheel drive if you run off the road, but take the bottle with you. Light a candle and share it with our mutual memories. Ready?" I stood.

"The check?"

"Paid in advance. You can do that when you know what you're going to order."

"How about the Buick?"

"I'll drop it at the airport, no problem."

Our waiter brought a paper sack, mashed the cork back into the bottle, bagged it, and handed it to Angie. I offered my arm and we marched outside. We stopped beside the Jeep and I opened the door.

"You go first, I don't want you to see a macho man cry."

We hugged, long, hard, intimate, loving. She slid into the Jeep, inserted her key, and fired the engine.

"Thanks for dinner, Alex. See you next trip." She backed out of the lot and drove away.

It was a long, cold, lonely drive to the airport.

To receive a free catalog of Poisoned Pen Press titles, please contact us in one of the following ways:

Phone: 1-800-421-3976
Facsimile: 1-480-949-1707
E-mail: info@poisonedpenpress.com
Website: www.poisonedpenpress.com

Poisoned Pen Press
6962 E. First Ave. Ste. 103
Scottsdale, AZ 85251